Goodbye
Cruller
World

Books by Ginger Bolton

SURVIVAL OF THE FRITTERS

GOODBYE CRULLER WORLD

Published by Kensington Publishing Corporation

Goodbye Cruller World

GINGER BOLTON

KENSINGTON BOOKS
www.kensingtonbooks.com

KENSINGTON BOOKS are published by

Kensington Publishing Corp.
119 West 40th Street
New York, NY 10018

All Kensington titles, imprints, and distributed lines are available at special quantity discounts for bulk purchases for sales promotion, premiums, fund-raising, educational, or institutional use.

Special book excerpts or customized printings can also be created to fit specific needs. For details, write or phone the office of the Kensington Sales Manager: Kensington Publishing Corp., 119 West 40th Street, New York, NY 10018. Attn. Sales Department. Phone: 1-800-221-2647.

Kensington and the K logo Reg. U.S. Pat. & TM Off.

eISBN-13: 978-1-4967-1190-9
eISBN-10: 1-4967-1190-4
First Kensington Electronic Edition: September 2018

ISBN-13: 978-1-4967-1189-2
ISBN-10: 1-4967-1189-0
First Kensington Trade Paperback Printing: September 2018

10 9 8 7 6 5 4 3 2 1

Printed in the United States of America

Acknowledgments

Many thanks to my supportive friends, including Krista Davis, Daryl Wood Gerber, who also writes as Avery Aames, Laurie Cass, who also writes as Laura Alden, Kaye George, who also writes as Janet Cantrell, and Allison Brook, who also writes as Marilyn Levinson. And then there are the Deadly Dames: Melodie Campbell, Alison Bruce, Joan O'Callaghan, Cathy Astolfo, and Nancy O'Neil, who are very good at laughing and making me laugh.

Thanks also to Sgt. Michael Boothby, Toronto Police Service (Retired), who advises me on what police officers do and don't do. Any mistakes my officers make are their fault, not Mike's. And mistakes are not the fault of the Writers' Police Academy, either, which was not only very informative but also lots of fun. With more practice, I'm sure I could drive around those traffic cones without knocking them down. Thank you to everyone who made WPA happen.

We never know where research might take us. Thank you to Dr. Sameh Youssef from First Aid 4U and to Nathan Riehl, EMS Instructor, Northeast Wisconsin Technical College, for sharing your knowledge.

I couldn't have written this book without the enthusiasm and help of my agent, John Talbot, and of my editor, John Scognamiglio. Thank you also to the rest of the Kensington team, especially Mary Ann Lasher, the cover artist, and Kris

Noble for the cover design. Production editor Paula Reedy worked overtime answering my questions and concerns, and publicist Karen Auerbach has been wonderful. Thank you to Lulu Martinez for the signing opportunity at Bouchercon 2017 and for lugging around all those books. Lauren Jernigan and her social media team have been great! And I thank the many other people at Kensington who worked hard to turn my manuscript into real books in real stores.

My family and friends put up with a lot from me, and I thank them.

Last but not least, thank you, readers. I think I can see you at tables in Deputy Donut. You're sipping beverages, eating sweet treats, and helping solve mysteries. . . .

Chapter 1

✼

The yelling began almost the second I started walking down the driveway between Deputy Donut, the café that my father-in-law and I owned, and Dressed to Kill, Jenn Zeeland's cute clothing boutique.

The loud argument wasn't going on inside Deputy Donut, where Tom was finishing the day's tidying. It was going on inside Dressed to Kill, where I was heading. I couldn't make out the words, but the women spewing them were obviously angry.

I almost turned around and went back to Deputy Donut.

However, it was nearly five. In ten minutes, Dressed to Kill would close for two weeks, and I needed the black jeans and white shirts that I'd ordered. Besides, what if Jenn was in danger?

I hurried to the front of Dressed to Kill.

I wasn't about to barge inside without peeking in first. Jenn's display windows were lovely, but I couldn't see beyond her hand-knit sweaters, mittens, scarves, and hats, and the cords and down-filled vests that went with them. The clothes were draped over antique skis, sleds, skates, and snowshoes. In one window, an electric fireplace sent warm hues rippling over the entire scene. It could have been very welcoming if women inside the store hadn't been screaming at each other only seconds before.

A red-faced woman burst out of Dressed to Kill. She muttered, "Don't go in there," budged past me, and raced south on Wisconsin Street.

My training kicked in. *Get a description, Emily.*

I guessed she was in her mid-to-late forties. She was tall and angular, with straight brown flyaway hair. Her mid-calf, flowing dress, a floral print in blue and white, hung several inches below an unbuttoned navy wool coat. She hadn't zipped up the sides of her tan knee-high leather boots. With their tops flapping and threatening to trip her with each step, she ran past the bookstore and the artisans' co-op, and then she turned right and disappeared. For a few seconds, I heard the clap, clap, clap of those unzipped boots.

I had never seen her before.

I again considered returning to Deputy Donut. Before Tom and I opened our coffee and donut shop, he had been Fallingbrook's police chief. Tom could handle whatever had gone on inside Dressed to Kill.

And so can you, Emily.

I pulled the door open. Tiny bells jingled.

Usually, unless Jenn was busy with a customer, she heard the bells, peeked around racks of clothing, and greeted me.

This time, she didn't. I was getting twitchy.

That shouting I'd heard earlier . . .

And now, this breathless quiet . . .

I told myself I was being overly dramatic. Jenn knew I was coming. Besides, she was probably immersed in wedding preparations.

I tiptoed into the store. I couldn't help touching, with one tentative finger, an emerald green velvet cocktail dress. It would be perfect for Jenn's reception the next night, but I was attending the reception late, only to keep the donut wall stocked, and I would be wearing my Deputy Donut uniform. The black jeans and white shirt would be new, though, if Jenn was here to give them to me.

"Jenn?" I called.

No answer.

I walked farther into the store, past a table of neatly folded sequined sweaters. "Jenn?"

Near the back of the store, a door slammed or something fell.

"*Jenn!*" I sounded a little frantic. "Are you here?" If she didn't answer by the count of ten, I was going back to Deputy Donut for Tom.

I got to eight, and then footsteps approached from the office beyond the dressing cubicles. Someone vigorously blew a nose.

Tall and slender, dressed in tight jeans and a luscious coral sweater that she must have designed, Jenn came out from between the dressing rooms. Her head was bowed, and her long blond hair hung down like curtains, concealing the sides of her face. "Hey, Emily," she mumbled toward her sweater. "I'll get the things you ordered." She walked away quickly, like she didn't want me to get a good look at her.

It was too late.

I'd already noticed her red and swollen eyelids.

The poor thing. She was only a little older than I was, in her mid-thirties, but the sad eyes aged her, and in less than twenty-four hours she was scheduled to wow everyone with her long white dress and the radiance that wedding guests expected from brides.

She returned, holding the clothes, which were on hangers, high, as if she were hiding behind them. She walked to the cash desk at the front of the store and hung the garments on a rack. I followed. Fiddling with receipts and invoices, she didn't meet my gaze. "These should fit," she said. "Teensy for you and muscular for Tom."

I tried to prolong the joking atmosphere. "You've changed the names of sizes?" She raised her face, and I couldn't ignore the tear rolling down her cheek. "What's wrong, Jenn?"

"*Everything*. I wish I had your curls."

I couldn't believe she was crying because she didn't have a crop of unruly dark curls.

"*And* those vivid blue eyes."

"Don't be ridiculous," I said. "Nearly everyone wants straight blond hair like yours, and your hazel eyes are beautiful. Besides, curls seldom behave the way I want them to." Plunking a hand on my Deputy Donut cap, a police hat with a faux-fur donut attached where the badge would ordinarily be, I accidentally pushed the cap down. It nearly covered my eyes. "It's a good thing I designed a hat to hide my hair at work." I shoved the hat up again. "The bad news is that when I remove it every evening I have a bad case of hat head."

"The blond is out of a bottle, but the straight is real. Without the help of chemicals, my hair is mousy brown. Like my sister's. Do you know Suzanne?"

She was jumping so quickly from subject to subject that I couldn't do much besides shake my head and clench my teeth to prevent my mouth from gaping open.

"She just left," Jenn said. "I thought maybe you saw her. She's my half-sister, really. We had different fathers. She's ten years older, and when our mother got sick, Suzanne promised to look after me. I was only nine. Looking after is one thing, but . . ." She blew her nose again. "Smothering is quite another. I mean, we work together *here* all right."

"Here? I never saw her before today." I didn't mean to sound skeptical.

"We own Dressed to Kill together, fifty-fifty. She does the books, usually at night, long after you've closed Deputy Donut. She doesn't like dealing with customers or ordering clothes, so I do all that. She says it would be different if we sold shoes. She loves shoes and knows just about everything there is to know about footwear."

Maybe wearing boots unzipped and flopping around one's ankles was the latest trend. Would knowledge about footwear make someone cry? "Did she upset you?"

Jenn wailed, "She told me to cancel the wedding. *Told* me!"

All I managed was, "Oh." Did Jenn's half-sister want Jenn's fiancé for herself?

Apparently not. "She *hates* Roger! She always has. She never gave him half a chance."

Still not knowing quite what to say, I mumbled something meant to sound sympathetic.

"I never should have agreed to marry him in the first place, but the wedding's tomorrow, and now it's way too late to change my mind."

Seriously confused, I held up a hand. "Wait. Don't you want to marry him?"

"Yes. No." She strode to the cash desk and grabbed a fresh tissue. "I don't know. To make matters worse, I haven't told Roger that I invited my old boyfriend to the wedding and reception. There was never a right time to tell Roger. And my old boyfriend and I are just friends, really, but he's one of my best friends."

I saw where this could pose a problem. "Maybe you should tell Roger before tomorrow. Or wouldn't a best friend understand if you uninvited him?"

She clicked long and shapely nails against the cash desk. "I couldn't do either of those things. Uninviting someone would be just too rude. And I don't want to make Roger angry tonight, the night before our wedding. I'll just have to trust that he won't make a scene tomorrow."

Some people were really good at causing problems for themselves. I suggested, "If you're not sure about marrying Roger, maybe you could postpone the wedding until you know what you want to do."

"I do know. Marry Roger. I'm just having pre-wedding jitters, I guess. They say every bride has them."

I'd never had the least doubt about marrying Alec.

As if I'd said it aloud, she apologized. "I shouldn't be reminding you. You must miss your husband."

"That's okay. I've finally reached the stage where thinking

about him brings back wonderful memories." Still, I couldn't help remembering the night that my detective husband was killed while on duty, and it still hurt. "Why did your sister wait so long to tell you to cancel the wedding?"

Jenn bowed her head again, letting her hair fall in front of her face. "She's been saying it all along. She told me to stop seeing him when we were first dating. Like it's any of her business, you know? And this afternoon, she went ballistic on me, screaming, yelling, the whole nine yards. For no reason, other than this last-ditch attempt to get me to drop Roger."

"Is she married?"

"No. Never has been. And I know she cares about me, really. It's just that . . ."

"Smothering," I repeated.

"She doesn't want me to move away from Fallingbrook, either."

"Are you going to? We'd all miss you—and your wonderful shop. I love how you turned your online knitting and knitwear design business into a bricks-and-mortar store." And I'd been buying a lot of sweaters. . . . "But you can run your online store from wherever you live, can't you?"

"I don't plan to close Dressed to Kill, but Suzanne says that Roger won't let me stay in business, period. She thinks he's jealous of my success. But how could he be? He's doing great as a life coach, even though he inherited so much from some distant relative that he doesn't have to work. Suzanne says that Roger has always moved around and he's not going to want to stay in Fallingbrook. She even uses his wealth against him, saying it will allow him to live anywhere." Jenn's face crumpled and tears welled in her eyes. "Just now, she accused me of being a gold digger."

"That's nonsense." Jenn seemed too sweet to marry a man only for his money. She had to care about him. "He used to live in Fallingbrook, didn't he? And he came back, so maybe he's ready to settle down, with you, here."

"I hope so. I don't think I could bear to part with Dressed to Kill." She gave a resigned little shrug. "But I might have to. The things we do for love." Her halfhearted attempt at a smile didn't reach her eyes. "And the things we do because we've already planned a wedding. Maybe I could have canceled it a year or even six months ago, but now it's too late. For instance, you and Tom—you wouldn't let me put down a deposit. You built that donut wall and you're planning to stay up tomorrow night to provide late-night snacks for our guests. You've probably ordered tons of extra ingredients for the donuts and crullers. I can't ask you to cancel *now*."

"It wouldn't be a problem. We can use that donut wall another time, and the ingredients will keep. But you'd lose your deposit on the banquet hall rental and the meals you ordered, and you probably can't send your dress back, and . . ." Why was I giving her excuses to marry someone who, I was beginning to suspect, might make her unhappy?

"Yeah, it's definitely too late. And I want to marry Roger. I do." She gave me a watery smile. " 'I do.' See? I'm already practicing my lines for tomorrow."

Chapter 2

✺

On Saturday afternoon, Tom and I closed Deputy Donut at our usual time, four thirty. Leaving Tom in the kitchen to make the dough we'd need for Jenn's reception later that night, I went through our dining area to our office and shut myself inside with my cat. When she was a tiny kitten, Alec had taken one look at the donut-like circles on her sides and had burst out laughing. "Deputy Donut," he'd said, "the perfect name for a cop's cat." Laughing as hard as he did, I'd agreed.

And then after Alec was gone, Dep had graciously allowed Alec's father and me to call our coffee and donut shop Deputy Donut.

Because of health regulations, Dep wasn't allowed in the kitchen or dining area, and we had designed our office as Dep's home-away-from-home. The room had windows on all four sides. Dep could perch on windowsills and supervise the kitchen, the dining area, the parking lot, or the driveway between Deputy Donut and Dressed to Kill.

She was curled up on our comfy couch. She stood and stretched. Her markings, including those cute circles, were tabby, and her coloring was tortoiseshell—black, cream, and ginger, which qualified her as a tortoiseshell tabby, also known as a torbie. I kissed the stripy orange patch on her forehead.

She and I usually walked to and from work, and her cat

carrier had been underneath the desk for days. However, she must have sensed that I was in a hurry and needed to drive her home. She scrambled up a carpeted "tree" to the multi-level catwalk that Tom and I had built for her above the windows. Darting up and down steps and ramps, she circled the room and picked up a catnip mouse she'd stored in a cranny.

"Come down, Dep," I urged.

I closed my mouth just in time. The slightly damp catnip mouse bounced off my chin.

I rattled her halter. That plus the catnip mouse at my feet must have convinced her to trot down her kitty-sized staircase. Grasping my warm fur baby, I pulled the cat carrier into the center of the office.

Despite a flurry of caterwauling and spread-out kitty toes, I managed to shut her into her carrier. I called goodbye to Tom, took the vociferous cat out to the garage in the back of our parking lot, and opened the overhead door.

Our Deputy Donut delivery vehicle was a restored 1950 Ford Fordor, a four-door sedan painted like a police cruiser, black with white doors and roof. However, the insignia on the doors was our Deputy Donut logo, the silhouette of a cat wearing a rakishly tilted Deputy Donut hat, faux-fur donut and all. Instead of a light bar, a large plastic donut lay flat on the roof. It was topped by dripping white "icing" and sprinkles that were actually tiny lights programmed to change colors and patterns in a zillion ways. A megaphone-shaped loudspeaker in front of the donut resembled an old-fashioned siren.

I buckled Dep's carrier into the back seat. During the entire eight-block ride, Dep commented loudly about the indignities she was suffering. I parked behind my own car in the driveway of our Victorian cottage, took the carrier inside, and let Dep out in the living room. "I'll come home and change around nine," I promised.

Switching her tail back and forth, she looked away.

My phone rang. Why was Detective Brent Fyne calling? I

knew it was silly, but I answered his call with the sort of pin-pricks of anxiety I would always feel when a law-enforcement officer called unexpectedly, even when he called from his personal phone. "Hi, Brent."

"Hi, Em. I'm on duty later tonight. I was wondering if I could bring over pizza and beer for a quick dinner."

"That sounds great, but Tom and I are providing the late-night snacks at a wedding reception, and I'll be working until the wee hours. How does tomorrow sound instead?"

He agreed, and we disconnected.

Brent and I were friends again despite my standoffishness during the first three years after Alec was shot. Brent and Alec had been best friends and had also been partners on the Fallingbrook police force, first as patrolmen and later as detectives. They'd been together the night that Alec was killed and a bullet grazed Brent's arm. I'd been a 911 dispatcher, but I wasn't working that fateful night. Out-of-town friends had been visiting only one evening, and I'd traded shifts with a new dispatcher so I could go out to dinner with my friends.

I would always feel guilty about going out that night. If I hadn't traded shifts, maybe I could have gotten emergency responders to Alec in time to save him. Brent had told me that I couldn't have sped the response. Brent had radioed police headquarters even before a witness phoned 911, and the ambulance had arrived almost immediately.

But I still felt guilty.

During those first three years, my raw grief had excluded Brent. I hadn't wanted to think about Alec and the night I lost him. However, just over a year ago, Brent's investigation of the murder of a Deputy Donut customer had forced me to spend time with Brent. Finally, I'd understood that both of us missed Alec terribly. Alec and I had often gotten together with Brent and whatever woman he was dating at the time. Brent was a good man, and he and I had lots in common, including the shared pain that we almost never mentioned to each other. We were friends again, but the friendship was tenuous, and the time we spent together was always casual, like a pizza and beer at my place before he headed off to an evening shift. Sometimes I wondered if Brent was visiting me or the cat he'd gotten to know when Alec was alive.

I said goodbye to Dep. Undoubtedly having figured out that I was about to abandon her, she ignored me.

I drove Tom's and my "police car" to Deputy Donut and went into the kitchen. In his black jeans, white shirt, sturdy white cotton apron embroidered with our Deputy Donut logo, and his donut-trimmed "police" hat slightly askew on his short salt-and-pepper hair, Tom was kneading the last batch of yeast dough. He patted it into a ball and put it into our proofing cabinet, where it would rise in controlled warmth and humidity.

Leaving his apron and hat behind, we locked up and climbed into his shiny black SUV, a powerful monster similar to vehicles he'd driven as police chief. I knew from experience that he still drove like he was on the way to a life-or-death emergency. I fastened my seat belt, gripped the armrests, and held my breath.

A few miles north of Fallingbrook, he had to slow down to negotiate the hills and curves on a two-lane road hemmed in by tall trees. On our left, the sun was low and already hidden from ground level by a forest of pines, but on our right, the crowns of maples glowed red and gold in orange light reflecting from clouds.

Jenn and Roger's ceremony in a cute Gothic chapel in downtown Fallingbrook should have ended. Had Jenn gotten over her jitters? And her puffy eyes?

Wind sent yellow leaves skipping across the road in front of us. Even though I was wearing one of the bulkier sweaters that Jenn had designed, a scrumptious turquoise, blue, and purple one, I shivered.

We crossed a bridge over a foam-flecked stream so dark it looked almost black. Tom sped up the next rise. Near the top, a carved wooden sign said LITTLE LAKE LODGE. The lodge's logo, a row of three pines—big, bigger, biggest—was carved in relief below the name and painted dark green. Tom slammed on the brakes, wheeled left, and zoomed up Little Lake Lodge's steep driveway.

We crested the hill. A cleared area sloped down to the lodge, a sandy beach, and Little Lake, bisected by a blinding pathway leading, it seemed, directly to the setting sun.

Little Lake wasn't actually little, unless you compared it to other lakes in the Fallingbrook chain. Shading my eyes, I could barely make out the far shore.

The lodge was *definitely* not little. It was about a hundred years old and built of logs. Its steeply pitched roof and wide eaves sheltered three stories of white-mullioned, red-sashed windows. The lobby entrance, capped by a peaked roof supported by substantial peeled tree trunks, faced the flat main parking lot and beyond that, lawns and gardens sweeping up the hill toward the road we'd left.

Following instructions Jenn had given us, Tom stopped at the south end of the lodge and backed into a parking spot near a rustic pine door labeled DELIVERIES ONLY. We carefully removed our blanket-wrapped donut wall from the SUV. Tom carried it while I brought his cordless drill and a box of screws.

The floor of the corridor inside was concrete painted deep red, while the walls were peeled and varnished logs. On the left, a closed solid pine door was marked RUFFED GROUSE. Applause sounded behind that door. Even though Tom was carrying the donut wall, he executed a comical bow toward the door, and I had to stifle a giggle. If anyone was behind the next door on the left, titled CALL OF THE LOON, they were silent. Farther, on the right, we found the door to the banquet hall. The name on that door was, as Jenn had told us, WILD GOOSE.

I opened the door, and we were in another sort of corridor, a dimly lit and narrow one between the log wall and sheeny white drapes hanging from the ceiling. To our right, cartons were stacked behind what had to be the reception's temporary bar.

Closer, but still on our right, masking tape outlined the back two-thirds of a square on the carpet's red, purple, and beige swirls. The drapes were semitranslucent, and we could sort of see into the more brightly lit banquet room. We lifted the hem of one of the curtains and found the rest of the taped square. We were supposed to center the table supporting our donut wall over that square.

I put the drill and screws down and helped Tom lean the donut wall against the logs. Next to the left side of the taped square, the edges of two curtains met. We widened the gap and peeked into the banquet hall.

Maybe Jenn hadn't been sure she wanted to marry Roger, but she had definitely created a dreamy setting for their reception. Lights were brighter than where we were standing, mostly behind the curtains, but they were still romantically low, and the entire room was draped, floor to ceiling, in those white curtains. The curtains themselves were decorated with swags of periwinkle tulle tied with gold bows trailing long ribbons. Rows of round tables were covered in white tablecloths overlaid by squares of sheer, glittery periwinkle fabric and set with white napkins and china. Crystal and cutlery sparkled, while simple white vases held purple and white flowers. On a dais to our far right, the long, rectangular head table faced the length of the room. Larger vases on the head table were empty, probably waiting for Jenn's and her attendants' bouquets. Although tables and chairs covered most of the flashy carpeting, the floor in front of the head table was a much calmer-looking parquet.

On the other side of the room from us, gold-backed chairs like the ones around the tables were in a semicircle behind music stands and microphones.

Beside the space obviously reserved for a band, a break in the white drapes revealed glossy pine double doors. A squarish red glow lit the white drapes above the doors.

"Well," my father-in-law grumbled, "I *guess* people will be able to see the exit sign after one of those candles on the tables tips over and the room fills with smoke." We turned around. The exit sign above the door we'd used wasn't clearly visible, either. We went out that way, into the service corridor. "There are lots of places to hide in that banquet hall," Tom commented.

I laughed. "Who's going to hide at a wedding reception?"

"The bride, if she's smart. Or anyone who needs a nap."

"You're such a romantic."

He held a hand over his heart. "A hopeless romantic. With the accent on 'hopeless.'"

I laughed again. And then I sobered and asked him, "Do you know something about Roger?" Maybe when Tom was police chief, he had arrested or charged Roger. . . .

"Who's Roger?"

"The groom. Roger Banchen."

"Nope. But I've seen grooms who've made *me* want to hide."

Outside, Tom opened the back of his SUV. Carefully, we removed the table that would support the donut wall. We'd painted the table periwinkle to match a swatch of fabric that Jenn had given me. We carried the table into the banquet hall and set it over the taped square, putting one-third of the table in front of a section of white curtain and the other two-thirds behind it. The curtain pooled on top of the table and drooped to the floor on both sides.

Jenn had left a periwinkle tablecloth on the bar for us. We refolded the tablecloth to fit the front third of the table, touching the floor on all three sides. We would have space underneath the table, behind the tablecloth and the white curtains, to stow things out of sight, including any napping reception guests.

Tom and I unwrapped the donut wall, which we had constructed of thick plywood with dowels sticking out the front. Each dowel was long enough to hold about three donuts. We had surrounded the plywood with a shadow-box frame and had painted the entire thing periwinkle.

Since I'd last seen the donut wall, my mother-in-law, Cindy, had painted a gold heart outline near the top of the donut wall and had written inside it, in gold curlicued script, *Jenn & Roger*. She'd also written *Jenn* above the top dowel on the right side of the wall and *Roger* above the top dowel on the left. I clapped my hands. "Tell Cindy I love it!"

To hold the tablecloth in place, we set the front edge of the donut wall on the back folds of the tablecloth. Then we lined up the holes in the braces at the back of the wall with holes that Tom had pre-drilled in the top of the table, and I steadied the wall while Tom used the drill to twirl the screws into place. I straightened the pooled hem of the white curtain and folded it neatly over the braces to make space for the boxes of donuts I would bring later that evening.

Jenn had also left several vases of flowers plus two three-tiered cake stands, china with lacy edges, on the bar for us. We set the flowers and cake stands on the tablecloth in front of the donut wall and then stood back to have a good look at our creation.

I couldn't help grinning. The donut station Jenn had ordered for her guests' late-night snacks was both pretty and fun, and later, after I loaded those dowels and cake stands with donuts, it would be even prettier and more fun.

I heard voices beyond the banquet hall's double doors. Both doors opened with unnecessary violence.

A short, thin man marched into the room. His thick eyebrows and heavily gelled black hair overshadowed a pointy nose and close-set shoe-button eyes. Judging by his outfit—black tux, white pleated shirt, and black bowtie—and the authority in his stride, he was the maître d' from the lodge's main restaurant.

Her makeup thick, her veil trailing, and her blond hair waving loosely around her face, Jenn attempted to maneuver her meringue of white ruffles and lace through the double doorway.

Behind her, a bony woman in a shoulder-baring periwinkle

gown frowned. Even though the woman's fine brown hair was pinned up and decorated with ribbons and flowers and she was wearing gold sandals with impossibly high clear heels instead of unzipped boots flopping around her ankles, I recognized her—Suzanne, Jenn's half-sister.

Suzanne fussed with Jenn's frills until Jenn popped through the doorway. Suzanne and two shorter and less peevish-looking women in gowns matching Suzanne's came in. They were wearing gold sandals, too, but theirs had short gold heels.

Three men—they looked like teenagers, actually—in gray tuxes with gray bowties followed the bridesmaids into the banquet hall and stopped, awkwardly shuffling their feet and staring around as if flummoxed by the silky draperies and bouffant tulle.

His shoulders back, the maître d' did what one of my friends called a short-man walk to the head table. The soles of his shoes smacked the parquet dance floor. He stopped, turned around, and beckoned to a harried-looking man with a camera bag. A colorless woman wearing a gray pantsuit and carrying a larger camera bag and a tripod followed the man toward the maître d'.

Jenn wound her way between tables to us. Her bouquet smelled like the old-fashioned roses, sweetness peppered with cinnamon and cloves, that had been my grandmother's pride and joy. "Your donut wall is beautiful!" Jenn crowed. "Thank you so much! You've done a wonderful job, more than I could have dreamed of." She picked up the smallest vase of flowers. "This would be perfect up here, don't you think?" She set it on the flat top of the donut wall's frame. It just barely fit.

With loud snaps near the head table, the photographer's assistant lengthened the tripod's telescoping legs.

The maître d' bore down on us and waved his hand at the shimmering white drapes. "What's with all this tent stuff, Jenn? You wanted to feel like you were inside someone's enormous nightgown?"

Jenn opened her mouth, but whatever she might have been

about to say was interrupted by the slam of the door behind the donut wall. The nearest sections of the "enormous night-gown" billowed and fluttered.

Behind me, Tom quipped, "Gown with the wind."

I bit off a snicker when I noticed that the man in the tux was glaring. His anger wasn't aimed at me, however. It appeared to be aimed at our donut wall. "More purple!" he yelled. "Whatever got into you, Jenn?"

Finally, she found her voice. "It's periwinkle."

Veins stood out at the side of the man's reddening neck. "It's *girly*."

Jenn stared toward where her feet should be underneath her own enormous gown.

I wanted to tell the man in the tux, *Wedding receptions tend to be girly*.

As if I'd spoken aloud, the man, who I was quickly deciding was *not* the maître d', scowled at me. "Where are the donuts?"

"I'll bring them before ten," I said.

"They should be hanging on that board *now*." He had to be Jenn's new husband. No wonder Suzanne had warned her against marrying him.

I regretted not having joined forces with Suzanne.

Jenn appeared to be pondering whether a dress the size of hers could sink through that gaudy carpeting and into the lodge's basement.

Obviously, she wasn't going to help me. I said, "Donuts would dry out if we hung them now."

Roger scolded, "You should have made some for now and some for later."

My face heated, but I managed to say coolly, "Our contract says they're to be served as late-night snacks, after dinner and speeches. During the dancing. At ten."

Tom moved closer to me. "We're about to go make them. They'll be fresh."

The man turned on Jenn. "You couldn't even write a contract right? Do I have to think of everything?"

Jenn set a tentative, perfectly manicured hand on his sleeve. "Roger . . ."

He shook her off and yanked a folded piece of paper and a chewed-on pencil out of a pocket in his tuxedo trousers. He stabbed the pencil down on the paper. Even in the romantically low lighting, I could see the dark marks he made. "I wrote right here that we were to have our pictures taken in front of that donut board." He pointed at our lovely donut wall. "But it's useless now." He stroked the point of his pencil angrily across the paper, and then narrowed those small eyes at his bride. "So, *Wife*, bring your bouquet. Let's see if you can set it into the vase where it belongs, and we'll *try* to have the head table pictures taken." He stomped toward the front of the room.

Jenn threw us an apologetic look. Clutching skirt fabric in one fist and her bouquet in the other, she minced away, brushing that voluminous skirt against gilded chairs. The scent of roses drifted from her.

The man in the black tux turned around and shouted, "Hey, donut people! You messed up. You missed a big promotional opportunity!"

Jenn pleaded, "*Roger . . .*"

In front of the head table, the three young men in gray tuxes took a run at the shiny parquet floor.

Suzanne flapped her hands and called out, "Boys!"

Arms out for balance, the young men slid from one side of the dance floor to the other.

My eyes wide, I turned to Tom. "They really are kids. The groomsmen. *All* of them."

Tom squinted at them for a few seconds as if memorizing their appearance in case he had to describe them to his former colleagues in the police department. "Take a good look at the two bridesmaids," he said. "Not the tall one, who seems to be the maid of honor."

"Probably. She's the bride's half-sister."

The shorter female attendants resembled grown women except for the way they giggled at the boys. My eyes opened wider. "The bridesmaids are teens, too!"

"Yep." Tom picked up his drill and box of screws. "Let's go make donuts."

Chapter 3

✼

Back at Deputy Donut, Tom mixed so-called unraised batter, the kind that relied on baking soda instead of yeast to rise, and I rolled and cut the yeast dough that had risen while we were out at Little Lake Lodge. Then Tom fried the yeast donuts and I made cruller pastry and piped bumpy circles of it onto parchment paper. Tom fried the crullers, I rolled and cut the unraised batter, and then he fried those donuts, too.

As the donuts cooled, I decorated some with confectioners' sugar and others with white or periwinkle frosting. I placed white sugar "pearls" on some of the periwinkle donuts, periwinkle sugar hearts on some of the white donuts, and dusted edible gold confetti on other donuts. I dipped the crullers in a simple honey glaze. The hills and valleys in their surfaces glistened. It all smelled delicious.

Tom grinned at my rapidly filling trays. "They're looking good."

We carefully arranged our finished donuts in bakery boxes, white with our Deputy Donut logo printed on them in black.

Shortly before nine, we stacked the filled bakery boxes into the trunk of our "police" car, and then we slid a stainless-steel cart, wheels up and swiveling lazily, into the back seat. I added a clean Deputy Donut apron, one of my Deputy

Donut hats, and a box of food handlers' disposable plastic gloves.

Tom shut the car's back door. "Would you like me to go instead, and cope with that wedding party, especially Roger-the-Rager and those kids they must have picked up from some stray prom?"

I laughed. "You just want to drive this car. But the gloves I packed are too small for you, and besides . . ." I dangled the car keys out of his reach. "I have the keys. I'll go party, and leave you to clean up." Tom deserved to spend what was left of the evening with Cindy.

He knew I was only pretending to be fierce. His slightly crooked smile reminded me of Alec's. "Call if you need me."

I agreed and drove home. With Dep batting at my hands and feet, I changed into the new black jeans and white shirt I'd picked up from Jenn. In honor of the formal occasion, I put on a pair of black suede flats with sprays of rhinestones across the toes.

I threw on a red down-filled jacket and picked up the peri-winkle step-on wastebasket that I'd trimmed with white lace and gold ribbon. "Goodbye, Dep," I said. "I'll be back really late. Don't wait up for me." She rubbed a paw over her head, flattening an ear. "Pretend you can't hear me, Dep," I teased. "I know you can." She flattened her other ear.

Driving that vintage car up and down the hilly, curvy road to Little Lake Lodge was even more fun than driving it in town. I turned on the "sprinkles" in the rooftop donut. Multicolored streaks darted across trees crowding the road. As I often did in the 1950 Ford, I played a soundtrack from 1950, but I didn't broadcast it from the loudspeaker on the car's roof. "The Cry of the Wild Goose" came on, and I burst out laughing at the coincidence—I was heading back to the Wild Goose Banquet Hall.

Millions of stars pierced the black sky. The way the rooftop "sprinkles" kept time to the music was whimsical, but the dancing lights seemed to disturb the peaceful drama of the otherwise dark forest. I turned off the lights but left the music on.

I sang along with "Harbor Lights" and "The Tennessee Waltz." Apparently, love and loss were popular themes in 1950.

I allowed myself to miss Alec intensely, but the songs from 1950 seemed to imply that there would be happy endings out there somewhere. The harbor lights would bring the lover sailing back, and the sweetheart would come to her senses and return from the "friend" who had stolen her away. The songs seemed more peculiar than sad.

Maybe it had something to do with the way I was singing them.

I drove down the slope to Little Lake Lodge. Ahead, those millions of stars twinkled, both in the sky and on Little Lake's calm surface.

I backed up to the delivery entrance, took the cart out, and loaded boxes of donuts onto it.

Behind me, someone slipped on a gravel driveway leading down the hill from the lot that Jenn had said was the staff parking lot. A woman asked, "Are you okay?"

"I'm fine," another woman answered.

I opened the lodge's delivery door.

One of the women on the driveway above me shouted, "Hold the door!"

Despite their high-heeled sandals, which weren't nearly as high as Suzanne's, the two women caught up quickly. They were wearing nice pants and frilly tops, but judging by the huge totes they were carrying, they weren't wedding guests. I couldn't place the perfume wafting from at least one of them, but I suddenly remembered being inside a store in Colonial Williamsburg when I was about eight years old and my parents had taken me on a road trip to Virginia. I glanced at the women's totes. They advertised *The Happy Hopers Conference—Goal Achievement Through Shopping!*

The slightly shorter woman, a sharp-featured one with close-cropped dark hair that feathered around her ears, held the door open for me. I wheeled my cart into the service corridor and had to veer left to avoid crashing into a security guard who, along with the chair he was on, had appeared since Tom and I left the lodge around six thirty. The security guard was sitting with his back to the door, obviously positioned to see down the length of the corridor and watch the doors leading to the backs of the meeting rooms. He wore a black uniform, complete with typical law-enforcement shoes and a red and yellow badge on the sleeve of his jacket, but no hat covering his gray hair. Leaning away from me, he pulled a newspaper out of a briefcase. The lace of his left shoe must have broken. It had been retied near the middle, leaving only enough string at the top for a meager knot that showed up against his white sock.

"I'm with Deputy Donut," I told him. "I'm bringing donuts to the wedding reception in the Wild Goose Banquet Hall."

He nodded.

The taller of the two women, the one with a serene face framed by wavy shoulder-length blond hair, asked him how to get to the Happy Hopers Conference.

"Go around to the front and in through the lobby entrance." His voice reminded me of toast being scraped with a dull knife.

The two women backed out. The door closed behind them.

Band music in the banquet hall put an end to my brain's constant looping of "The Tennessee Waltz." I left the cart in the gloomy narrow space between the log walls and the draperies, out of sight of the people talking and laughing beyond the white curtains, and then went back out to the service corridor. Jenn had said that after I unloaded I could park in the staff parking lot. She'd expected the front lot to be filled with vehicles belonging to hotel and wedding guests.

The security guard was reading his newspaper. "I'm just going to park my car," I told him.

He grunted.

"Will this door still be unlocked when I get back?"

"Far's I know."

The Happy Hopers were standing outside the delivery entrance. They stopped chatting, and the brunette pointed at the old Ford. "Nice car!"

I pointed at my head. "It goes with the hat."

She smiled. Her friend continued looking serious, as if she couldn't quite approve of decorating cars and hats with fake donuts.

I drove the Fordor up the gravel driveway and parked in a lot hedged in by slightly scraggly pines. Shivering, glad I was wearing a warm jacket and my Deputy Donut hat, I carried my decorated wastebasket, apron, and box of disposable gloves down the driveway. I understood why one of the Happy Hopers had slid on it a few minutes before. The "gravel" was actually rounded stones that rolled underfoot.

Both women were still downhill from me, near the delivery entrance. The brunette looked up, pointed at me, and said something to the blonde. Their heels clip-clopping on the concrete pathway, they hurried away, toward the lodge's front door.

Some of their fragrance had lingered. As I recalled, it had a name I'd found funny when I was eight. This heady fragrance smelled like roses, lavender, and citrus, with overlays of exotic spices.

As the security guard had sort of promised, the delivery door was unlocked. He was snoozing over his newspaper. I set my cute flats down quietly, but if he was sleeping through the band music, my footsteps and the slight rattling of the lace-embellished wastebasket weren't likely to awaken him.

Inside the banquet hall, I set the wastebasket behind the curtains and put my apron and the box of gloves on our table. I stuffed my jacket underneath, where it would be hidden from reception guests by the tablecloth and draperies. Deputy Donut aprons were too long for me. I looped the strap over my head, made a tuck at the waist, crossed the strings in back, tied them in front with a bow, and folded the tuck over the bow. I slid my phone into one of the apron's large front pockets.

Straightening my hat, I peeked between the curtains to the slightly brighter reception. The meal had been cleared away, many of the tables had been removed, and chairs had been pushed back. The parquet dance floor was larger than it had first appeared. Dancers were smiling, including Jenn, dancing with Roger. He wasn't smiling. I wondered if he ever did.

I wheeled the cart in front of the curtains and parked it next to the donut wall. After I pulled on a pair of plastic gloves, I could finally do what I'd been anticipating ever since Jenn had first asked for a donut wall. I decorated it with donuts.

Jenn's favorite honey-glazed crullers went on the dowels underneath her name, and Roger's favorites, raised donuts coated in confectioners' sugar, went on the dowels underneath his.

After I hung those, I did the most fun part. Varying frosting colors and designs, I stocked the middle dowels. I also arranged donuts on the tiered cake stands. Stepping on the wastebasket's foot pedal, I threw out the first of what would probably be many pairs of gloves that night. I tweaked the positions of the vases of flowers and then I tried not to be too obvious as I used my phone to photograph the enticing donut wall and the tulle-festooned white curtains on both sides of it.

I was wheeling the cart, with newly flattened bakery boxes stacked on its lower shelf, behind the curtains when the music stopped.

Roger announced, "The donuts are here, folks. Finally."

It was exactly ten.

I parked the cart underneath the table. Smiling, I returned to the front of the donut wall. Roger said into the microphone, "Go help yourselves." The band began playing again. Roger stalked toward the head table. Jenn and her periwinkle-gowned attendants were near the table, but where were the boys in gray tuxes?

At the end of the banquet hall opposite the head table, the white curtains bulged and rippled. Either the room was suffering another bout of gown with the wind or the boys were racing around the room behind the curtains.

Guests mobbed the donut wall, taking selfies with it and raving about it and the donuts.

I didn't know that Fallingbrook's fire chief, Scott Ritsorf, was at the reception until he gave me that adorable grin and a quick hug. His hard chest almost knocked my cap off. Although whipcord thin, he was the super-fit kind of person you'd want rescuing you from a fire, except I didn't like the idea of his endangering himself by entering a burning building any more than I liked the idea of being trapped inside one. In a dark blue suit, white shirt, and fire-engine red tie, he was every bit as handsome as he was when he showed up in Deputy Donut wearing his fire department navy blue pants and shirt.

Was he at the reception with a date, and if so, who was she?

I had designs on Scott.

Not for myself. I liked him a lot, but I wasn't interested in dating and didn't know if I ever would be. Scott was perfect for one of my best friends, Misty, an officer with the Fallingbrook Police Department, and not only because they were both tall and blond like their Scandinavian ancestors. They were also smart, funny, and kind. As far as I was concerned, they belonged together. I was almost certain that Misty was on duty that night, though. Who was Scott's date?

Questioning him about it might give him the impression that I was interested in him for myself. Instead, I asked, rather inanely, "How do you like the way the exit signs are hidden?"

"I don't."

"I bet you already picked up that mic and made certain that everyone at the reception knows where the exits are."

"I did. Before dinner was served. How did you know?"

I laughed up at him. "I guessed."

"Can you dance, or do you have to work?"

"Jenn said I should join the party beginning at midnight. Sort of like Cinderella, only backward, and no fairy godmother brought me a ball gown."

"How about a coach?"

"It's black and white with a donut on top, and its horses won't turn into mice."

"That is one great coach." And he had one great smile. He asked, "Save me a dance at midnight?"

Behind the donut wall, feet scuffled and someone stage-whispered, "Sh!"

I ducked between the curtains. The three boys in tuxes were slinking away with a bakery box. I'd brought donuts to the reception to be eaten. No one needed to be sneaky about taking some.

Scott had followed me. He loped after the boys. They slowed behind the bar, near the cartons of wine and beer. The boy carrying the donuts turned around, saw Scott behind him, and heaved the box toward him.

As if in slow motion, the box went up in an arc, and the lid started opening, revealing rows of Roger's favorite donuts. I imagined a dozen powdered-sugar-coated donuts flying out and rolling around leaving trails of sugar on the gaudy carpet.

Scott caught the bakery box with both hands, neatly clamping the box closed and saving the donuts.

That must have impressed the boys. They let him walk right up to them. He opened the box. They each took a donut. He watched them until they passed the bar, and then he came back and set the box and the nine donuts left in it on the periwinkle table. "Did you bring a purse tonight?" he asked.

"Only a thinned-out wallet, with my driver's license, credit card, and a couple of small bills."

"Where is it?"

"In my jacket, under the table."

"Is it still there?"

A sleeping security guard out in the hallway was not particularly reassuring. "I . . . hope so."

"Want me to get your jacket for you? Or are food handlers encouraged to crawl around on floors in the middle of their food handling?"

I had to laugh. "We weren't, last I knew." I grabbed the cart's handle. "Here, I'll move this out of the way." I pulled it out into the space between the table and the room's back wall.

He folded that lanky body underneath the table and handed me the jacket.

My wallet was safe. Thanking him, I slipped it into my apron pocket with my phone. "I should have thought of that myself."

He put the jacket where he'd found it, stood, and brushed the knees of his pants. "No problem."

"And thank you for rescuing those donuts from certain death. I owe you a dozen, any kind." Despite being one of our best customers, Scott never seemed to gain an ounce.

He shot me that grin again. "I'll take it in dances after midnight, Cinderella." Giving me a thumbs-up, he went out between the curtains.

Chapter 4

✼

Scott went to the opposite side of the room and sat down. Even standing on tiptoe, I couldn't tell which of the women at his table might be his date.

I parked the cart underneath the table again and then spent the next hour and a half chatting with reception guests and restocking the donut wall. Several guests asked if we could provide donut walls for their events. "We'd love to," I said.

Scott danced with Jenn at least twice. I'd known who Scott was in high school, and Alec had liked and admired him. Scott and I had become friends a little over a year ago, after police officers and firefighters had begun flocking into Deputy Donut for their breaks. So far, my attempts to throw Scott and Misty together had fizzled.

Could Scott be the ex-boyfriend Jenn said she'd invited to the wedding and reception?

At nearly midnight, I was hanging more donuts on the wall. I didn't know that a man had come up behind me until he asked, "What do you recommend?" His deep voice carried without apparent effort.

I turned around.

He was almost as tall as Scott, but not as wiry, and his gray suit looked brand-new and perfectly tailored. As if he'd run out of time to have a haircut before the wedding, his thatch of brown hair drooped over one eye. He brushed it aside. His eyebrows slanted downward toward the outer corners of his eyes, giving him a look of amusement.

Maybe he had a good reason to be amused. I might have been the first person in history to wear a fuzzy donut glued to the front of a police hat at a wedding reception.

"What do you like?" I was becoming hoarse from talking over the band. "Light, eggy crullers or donuts? Raised or unraised? Frosting or confectioners' sugar?" I didn't ask him about sugar pearls versus periwinkle hearts or gold confetti.

His grin broadened, and his warm dark eyes seemed to take in my entire face. "I like it all."

Oh. A flirt.

He held out a hand. "I'm Chad," he said.

I stripped off my plastic gloves and shook his hand. His grip was firm and warm. "I'm Emily." I ducked behind the curtain, added the gloves to the growing collection in the wastebasket, and returned to the front of the table.

Chad was still there. He hadn't taken a donut.

One of the groomsmen ran past, with another one close behind. Both boys had removed their jackets. Their shirts were untucked.

Chad reached out and tapped the second boy on the elbow. "Whoa. Let's slow down before we cause an accident."

The boy stopped and looked down at his feet, and the other boy came back to stand beside him. The boy who had been winning the race asked Chad, "Can you get us some beer from the bar? We forgot our ID."

Chad shook his head. "Afraid not. The bartender will serve you soft drinks, won't he?" Chad was not a bad sort, even if he was a flirt.

The boys tried me. "Can you?"

"No," I said firmly. "Have a donut."

They each grabbed one. One of the boys pointed at the

double doors. "Hey, guys, Dad's already here to drive us home. It must be midnight. Let's go." He turned back to me. "Can I have a donut for my dad, too? And my mom?"

"Sure. Help yourself."

He took two more, and both boys hurried away, not quite running.

I asked Chad, "Why are the groomsmen and the two bridesmaids so young? Are they Jenn and Roger's relatives?"

"Jenn and Roger hired them. The Fallingbrook High soccer teams are raising money for new uniforms and equipment."

I managed not to gape. "Jenn's half-sister is her maid of honor. Is one of those boys Roger's best man?"

"Yep."

"Why didn't he ask a friend? You, for instance."

Chad threw back his head and laughed. "That would be the day."

Chad probably didn't realize that Roger had crept up behind him. Jostling Chad out of his way, Roger shook an index finger toward my nose. "You're supposed to be working for me, not flirting with my guests." He glared at Chad. "My *party crashers,* I should say. What are you doing here? Get out." He tilted slightly, grasped the edge of the table, and regained his balance.

Chad folded his arms and looked down at Roger. "Jenn invited me. If she wants me to leave, she'll tell me."

Roger swore, grabbed a cruller off one of the dowels beneath Jenn's name, crushed it in his fist, and stuffed the entire smashed cruller into his mouth, pushing the last bits in with his fingers while he chewed. Weaving back and forth, he stumbled toward Jenn. Roger-the-Rager was rapidly becoming Roger-the-Tipsy.

"Dance?" Chad asked me.

I checked my phone. It was one minute after midnight. "Sure. Just a second." I dodged between the curtains, took off my hat, and set it down with its fuzzy donut facing the

back wall. Two unopened bakery boxes were on the table behind the donut wall. If anyone wanted more deep-fried goodies, they might find them there.

I attempted to fluff my flattened curls with my fingers. My
phone and wallet were in my apron pockets and wouldn't fit
in my jeans pockets, so I left my apron on and pushed my
way through the curtains.

The two bridesmaids and the three boys, wearing their
tuxedo jackets rather haphazardly, followed the chauffeuring
father out between the open double doors leading to the
lobby. One of the boys held his forefingers, each of them inserted into a donut, straight up. I expected him to start the
donuts spinning.

With a theatrical bow, Chad offered me his arm. His aftershave was spicy, like cinnamon, and I thought I detected the
fragrance of the roses in Jenn's bouquet. He must have danced
with her. I couldn't help pulling at his arm until he leaned
down toward me and I could say, close to his ear, "Jenn had
doubts about this."

One of the slanted eyebrows went up. "About what?"

"Marrying him."

He patted my hand. "She knows what she's doing."

"She should have married you!"

He swung me onto the dance floor. "But then, I might not
have met *you*." The music was slow and romantic.

I grinned up at him in a way that I hoped showed I wasn't
taking him seriously.

He smiled, but a bleak shadow passed through his eyes, so
quickly that I wasn't certain I'd seen it.

I told him, "You could win her back."

He pulled me closer. "Maybe I don't want to. She and I are
friends. Good friends. Are you always such a matchmaker?"

"I . . ." Was I? "I guess so."

"Always looking out for others, and not yourself?"

"Always looking out for myself."

"Are you dating anyone?"

This guy moved quickly, and I wasn't talking about dancing. "No, and I'm not trying to." Planning one of Brent's and my pizza and beer dinners the next night didn't count. I asked Chad, "Do you know who Alec Westhill was?"

Lips thinning as if he guessed what was coming next, he nodded.

"He was my husband."

Chad didn't say anything for a few beats. With a sigh, he tightened his arm around me. "I'm sorry, Emily. That was a senseless tragedy, and Detective Westhill was a great loss to the entire community. I know, kind of, how you feel. Before I dated Jenn, my girlfriend died in a collision with a drunk driver."

"I'm sorry. Did Jenn feel like she never quite measured up?" Ordinarily, I wouldn't ask a stranger a personal question, but maybe I was vulnerable after working alone all evening, being at the reception but not actually part of it, or maybe his flirting and his own sad history were encouraging me to take chances.

He looked down at me, and I saw compassion in those brown eyes. "Could anyone ever live up to Alec Westhill?"

"I really don't know. But I don't think we can compare people that way. We have different reasons for how we feel about different people. Jenn isn't the girlfriend who died, but—"

"She's Jenn, and loveable in her own way."

Suddenly uneasy, as if I'd confided all of my secrets to a stranger, I clammed up.

Both Chad and I were probably relieved when Scott tapped Chad's shoulder. "Sorry," Scott said, "but this lady is promised to me for the next four dozen dances."

Letting me go, Chad promised to see me sometime at Deputy Donut. "Lady in Red" ended.

Standing face-to-face with Scott, I smiled up at him. "Four dozen dances?"

"Or more. You said you owed me a dozen donuts. Each donut must be worth at least four dances."

"*What?* It's after midnight. There won't *be* forty-eight more dances."

But the music started again, fast, this time. Chad and I had been mismatched in height, and Scott was even taller. But he was a good dancer, and he kept me laughing so much that my cheeks hurt.

When that dance was ending, Chad went out through the double doorway leading to the lobby. Had Roger-the-Rager forced Jenn to send Chad away?

Another fast dance started. Suzanne helped Jenn and her froth of white frills leave the banquet hall.

I caught a glimpse of Roger plucking a cruller from the donut wall. Not wanting him to catch me watching him and maybe tell me, when Jenn wasn't in the room, that I was supposed to be working, I looked away and threw myself into frenzied dancing. Six fast dances later, I started wondering if I would last through even *one* dozen dances.

The band let us catch our breath with—of all things— "Harbor Lights." I told Scott about playing a 1950 sound-track on the way to the lodge, and getting "The Tennessee Waltz" stuck in my head. He laughed down at me and pulled me closer. He knew my story, and that I wasn't ready to start dating. He didn't officially know about my plans for him and Misty, but I'd probably been obvious at times, and he could have figured them out.

Suddenly he stopped dancing. Concern on his face, he stared at something behind me. He said, "Sorry," and then dashed toward the donut wall.

I turned around. The small vase on the donut wall's frame had fallen on its side, spilling water and flowers on the donuts below it.

That little accident couldn't have caused Scott's abrupt departure.

People standing near the donut wall were looking down toward the floor and covering their mouths with their hands. Above the pounding music, someone yelled, "Help!"

I ran to the donut wall.

A man was curled on the red, purple, and beige carpeting. His head and shoulders were underneath the table and hidden by the periwinkle tablecloth, but I recognized the black tux, and earlier in the evening, before the reception started, I'd heard the hard leather soles of those shiny black shoes smack the dance floor when he walked.

Chapter 5

※

Roger wasn't walking now.

Scott was beside the donut wall, in front of the spot where the edges of two curtains met. Crouching, Scott lifted the lower edge of the tablecloth. One of Roger's shoulders was on the taped line on the carpet.

Scott pushed the tablecloth behind Roger's head. Roger's eyes were closed and his thick eyebrows were dark against his too-pale forehead. Scott positioned his fingers on Roger's wrist.

I eased around the crowd to stand next to the curtains, right behind Scott. Around us, wedding guests murmured about people who drank too much, especially at their own receptions. Scott pulled his phone from a pocket and dialed 911. Although I hadn't smelled garlic around Scott or Roger before, I was catching whiffs of it now. Scott said into his phone, "Send an ambulance to Little Lake Lodge. A man in the banquet room is unconscious and breathing more slowly than he should be. . . . Yes, I'll stay on the phone." Using his shoulder to hold the phone against his ear, Scott quickly undid Roger's bowtie, removed the studs from the top of his shirt, and loosened his waistband.

I placed my hand on Scott's shoulder. He looked up into my face and gave me a grim nod as if thanking me for being there.

As far as I could tell, Jenn had not yet returned to the banquet hall. Oblivious to the mini-drama going on near the donut wall, many guests were on the dance floor, still dreamily dancing to "Harbor Lights."

It was possible that Roger hadn't collapsed from drinking. Could someone have knocked him out?

Remembering Tom's comment about people hiding in that vast room, I edged between the curtains to the narrow, dim space near the log walls.

It was bright enough for me to be certain that no one was near our donut wall. Our stainless-steel cart was still underneath the table, too far from the tablecloth bulging behind Roger's head for Roger to have hit his head on the cart as he fell, although he could have crashed into the table.

When I'd put my hat down on the table before dancing with Chad, the two boxes of donuts near it had been closed. Since then, one of them had been opened. The flaps were no longer inserted in the front and sides of the box.

Also, my hat had moved. I was sure I'd set it down with the donut facing the back wall. Now the donut was facing the bar.

A gust of air came from the corridor. Surprised, I glanced toward the room's back door.

It was standing open.

It had been closed when I went off to dance with Chad. Had someone clobbered Roger and then fled?

That corridor and the rooms off it had to be checked, and not by allowing hordes of wedding guests to race around covering the tracks of anyone who might have rushed out of the banquet hall. Because lights were brighter in the banquet hall, I could just barely make out the people nearest the draperies. Scott was still sitting on the floor. No one out there would be able to see me in the gloomy space near the room's back door.

Careful not to touch that door, I slipped into the corridor. The security guard's chair was beside the delivery entrance, but the man, his newspaper, and his briefcase were gone.

I tiptoed down the hallway in the other direction, toward the lobby.

A round window near the top of the last door on the left was partially steamed up. Another time, I'd have liked a tour of the kitchen, but I ran past, opened the door at the lobby end of the hallway, and peeked out. In the well-lit and noisy lobby, people I'd seen enjoying donuts and crullers were heading to and from restrooms and greeting one another with the slightly brittle cheer that went with the wrapping up of a wedding reception, when everyone's tired, folks are saying goodbye to nearly forgotten cousins, and a few people are beginning to regret some of the ways they partied.

Feeling conspicuous in my logo-trimmed white apron, I backed into the service corridor, let the door close behind me, and trotted down the hall, past the kitchen and the back door of the banquet hall.

The door labeled CALL OF THE LOON was unlocked. The room was dark and quiet, with rows of tables lined up and chairs pushed neatly underneath them. Below a red exit sign on the room's opposite wall, double doors leading to the public hallway to the lobby were closed. I heard nothing besides clanks from the kitchen and the music, fast and loud, from Roger and Jenn's reception.

Much earlier, applause had come from the room labeled RUFFED GROUSE. That door was also unlocked. Inside, tables and chairs were knocked every which way and a wastebasket near the door was overflowing with packaging materials, as if someone had been rehearsing for Christmas two and a half months early. The room smelled strongly of the fragrance that the two Happy Hopers had been wearing. Beyond a podium on a low stage, a banner read: *Happy Hopers Conference—Goal Achievement Through Shopping!*

Again, I pictured my eight-year-old self in Williamsburg, and the name of that particular fragrance came back to me.

At least one of those women with a tote bag from this conference must have been wearing a perfume resembling the potpourri I'd smelled in that store in Williamsburg.

What had become of the two women during the more than two hours since I'd encountered them? The room's front door, the one leading to the public hallway, was closed.

I shut the room's back door and tiptoed as quickly as I could down the hallway to the delivery entrance. The security guard had not returned.

Cautiously, I opened the delivery door, gripped its edge tightly, and leaned out. No one was on the concrete walkway or the gravel lane leading to the staff parking lot on the hill. No headlights moved between trees surrounding that secluded lot, and I heard no engines up there. To my right, Little Lake was calm and nearly silent. To my left, the main driveway was empty of vehicles. A whiff of exhaust fumes hung in the air.

If an ambulance was racing toward us with sirens blaring, the sound was blocked by hills between here and Fallingbrook.

I didn't realize I'd been holding my breath until I exhaled, creating a small cloud of fog. Shivering, not only because of the nearly freezing temperature, I let the door close and ran up the corridor toward the banquet hall. Again not touching the door marked WILD GOOSE, I eased into the space between the curtains and the banquet hall's log wall.

I stared at my Deputy Donut hat. Why had it moved?

Biting my lip, I grasped the fuzzy donut between my thumb and forefinger and slowly raised the brim of the hat off the periwinkle-painted table.

Someone had left an ironstone saucer underneath my hat. The saucer was off-white with the Little Lake Lodge logo—three dark green pines, small, smaller, smallest—printed on the edge.

White powder resembling confectioners' sugar covered the

middle of the saucer. A donut-sized circle dented the layer of sugar, and there were ridges in the dent.

It was exactly how confectioners' sugar would look after someone dipped a cruller in it.

I would have coated a cruller that way if I didn't have a sieve.

That night, I had not decorated any crullers with plain confectioners' sugar.

And, except for the sugar already coating Roger's favorite raised donuts, I had not brought confectioners' sugar to Little Lake Lodge.

Chapter 6

There was absolutely no reason for anyone to have left confectioners' sugar on that table, and even less of a reason to hide a saucer of it underneath my hat.

Afraid that the white powder wasn't sugar, I wanted to scream and let go of my hat, but screaming wouldn't have accomplished a thing, and dropping my hat might have disturbed the powder and sent a possibly dangerous substance into the air we were all breathing.

Careful not to inhale, I lowered the hat to cover the saucer. Cautiously, I lifted the lid of the bakery box that had obviously been opened. We had packed a dozen donuts or crullers in each box. This box now held seven crullers.

I peeked out between the curtains. People were still standing around Roger and Scott, staring down at them and offering Scott suggestions. If Roger had moved, he had only tightened his fetal position. Scott was now sitting on the carpet, his long legs crossed and one hand clasping Roger's wrist.

No one was eating a donut or a cruller. I'd seen Roger taking a cruller after I left my post at the donut wall. . . .

Brent had said he'd be on duty. I positioned myself between the curtains so I could watch both the front of the table supporting the donut wall and the back of the table where my cap was concealing the saucer of white powder.

I'd known the number of the police station ever since I started dating Alec, years ago. But Brent's personal number was on my speed dial, and by calling him directly I would avoid having to wait for a police department operator to connect us.

Brent answered right away. "Em? It's late. Is everything okay?"

I took a deep and wavering breath. "No. I'm still at the wedding reception. It's at Little Lake Lodge. The groom, Roger Banchen, collapsed. Scott Ritsorf called an ambulance, but I think this might be a police matter also." In a voice barely above a whisper, I told Brent about the white powder.

"Did you touch the white powder?" Brent's voice was unusually sharp.

"No."

"Taste it?"

"No."

"Sniff or inhale any of it?"

"No."

"Eat donuts or crullers?"

"No."

"Did any of the white powder transfer to your skin or clothing?"

"I don't think so."

He let out a long breath. "When did Banchen collapse?"

"About ten minutes ago, around twelve thirty."

"Is anyone else showing signs of illness?"

"Not that I can tell, but some guests have left the reception and might get sick on their way home. I'm staying near the powder to make certain that no one goes near it."

"Emily, get away from that powder."

"I covered it with my hat again. Carefully, so that none of it blew around. And it could actually be sugar, and Roger could have passed out from drinking too much. He was pretty sloshed at midnight."

"I . . . listen, Em, get everyone out of that room. Scott can quickly authorize evacuating the entire lodge, hotel rooms and all, and turning off the ventilation system, so tell him to do that. If you can corral the wedding guests in one spot outside, please do, but the important thing is to make certain that everyone, including you and Scott, goes outside. Have you told anyone besides me about that white powder?"

"No."

"Good. Tell Scott, but no one else. Okay?"

"Okay."

"And don't take chances."

I repeated, "It could actually be sugar."

"Assume it's not, and stay away from it. I'll be there in a few minutes." He disconnected.

People around Scott were still chattering, and Scott was on the phone with the 911 dispatcher. Not knowing if Scott had heard anything from my end of the conversation with Brent, I bent over and whispered into his free ear. I told him what I'd found and gave him Brent's instructions. I added, "And no one should leave this room by the back door. It's too close to the white powder."

With quick grace, Scott stood up. I held out my hand for his phone. He relinquished it and strode across the room to where the band was playing.

Brent had told me to leave, but with 911 on the phone, I needed to stay near Roger. I also had to keep an eye on my hat and the saucer of white powder underneath it, and on the front of the donut wall to prevent people from helping themselves to possibly contaminated donuts and crullers. The only place where I could monitor all three areas was the gap between the white drapes next to the donut wall, so I stayed where I was, trying not to shiver in the draft eddying in from the service corridor. The sides of the drapes tapped at my sleeves.

Except for random twitches, Roger wasn't moving.

Scott talked to the bandleader for a few seconds. The leader brought "The Way You Look Tonight" to an early close, and

Scott took over the microphone. "We've been asked to evac-
uate the hotel. There's no need to panic. Please leave by the
front doors, and stay together in the south end of the front
parking lot. That will be to your right as you exit the lodge's
main doors." He pointed toward me. "Emily and I will join
you there."

I waved my free hand high in the air, but I wasn't certain
that anyone was watching me. People were gathering belong-
ings or looking at Scott, and some were already leaving. No
one came toward me or the room's back door.

Scott added, "If anyone feels ill, please tell Emily or me, or
call 911, or go straight to Emergency." That speech came
close to negating his earlier instructions about not panicking,
but, with a few exceptions, everyone was filing out in a semi-
orderly way. Scott handed the mic to the bandleader and then
strode toward the lobby.

The bandleader returned the microphone to its stand.
Cradling instruments in their arms, band members followed
wedding guests into the hallway.

The fans in the ceiling juddered to a halt, the drapes stopped
their constant tip-tapping at me, and the hotel's PA system
blatted out a series of squawks loud enough to awaken the
lodge's heaviest sleepers. A woman's voice announced that
everyone should leave the building and assemble in the front
parking lot to await instructions.

The 911 dispatcher must have overheard some of the
racket. She asked how the patient was.

"Unchanged." *And he doesn't seem aware of the clamor
surrounding him. . . .*

Scott returned to the nearly empty banquet hall and removed his phone from my stiff fingers. "You're supposed to
leave, Emily."

"You are, too." Ordinarily, both of us would stay with a
stricken person, but rules and common sense dictated that
we leave a situation where our own health and lives could be
in danger.

"The ambulance is almost here. I'll stay with him. You go outside and try to keep wedding guests together."

"I . . . you . . ." I folded my arms. "If it's not too dangerous for you to stay, I'll stay, too."

"I'm fire chief and I'm ordering you to leave." There wasn't even a hint of a smile on his face.

I frowned back at him. "I'll get revenge someday, Scott."

In the distance, sirens wailed.

"Go," Scott insisted. "Until I join you outside, it will be up to you to keep an eye on everyone out there and call Emergency if anyone else seems ill. Do you have a phone?"

I nodded, but my frown turned into a glower. Scott knew exactly how to make me leave him alone with a sick patient and a saucer full of potential danger. "Don't take chances," I told Scott.

"I'm not." Now that the ventilation system had been turned off and everyone else had left the room, Scott was able to speak softly.

My jacket was underneath the table, but if that white powder was dangerous, my jacket could have been contaminated. I left it behind, crossed the room, and went out between the wide-open double doors. In the brightly lit lobby, the red, purple, and beige swirls in the carpet seemed to leap up and smack me in the eyes.

Not surprisingly, the temperature outside was still barely above freezing. At the nearest edge of the parking lot, hotel guests were standing around in nighties and pj's covered in bathrobes, coats, and blankets. Some were barefoot. I was wearing jeans, a long-sleeved shirt, an apron, and shoes, and I was shivering.

Corralling wedding guests or even keeping an eye on them was going to be impossible. Most of them had gotten into cars and were driving away, a steady stream of vehicles inching up the hill toward the road. I stayed near the main doors so I could direct the Emergency Medical Technicians to the banquet hall where Scott waited with Roger.

Fortunately, the lodge's driveway was wide enough for the ambulance to speed in past departing cars. Lights flashing and siren howling, the ambulance stopped in front of the lodge's main entrance. The lights continued strobing and the engine continued running, but the sudden silence of the siren pulsed against my ears.

Wearing a reflective parka and a black EMT stocking cap that covered most of her pink-streaked dark brown curls, my friend Samantha climbed down from the driver's seat. I ran to her. She was taller than I was, mostly because of her thick-soled boots. "You'll need hazmat gear," I told her.

"Brent radioed us about a mysterious white powder that might be poison." She quickly assessed my face in the on-again-off-again lighting. "And he said to take you to the hospital if you showed any signs of illness."

"I'm fine. But Scott stayed in there with the patient."

She looked worried. "He's not supposed to."

"I know. He wouldn't listen. He seemed okay a few minutes ago."

"We'll look after him. When you get home, change your clothes and take a shower, just in case. Where's the patient?"

I pointed. "In the Wild Goose Banquet Hall. Go in through these doors, turn left, then take the first right."

Samantha and her partner, a strong-looking guy possibly ten years younger than Samantha and I were, quickly covered their black uniforms with hazmat suits and removed a wheeled stretcher covered with cases of lifesaving equipment from the ambulance. Running, Samantha and her partner wheeled the stretcher into the lodge.

Only seconds later, Scott joined me. He wasn't wearing a coat over his tailored blue suit. "How are you?" he asked.

"Physically fine, but stressed. You?"

"I'm not sick or anything." He paused, then added, "I'm used to this kind of thing."

A woman's voice behind us quavered, "What's going on? Is someone hurt?"

I turned around. A ghostly cloud of white cloth floated toward us. Jenn. She must have come from the south end of the building, where the delivery entrance was, and although my shivering was becoming more violent, she didn't look cold in her strapless wedding gown, maybe because of the yards of fabric in the skirt. Although she wasn't carrying her bouquet, the smell of roses surrounded her.

I put a hand on her surprisingly warm arm and said, as gently as I could, "Roger fainted."

"Where is he?"

"Inside. They'll look after him and bring him out."

"Is he okay?" Her voice was shrill and her face looked pinched.

Scott and I took too long to answer, which she probably interpreted correctly. *He doesn't look good.*

Her eyes rolled back in her head and her neck listed to one side. Like a marionette whose handler had dropped the strings, she sagged toward the ground.

Chapter 7

Grasping Jenn's arms, Scott and I eased her and her trailing veil and froth of fabric onto the pavement.

Scott felt Jenn's wrist. "Her pulse is strong." Strobing lights from the ambulance colored and recolored the planes of his face.

The ambulance's engine rumbled. Exhaust curled from the tailpipe. Scott had to be making more sense of the garbled strings of words blatting from the radio than I was.

Colder and colder, I could no longer control my shivering.

Scott gave me an assessing look and then jumped to his feet. "Stay with her." He ran to the back of the ambulance, returned with three folded white blankets, and handed me one. "Wrap it around yourself."

I did, and it helped, although cold air crept in between the blanket's loosely woven fibers.

Scott slid one blanket, still folded, underneath Jenn's head and spread the other over her. With one hand, I held the edges of my blanket together at my throat. With the other, I helped Scott tuck Jenn's blanket around her shoulders.

"What about you?" I asked him.

"I'm dressed warmly enough."

Right, in a suit with no coat over it. *Men.*

High heels hammered across the pavement from the direction of the lodge's main entrance, and then Suzanne towered over us. The ambulance lights turned her slinky periwinkle gown first dull gray and then blinding white. Her cheek and collarbones cast purplish shadows on her skin. She demanded, "What did you two do to my sister? I was in the ladies' room and couldn't come out when they told us to, and now look what's happened!"

"She's okay." Scott was apparently accustomed to speaking in reassuring tones. "I think she only fainted. She's coming around."

"Then why is an ambulance here?" Suzanne's voice was about an octave higher than it had been the few times I'd heard her speak, and her eyes were showing a lot of white, but she didn't seem about to topple over.

Remembering my 911 training, I tried to sound as reassuring as Scott had. "It's for Roger. He collapsed."

"I told Jenn he was getting drunk and she should make him stop." Suzanne did not sound any fonder of her new brother-in-law than she had before he became her brother-in-law.

I asked, "Are you okay, Suzanne?"

"Why wouldn't I be?"

I pointed out, "You must have spent a long time in the ladies'—"

Jenn struggled to sit up. "Whuh?"

Suzanne bent over her. "You're okay, Jennifer. You just fainted. I told you that bodice was too tight." She brushed Jenn's veil and hair back and helped her sit. I was ready to prop Jenn's shoulders, and I could see Scott trying to figure out where he dared place his hands on a woman displaying so much flesh, but Jenn seemed to be holding herself up and didn't need Scott's and my assistance.

Samantha and her partner, still in their white hazmat suits, wheeled the stretcher outside with Roger strapped to it, white blanket and all. Roger's face looked almost as gray as Suzanne's dress appeared.

Jenn shouted, "Roger!"

No one answered.

Samantha and her partner loaded the stretcher into the ambulance and then stripped off their hazmat suits and stuffed
them into plastic bags. Samantha's partner clambered into the
back of the ambulance. Samantha ran to us.

I told her, "This is the bride."

Samantha turned those dark, often humor-filled eyes on
me. "I figured." Having known each other since junior high,
Samantha and I were used to each other's sarcasm.

"I mean, she's married to the man you just put into the
ambulance. He's the groom."

"I get that, too. Are you sure you're okay, Emily?"

"I'm sure."

Scott looked skeptical.

"I *am*," I told him, jutting my chin out and looking up into
his face.

Samantha turned to Jenn. "Do you feel strong enough to
stand if we help you?"

Jenn nodded.

Samantha touched Jenn's wrist. "You can ride in back with
your husband. My partner will keep track of both of you." I
wasn't familiar with the voice Samantha used while working.
She truly was as kind as she sounded, but the laughter that
usually spilled through her sentences was absent.

"I'm her sister," Suzanne stated. "I'm coming, too."

Samantha's attention snapped to her. "Are *you* okay?"

"Of course. I didn't drink anything besides sips of champagne for the toasts, hours ago, and *my* clothes are not too
tight."

Under Samantha's direction, Scott, Suzanne, and I helped
Jenn to her feet and into the back of the ambulance. Samantha's partner was hanging an IV bag on a hook above Roger.
Samantha pushed at the yards of ruffles in Jenn's skirt and
closed the back door of the ambulance.

She handed Suzanne the folded blanket that Scott had
placed under Jenn's head. "Wrap yourself in that and ride in
front with me." A furrow between her eyebrows, Samantha

told Scott and me, "You two, look after each other, and call if you need us again."

In seconds, Samantha and her entourage were gone. The ambulance had been at Little Lake Lodge for about five minutes.

Its siren masked the siren of an arriving police car until the police car was near us. Instead of the unmarked car he usually drove, Brent had commandeered a cruiser. He must have driven it at speeds rivaling Tom's.

Brent shut off the siren and strobes and leaped out of the driver's seat. He was a big man, about six feet tall and muscular. He didn't shut the cruiser door, and he wasn't wearing a coat over his charcoal gray suit. His unbuttoned jacket and dark striped tie flapping, he sprinted to Scott and me. "Are you two okay?"

We both nodded, but another approaching siren prevented our replies from being audible.

Misty was at the wheel of the cruiser. A patrolman I'd never seen before rode shotgun.

As Brent had, Misty and her partner jumped out without closing their doors. The two patrol cops were dressed for the weather, with Fallingbrook Police Department parkas over their uniforms. Unlike Samantha, they wore billed caps similar to the Deputy Donut cap I'd left on the table behind the donut wall, but their hats sported proper badges instead of fuzzy donuts. Misty's blond hair was tied back in a low ponytail. She and her partner clomped to us in their substantial police-issue boots.

Misty asked Scott and me if we were okay, and we again said we were. Brent told Misty to talk to the wedding guests who had not yet driven away and then to get Scott's statement.

I controlled a smug grin. For once, I didn't have to be the one to throw Misty and Scott together.

Brent said he'd take my statement.

Turning away from Brent, Misty aimed an almost-smug grin at me.

Ha, I thought. Misty could do all the matchmaking she wanted, but it wasn't going to work. She knew perfectly well that I was not interested in dating and might never be. She told Scott to stay with her and point out reception guests.

Misty was almost as tall as Brent, and Scott was even taller. Lips twitching as if he was trying not to smile, Scott gazed down at Misty's upturned face. "I'm fine, you know."

"Stay that way," she answered, all business. "Let's go." They strode off together toward a cluster of formally dressed and anxious-faced people.

Brent told Misty's partner to tape off the lodge's entrances and then write down the license numbers of the cars in the parking lot. Misty's partner nodded and opened the trunk of his and Misty's cruiser.

Brent turned to me. "I don't see your donut car, Em. How did you get here?"

I pointed. "I parked my *cruiser* in the staff parking lot."

He stared toward the tree-rimmed rise. "Another parking lot? You can show it to me after I get your statement."

"Do you want to see where Roger was? And my hat?"

"Hazmat investigators in protective gear will do that. They'll photograph that saucer from all angles under different lights, so we'll probably get a good impression, no pun intended, of what you saw. Meanwhile, the EMTs should have taken a sample of the powder with them. It'll be analyzed in the lab at the hospital." He took out his notebook and pen. "Did you notice anyone near your donut wall around the time that the saucer appeared underneath your hat?"

Absentmindedly, I watched Misty's partner string tape around the peeled tree trunks holding up the roof over the lodge's main entryway. "Roger's the only one I specifically noticed, twenty minutes or so before he fell."

"Eating anything?"

"I saw him take a cruller, but I don't know if he ate it. He'd been drinking. He was belligerent right before midnight while I was talking to Jenn's—that's the bride—while I was talking to her ex-boyfriend, Chad. Roger told Chad to leave. Chad didn't, not right away. I danced with Chad a couple of times, and then Scott cut in, and Chad left the banquet hall. I never saw Chad come back, and he wasn't among the guests milling around the parking lot after the hotel was evacuated. He seemed nice, but . . ."

"Did you get Chad's last name?"

"No, sorry. Jenn and her half-sister, Suzanne, left the reception about the time Chad did. Unlike Chad, those two did come back, but by the time Jenn returned, it must have been about twenty-five minutes after Roger fell, and several minutes after everyone in the lodge was told to go outside. The ambulance was already here. Suzanne showed up shortly after Jenn did. They both came from, I think, inside." Pointing at Misty's partner, the roll of tape over one arm, heading toward the south end of the building, I added, "Jenn came from that direction, and although her gown was strapless, her skin was warm when I touched her arm, so I think she'd been inside only moments before. She could have come from the delivery entrance. Suzanne showed up a couple of minutes after Jenn did, shortly before you arrived." I pointed at the lodge's front doors. "Suzanne came from those doors. They lead to the lobby. She said she would have come outside sooner, except she was in the ladies' room."

Brent apparently thought the same thing I had. "Sick?" he asked.

"She said she wasn't. But she also said she was in the ladies' room when the evacuation announcement was made, which means she was in the ladies' room for around ten minutes. But it could have been more. She and Jenn left the reception about ten minutes after midnight and came back shortly after the ambulance arrived, around ten to one."

Brent looked up from writing in his notebook. "Were the bride and her sister carrying anything?"

"Not when they came back. When they left, it looked like they needed all four of their hands to tame the wedding gown and force it through the doorway leading out of the banquet hall."

"What about the ex-boyfriend?"

"I didn't notice him carrying anything. But maybe there's a coat check? Chad could have gotten something from his coat or his car, and returned inside through the delivery entrance."

"Did you see other people leave the reception around the time you put your hat on the table behind your donut wall?"

I tightened my grip on the blanket. "People were coming and going all the time. I didn't know anyone at the reception besides Scott and Jenn. I'd seen Suzanne once before, very briefly, last night, I mean Friday evening, when she was coming out of the clothing shop that she and Jenn own across the alley from Deputy Donut. I didn't notice who all had left and who was still at the reception at midnight."

Brent's gaze swept the main parking lot. "I don't see anyone dressed like a bride."

"She and Suzanne left in the ambulance. Suzanne was okay, but Jenn fainted when I told her that Roger had collapsed."

"How long was Jenn passed out?"

"About a minute."

"And you're sure you're okay?" Brent had a super-stern expression that he probably reserved for interrogating desperate criminals. Now he was using it on me.

"I'm fine." Wondering how Scott was, I glanced toward where I'd last seen him. He was standing with other reception guests, and he looked both relaxed and alert. Misty was a little distance away from him, interviewing another man.

"Tell me right away if you start feeling ill, Em," Brent demanded.

"Okay."

"Can you show me how to get to the delivery entrance you mentioned without going inside?"

"Sure." We walked toward the south end of the lodge.

"Are you warm enough?"

I tried to hide my trembling. "Yes." Technically, it wasn't a lie. I was warm *enough*. Warm enough not to freeze, anyway.

Chapter 8

Misty's partner had already strung police tape across the delivery entrance, but he was gone, probably taping off entrances along the section of the lodge facing Little Lake.

Standing behind the police tape, I told Brent, "This door was unlocked during the early part of the evening, until ten, anyway. A security guard was posted on a chair just inside it, but after Roger's collapse, when I noticed that the banquet hall's back door had been left open, the security guard was gone. I was able to open the door from the inside without unlocking it."

"I should hope so, for fire safety. Tell me about the security guard."

Brent positioned himself underneath the light above the door and wrote in his notebook while I described the security guard, complete with briefcase and broken and retied shoelace.

"A security guard with a briefcase." Brent said it with almost no inflection, but knowing him, he was pointing out that it might be unusual for security guards to carry briefcases while on duty.

"I saw him take a newspaper out of it. The other times I passed him, he was either reading the paper, nodding off over it, or possibly sound asleep. Shortly before ten, he told a couple of women that they shouldn't go to their conference through this door. He told them to go through the lobby, but they didn't, at least not right away. They were still here a few minutes later when I was coming down the hill from the staff parking lot. One of the two women pointed at me, and then both of them hurried off in the direction the security guard had told them to go. At least one of the two women was wearing a scent like potpourri—"

"Like what?"

I spelled it for him. "It's made of dried plant material, like flower petals. It was used as a fragrance and as an air freshener in colonial days, and people still make it. What these women were wearing was extra-strong and smelled like it was composed of dried roses and lavender, some citrus, and spices like cinnamon and cloves. Other scents, too, that I couldn't quite place and probably don't remember."

"Were those women among the people in the parking lot when I arrived?"

"No, and while I was looking in the corridor for the person who had left the banquet hall's back door open, I peeked into the two meeting rooms across from the banquet hall. One room was empty and clean, but a banner with the name of their conference on it was in the other one. No one was in that room, but the smell of potpourri was almost overwhelming."

"Did the area around your donut wall, where you saw the white powder, smell like potpourri?"

"I didn't notice it. There were flowers on the donut wall, but none of them had noticeable fragrances. Also, the banquet hall is much larger than the room that smelled of potpourri. The banquet hall's front double doors had been open from at least ten, and its back door must have been open for a few minutes, so the banquet hall could have aired out. Both of the doors to the meeting room were closed, though. The potpourri aroma could have lingered in that room after someone wearing it left." I told him about the two Happy Hopers and the wording on their totes.

" 'Goal Accomplishment Through *Shopping*'?"

"Yep."

He made one of his noncommittal comments. "Mmp. So . . . the security guard had a briefcase, and each of the two women had totes. How big were the totes?"

"Big enough to conceal a package containing a half cup or so of the mystery powder that I hope turns out to be sugar."

"That's how much powder you saw?"

"I didn't measure it—"

"I hope not!"

"But I'm guessing it was about a half cup."

He said dryly, "I suspect that your guesses about volumes of powders resembling baking ingredients are probably closer than most people's. Did you see anyone else besides the security guard and those two women in the service corridor or near this door?"

"No, but when Tom and I brought the donut wall around six this, I mean *last* evening, Saturday, people were clapping in the room that now smells of potpourri. And every time I was in the service corridor, I heard pots and pans being banged around in the kitchen. There's only one door from the banquet hall to the service corridor, and it's near our donut wall." I described the banquet hall and the drapes that formed a sort of tent inside it. "Tom and I set up the donut wall and were about to go back to Deputy Donut to make the donuts when the wedding party came in for a photography session. Roger was talking—if you can call it that—to us when the banquet hall's back door opened and then slammed shut." Tilting my head back, I looked into Brent's eyes. I knew they were gray, but they looked dark in the dim light. "The lodge has a strange, space-wasting layout, with three hallways paralleling each other down most of the length of the building. The meeting rooms and banquet hall all have front entrances into the outer hallways and back entrances into the middle hallway." I pointed. "That's the one just beyond this door. The draft that opened and slammed the banquet hall's back door could have come from here, from the door near the lobby, from a meeting room, or from the kitchen. The two meeting rooms and the kitchen are across the service corridor from the banquet hall."

Brent looked up toward the star-filled sky. "You're telling me that there are many ways that someone could leave a meeting room or the kitchen and disappear into another room or hallway?"

"And from there, outside. Plus, as Tom prophetically pointed out, anyone could hide behind those drapes hanging around the inside of the banquet hall."

Brent returned his gaze to me. "Did anyone?"

"The three groomsmen. They raced around behind the curtains for, I think, the fun of it. Jenn's sister was the maid of honor, but the groomsmen and the two bridesmaids were high school kids. They participated in the wedding as a fundraiser for Fallingbrook High's soccer teams."

Brent ran his hand through his thick light brown hair. "That's creative."

"One of the boys' fathers took all five of the kids away shortly before midnight, before I set my hat on the table. Unless the kids came around the lodge and snuck in through this door, I'm almost positive that they did not leave that saucer of powder on the table behind the donut wall."

"Did you see the vehicles that the security guard with the briefcase and the two women with the totes were driving?"

"No." I turned and pointed up the hill. "When I was coming back from parking in the staff lot, the two women walked down the hill behind me. If they parked there, it was odd. According to Jenn, lodge and conference guests were supposed to park in the lot in front."

"Let's have a look at the staff lot."

Using our phones' lights, we walked up the stony lane. At the top of the rise, we passed the straggly line of pines.

Brent deadpanned, "I can't see *your* car in all of this."

Although the Deputy Donut car's gleaming white-frosted donut was mounted flat on the roof, it stuck up above other cars and was about the most obvious object in the dark parking lot. I moaned, "If only I had a remote for the lights in the donut, then we'd find my *cruiser*."

He laughed.

We examined every single vehicle. Brent made a note of each license plate, including the Fordor's, and shined his light inside all of them. No one was in any of them, although the windows of a black sports car were fogged up. Whoever had been in the car had left, however. I hovered my hand above the hood. It wasn't warm.

Brent's phone rang. He answered it. "Okay. . . . Yes. I see. . . . Okay." He disconnected, turned to me, and took a deep breath. "The lab at the hospital has confirmed your guess. That white powder was poison."

I pulled the blanket up around my ears so I could clutch at the sides of my head. "No. . . ."

"The preliminary findings are that it was the tasteless form of arsenic known as 'white arsenic.' "

"How is Roger? And Jenn and Suzanne?"

"Jenn does not appear to have ingested any arsenic, but they'll keep her overnight for observation, and her sister is fine. She can go home. Mr. Banchen, however . . ." He rubbed the toe of a shoe against loose pebbles. "My investigation into a mysterious white powder that might have made someone sick is now an investigation into a suspicious death."

Chapter 9

✻

I gripped the edges of the blanket so tightly around my throat that I nearly choked myself. "The arsenic *killed* Roger?" Above us, the tops of pines sighed in a breeze I couldn't feel.

Brent aimed his phone's flashlight at the ground. "They gave him an antidote, but it was too late. His heart stopped and they couldn't restart it. I'm sorry, Em. Do you know his bride well?"

"Not socially, but I've talked to her a lot in her store." The flashlight in my hand wavered, shining at Brent's knees until I tamed it back toward our feet. "I met Roger for the first time here, when Tom and I dropped off the donut wall. Maybe Roger was under stress, but as far as I could tell, he was rude to everyone. Friday afternoon, Jenn was in tears because her sister told her not to marry him. Jenn said that Suzanne never liked Roger, so I wouldn't be surprised if Roger was boorish before the wedding, too. Suzanne accused Jenn of being a gold digger."

"He was wealthy?" Our lights reflected upward, casting odd shadows on Brent's face that could have made him appear devilish, but all I saw besides his suddenly alert expression was his kindness and concern.

Hoping the lighting didn't make *me* look scary, I said, "According to Jenn, he inherited. I think she said it was from a distant relative."

Brent didn't say anything.

I filled the silence. "I like her. I'm sure she's not a killer. Friday evening, she wasn't even sure she wanted to marry Roger."

Brent stared down at me in the darkness as if willing me to draw my own conclusions.

"Jenn could have simply refused to marry him," I pointed out. "Going through with the wedding and then killing him at the reception makes no sense."

"That depends on how his will was written. And if he didn't have one, his wealth would go to his next of kin."

"A wife, but not a fiancée?"

"Possibly."

"Jenn's a talented knitwear designer." I bent slightly to peer beyond the hem of my apron to my jeans-clad shins and then quickly straightened to look into Brent's eyes again. "Also, Tom and I buy the clothes we wear at work from her." I couldn't help smiling at my lack of logic. "Talent and good taste in clothes—that proves that Jenn can't be a killer, right?"

"Right." He knew I was joking.

I became serious. "Roger's death could have been accidental. Maybe someone mistakenly believed they'd found sugar and decided that Tom's and my crullers needed additional sweetening."

Brent reminded me, "Someone covered the saucer of arsenic with your hat."

I frowned, thinking back to that saucer and my hat. "When I discovered that someone had moved my hat, one of the bakery boxes that had been closed was open. It originally held twelve crullers, but five were missing. I suspect that your investigators are going to discover that someone purposely dipped at least one of those crullers in that powder." Not wanting to believe that anyone could have died from eating Tom's and my crullers or donuts, no matter how the poison had been added, I asked, "Are they sure that it was arsenic that killed Roger? Flowers can be poisonous, too. Maybe some of the purple flowers at the reception were monkshood, and Roger ate some of them."

"Monkshood is bitter. People usually spit it out as soon as they taste it."

"But will the investigators take the bouquets and flowers to check?"

"They'll take everything that might hold a clue."

"Like the leftover donuts, the boxes that I brought them in—most of them are flattened and piled on our stainless-steel cart—and my hat?"

"Yep."

"And the donut wall, and the table it's attached to?"

"Probably."

"And my down-filled jacket, which is on the floor underneath the table?"

"That, too. Sorry."

"It's okay. I don't think Emergency Medical Services is going to come after me for this blanket before I get home. Another thing your investigators should take is the periwinkle step-on wastebasket that I decorated with ribbon and lace. All evening, I was throwing plastic gloves into it. Maybe whoever put arsenic in the saucer threw something into my wastebasket or wore a pair of my gloves. There was a box that still had fresh gloves in it on that table near my hat."

"They'll take the wastebasket and the box of gloves, too."

I nodded toward the Fordor. "I suppose you'll need to check my car for arsenic."

"And your shop. Personally, I don't suspect you and Tom, but . . ."

"I understand." Checking food sources when food was suspected in a poisoning case was normal. "The sooner you clear Tom and me, the better. How do we do this?"

"You'll give me your car keys, and I'll have your car taken on a flatbed to Forensics. We'll seal your shop doors. Investigators will search your shop but not until after the lodge is thoroughly checked."

"Okay." I pulled the Fordor's keys out of my pocket and gave them to him. "Want the shop keys, too?"

"I'll call you when we need them. You know we could find arsenic in your shop, no matter what. It can be in poisons used to control vermin, and it's often found in old buildings."

I shuddered. "Ugh. I hope our renovations were thorough enough to remove anything like that. We've never used or needed rat poison since we opened Deputy Donut."

"Good to know. I'll have the doors sealed immediately, so no one can accuse you and Tom of going in there and destroying evidence."

"And because I'm giving you permission to search Deputy Donut and our car for arsenic, you won't need search warrants for them, right?"

"Right. And we'll get Tom's permission, too. How many outer doors does your shop have?"

"Three—the front door on Wisconsin Street and two in the back. You've used the one that goes into the office. And you've probably seen the other one. It's at the loading dock and goes into the storeroom."

He wrote some more and then we started down the hill. I lit the path ahead of us with my phone. The light bobbed around because I was also texting Tom about what had happened. I heard Brent tell someone in the police department to put seals on all three of Deputy Donut's doors.

Apparently, Tom was still awake. He texted, "Tell Fyne it's fine."

I showed Brent the text. "There, Tom's consented."

Tom added, "Might be too late to stop mop cops." The retired cops who cleaned Deputy Donut and changed the oil in the fryers each night around midnight called themselves the Jolly Cops Cleaning Crew, but Tom liked to call them cops with mops and mop cops. Seconds later, Tom sent another text. "They were almost done. They're leaving now. Take care of yourself."

Brent put his phone in his pocket. "There. An officer is going to seal Deputy Donut's doors."

I thanked him and told him that our cleaning crew had nearly finished their nightly cleaning but were leaving.

Brent grimaced. "I'll add them to my list of people to interview."

"What about our donut car?"

"I'll arrange that when I get back to the office." He must have picked up on my apprehension about leaving the fun vintage car in an isolated parking lot. He added, "Your car won't be here long. I have to go back into town soon."

"Okay." We managed to arrive at the foot of the driveway without sliding on pebbles. Lights on the outside of the lodge weren't plentiful, but they were enough. I turned off my phone's flashlight.

Brent asked me, "Do you have any idea why the victim's pockets were stuffed with crullers?"

"*What?* That makes no sense. Crullers were the favorites that Jenn specifically ordered for herself. Roger asked for raised donuts coated in confectioners' sugar."

"Interesting."

"Did the crullers in Roger's pockets have arsenic on them?"

"That'll be tested. Obviously, he didn't ingest those particular crullers."

"Maybe someone saw him taking crullers and that's why they dipped a cruller or two or five in arsenic and put them where he'd find them."

"Or . . . ?" He stared into my face.

"The poison was meant for Jenn," I concluded.

We walked toward the lodge's main doors. Several fire department vehicles were idling in front. Engines rumbled, exhaust fogged the chilly night air, and radios blared mostly unintelligible words and phrases. If I'd heard the Red Cross van and the yellow school bus arriving, I'd assumed they were investigators' vehicles or fire trucks. Lights were on inside the bus, people were in the seats, and the windows were steaming up. I asked Brent, "When will the hotel guests go back inside?"

"After the hazmat team gets here. They'll have to check the area around your donut wall, photograph the white powder, seal it and the saucer and your hat in evidence bags, and test the air in the banquet hall and the rest of the hotel. If they need to, the fire department will ventilate the entire building, and then the overnight guests will be able to go back to their rooms. The guests will probably be on that bus for several hours, at least."

In the dimly lit main parking lot just beyond the vehicles clustered outside the lodge's main doors, Misty and her partner were standing a short distance from each other, interviewing reception guests. Scott glanced over the heads of guests who were probably waiting their turns, met my gaze, and nodded. Neither of us smiled.

An odd pang jabbed at my midsection. The folks who had attended that reception to celebrate a wedding couldn't know that the groom had died. Scott wouldn't know, either, although he could have guessed, both from Roger's deteriorating condition and from Brent's and my solemn expressions and our body language. Although I was mostly hidden inside the blanket, my drooping shoulders and stiffer-than-usual gait were probably noticeable. Maybe I wasn't scowling as much as Brent was.

Brent opened the passenger door of the cruiser he'd driven to the lodge. "I'll take you home, Em."

"I could call a cab, and Scott's still here."

Brent gave his head a definite shake. "I don't want you contaminating a cab or Scott's car."

"Only your cruiser?"

"It'll be cleaned."

"What about you?"

"I'm washable."

"Okay, as long as you don't turn on the cruiser's fan."

"You drive a hard bargain, considering that neither of us is wearing a coat."

I clutched the blanket more tightly around myself. "I can get you a deal on the latest style in durable blankets."

He smiled. "Thanks."

I didn't realize how exhausted I was until I fell into the front seat of the cruiser.

Brent shut the passenger door, got in behind the wheel, turned the cruiser around, set the heat to high without turning on the fan, and drove at a speed rivaling Tom's. He didn't slow much on hills and curves.

I asked, "Are you going to turn on the siren and strobes?"

He laughed. "You should have gone back to Fallingbrook with Samantha. She was using hers."

"You were using yours on the way."

"I was in a hurry, then."

I wondered what he called this speed, if it wasn't a hurry. Finally beginning to thaw, I loosened the blanket and asked, "Do you think your chief will bring in the DCI again?" During the previous year's murder investigation, Fallingbrook's police chief had called in the Wisconsin Division of Criminal Investigation to take over a case that Brent had been supervising quite competently.

"I can almost guarantee it."

"Maybe this time the DCI will send a different detective."

"Let's hope so."

Last time, they'd sent Detective Yvonne Passenmath. Yvonne had been a patrol cop in the Fallingbrook Police Department when Tom was chief. She had failed the examination to become a detective, while Brent and Alec hadn't. Tom had promoted his son and his son's best friend, and now, even though Yvonne had eventually passed the exam and become a DCI agent, she had never forgiven Tom, Alec, or Brent. To make matters worse, although Alec had never been interested in her, Yvonne seemed to believe that I'd stolen him from her. Alec, Misty, and Tom had all told me that Yvonne's police work was shoddy, and I had discovered that if she saw or imagined evidence linking me to a crime, she focused on that and ignored more pertinent clues, and if she couldn't pin the blame on me, she rushed to judge others.

If anything, the thought of Yvonne Passenmath made Brent drive faster. We made it to my place in just over fifteen minutes.

I got out of the car and started up the walk toward the house and the warm and welcoming light streaming onto the front porch from the living room window. Brent called me back to his cruiser. He opened the trunk and handed me a large brown paper evidence bag with a self-sealing glue strip near the top. "I'll go in first and take Dep outside so she'll be safe from any arsenic drifting off you," he said. "Then you can go inside, shower, put your clothes, shoes, and that blanket in the bag, and seal it. I'll take them to be analyzed."

"These jeans and this shirt are new! Will I get them back?" I knew that evidence could be kept for a long time.

"Yes, unless they're covered in arsenic."

"They'd better not be!"

"Hope not."

I accompanied him as far as the porch, unlocked the door

for him, and took a couple of steps back. It felt a little strange to stay on the porch and watch Brent go inside without me. Meowing, Dep trotted to him. I could tell she expected him to do what he usually did, scoop her into his arms. Instead, he urged, "Come on, Dep," and strode toward the back of the house. Meowing, her tail up and her feet thumping on the pine plank floor, she followed him.

Still on the front porch, I heard more kitty exclamations and then encouraging mumbles from Brent. The back door opened and shut, and I heard no more from my cat or my friend.

Back in the 1890s, the cottage's original owner had surrounded the entire yard with a smooth brick wall, with no breaks or gates. It was marvelously secure, for both cats and humans, which was one reason my law-enforcement officer husband had wanted to buy this particular house. Dep, who'd been a kitten when we moved in, had quickly discovered that the fun of climbing up trees wasn't worth the difficulty of attempting to run down headfirst, which, with backward-curling kitty claws, ended in landings that were apparently far too undignified to suit her. Clever cat that she was, she stopped climbing trees and never discovered that those backward-curling kitty claws would actually allow her to *back* down tree trunks. In addition, the shrubs near the wall hadn't held her weight then and certainly wouldn't now.

However, a cat-sized tunnel had been incorporated in the wall when it was first built. At some point, that tunnel had been blocked with a stone. Just over a year ago, the woman in the house behind mine had moved the stone and Dep had taken the opportunity to pay visits to, and accept treats from, my cat-loving neighbor. That house was now vacant, and I had plugged my end of the tunnel with a couple of bricks. I knew that Dep would be, as always, perfectly secure in my yard. Besides, Brent would keep a watchful eye on her.

I eased into the living room, set my keys, wallet, and

phone down, locked the front door, and went upstairs to the pretty white-tiled bathroom that Alec and I had renovated. I sealed the blanket and my shoes, clothes, and apron into the bag that Brent had given me.

I might have lingered with shampoo and bath gel if Brent hadn't needed to return to work. Leaving my hair wet, I threw on flannel pj's and a thick terry robe the same blue as my eyes. Barefoot, I carried the bag down the stairs to the silent main floor.

Beside the front door, I gripped the bag by its top. "Brent? Dep?"

Neither of them answered. I set the bag on the front porch. Brent's cruiser was still beside the curb, probably causing any neighbors who were awake at a little after two in the morning to fret.

I padded through the unlit dining room, kitchen, and sunroom, and found Dep and Brent outside underneath the lit timber pergola on the deck. Still not wearing a coat and probably feeling the cold, Brent was sidestepping Dep's attempts to climb him as if he were a tree, a kindly one that would set her down whenever she demanded. Laughing, I opened the door. "Come on, Dep."

She sat down and scrubbed at her whiskers.

Brent smiled at her, but when he turned toward me, he looked past me into the dark sunroom, and his eyes were shadowed, as if another suspicious death in Fallingbrook worried him. "I'll leave her to you, now," he said.

I held the door open for him. "Thanks for looking after her. The evidence bag is on the front porch."

"Great. Thanks, Em."

"Do you think you can still make it to dinner tomorrow?"

"I hope so."

"Since Deputy Donut will have to be closed, I'll have the day off. How about if I cook, and take a raincheck on the pizza and beer?"

He flashed a quick smile at me. "That's an offer I can't resist." He headed toward the front of the house. "I'll be in touch. Call if you think of anything. Any time. And take care of yourself, Em. I'll let myself out." He headed into the sunroom.

Now that I was clean, Dep didn't want the hugs I was ready to give her. She strolled off the deck and pounced on something in the grass. I heard Brent close the front door.

Leaving the back door open for Dep, I went through the sunroom and turned on lights in the kitchen. I loved my sleek kitchen with its stainless-steel two-oven range and oversized fridge, its granite countertops and the pine cabinets that Alec and I had installed to go with the woodwork in the rest of the Victorian cottage. I opened the lower cabinet where I stored Dep's food and treats. Outside, the engine of a car thrummed.

I added kibble to one of the ceramic bowls that Alec's mom had hand-crafted, chocolatey brown with kitty paw prints and Dep's full name, Deputy Donut, in white. I refilled another one with water. Dep bounced in and skidded to a stop on the terra-cotta tile floor. Instead of eating or drinking, though, she stared at the bowls as if wondering what kibble and water were. I hurried to close the back door before she could decide to do more wee-hours prowling in our walled-in yard.

When I walked from the sunroom into the kitchen again, Dep pretended she hadn't been eating. She strolled toward the front of the house. I turned out the lights, bumbled through the dining room in the semidarkness, and switched off the light in the living room. I peeked out the front window. Brent's cruiser was gone. I could almost hear him ordering me to lock the door with the dead bolt. I obeyed.

I never understood why staying up late made it harder, not easier, to fall asleep. However, having seen Roger alive, and then drunk, and then comatose, and finally hearing that he'd died was enough to keep anyone awake.

More than that, I ached for Jenn.

I also worried about Brent. If investigating another possible murder was bothering him, maybe I hoped that the police chief *would* bring in the DCI, even if the lead investigator was Yvonne Passenmath.

Chapter 10

✺

I slept in as long as Dep would let me, about five minutes more than most mornings, which meant we were exploring outside in the dark around five fifteen. After breakfast and a mug of delicious Maui coffee, I was almost awake. I made sheets of pasta from scratch and then assembled a couple of lasagnas. I refrigerated one, froze the other, and took the opportunity of an unexpected day off to do some extra housework. And to lounge around with a book and a cup of tea.

Midway through the afternoon, Brent called. The investigators were ready to search Deputy Donut. I pulled a cheerful red sweater on over my light blue shirt and blue jeans and went outside.

It was one of those glorious midwestern autumn days, with a bluer-than-blue sky and a tang of dry leaves in the air. Walking to Wisconsin Street without my goofy cat doing her own rather thorough investigations took less than ten minutes.

The front windows of Dressed to Kill hadn't changed since Friday afternoon. A sign taped inside the glass front door announced that the store would be closed for two weeks. Jenn had added I'LL BE ON MY HONEYMOON!!! and had surrounded her handwritten note with hearts. I couldn't help glancing through the door above the sign. The store looked empty and forlorn. Sympathy for Jenn welled in my heart. I wondered if she and Roger had planned an exciting trip.

Brent was standing on the closer of the two patios flanking Deputy Donut's front door. Knowing him, he had walked from the police station, which was on the town square, a few blocks up Wisconsin Street. Maybe to some people, Brent would have appeared intimidating in his black jeans, black T-shirt, and black blazer, but I had seen how gentle he was with my cat and with the women he'd brought on double dates with Alec and me. Sunlight glinted gold and auburn in his light brown hair. Although I suspected he'd been up most of the night, he didn't look as tired as he had when he left Dep and me at our place early that morning.

Smiling, he walked toward me, and then we both stopped, still an arm's length apart. When Alec was alive, Brent and I had frequently given each other casual hugs, but after Alec was shot and Brent was grazed, I'd avoided anyone and anything that reminded me of that terrible night. And then, in the courtroom right after the guilty verdict, I'd thanked Brent for helping put Alec's killer behind bars. He'd again told me to get in touch if I needed anything, and I'd blurted that Brent wasn't the only person whom others could lean on and that Brent could lean on me. My outburst had shocked me so much that I'd continued avoiding Brent. It must have shocked or at least dismayed him, too, and we'd drifted even further apart.

Then, just over a year ago, when I'd inadvertently become involved in a murder investigation, I'd realized that Brent and I could become friends again. We'd begun giving each other the kinds of quick hugs that people naturally give friends, mostly when Brent wasn't on duty.

Now, although the sunlit afternoon seemed entirely different from the cold, the dark, and the horror of the night before, when I hadn't known whether or not I was covered with poison and would not have hugged my worst enemy, not that I usually went around hugging enemies, Brent was on duty. I tried to cover the awkwardness of the chasm between us by quickly apologizing for the lack of chairs on the patio and asking, "Are the investigators here?"

"They're out back."

A neat notice was taped to our door announcing that Deputy Donut was closed for the day. There was no mention of a criminal investigation. I figured that was a good thing. I nodded at the sign. "I should have thought of that. Did you put it there?"

Brent headed toward the driveway. "Yes, after I left you last night. I went to the office and printed it, and then I brought it here and taped it to your door. Doing something like that actually helps me think about whatever problem I'm trying to solve."

And he was naturally kind and thoughtful, besides. Walking up the driveway with him, I thanked him. "Did you figure out who killed Roger?"

He cast a humorously rueful look down at me. "Afraid not."

In our parking lot, two officers in hazmat gear were unloading equipment from a sinister-looking windowless black van. Brent waved to them, and they followed us to the door leading into Deputy Donut's office. Brent removed the seal.

With him and the two investigators watching my every move, I unlocked the door, stepped inside, disarmed the alarm, and turned on the lights. I couldn't tell that the Jolly Cops hadn't finished cleaning. The dining room sparkled. The Jolly Cops had swept and mopped the wood plank floor, taken the chairs off the tables, and scrubbed the tabletops, which were shiny slices of large tree trunks, complete with growth rings and variations in size and shape.

I went outside and held the door open for the two hazmat-suited officers and their cases of equipment. In their bootie-covered footwear, they shuffled inside. Brent followed in his civilian clothes and no hazmat gear.

"Sir?" one of the officers asked through his mask.

Brent was already removing a notebook from an inside pocket in his blazer. "I don't expect to find noxious substances in here."

I thought I saw a shrug inside one of those bulky coveralls. The officers began unsnapping the latches on their cases.

Brent turned toward me. "I'll call you when we're done."

I walked home. As soon as I went inside, Dep ran from the sunroom and twined herself around my legs. I picked her up, hugged her, and took her outside. I texted Tom that the investigators had arrived at Deputy Donut. Dep rolled in the grass and ended up on her side, blinking in the light. I pruned forsythia in the October sunshine. Dep found a warm spot on the patio and hunkered down to watch me work.

After about two hours, my shrubs were trimmed and my grass was mowed. My phone rang. Brent was waiting for me at Deputy Donut. "You're clear," he added. "Not a speck of poison of any sort. The hazmat guys were a little disappointed." I heard a smile in his voice.

Dep was reluctant to leave her patch of sunshine, but I managed to lock her inside so I could walk back to Deputy Donut.

Brent was sitting on the stoop outside the office. He stood and thrust his phone into a pocket of his blazer.

I asked him, "Did the guys make a mess in there?"

"No. They're careful not to spill things like flour and powdered sugar that might contain poisons, and we weren't taking fingerprints, so you won't need additional cleaning."

I went into the office, called the Jolly Cops, and left a voice message that they could skip cleaning Deputy Donut that night. Then I reset the alarm and joined Brent, now standing on the porch. He watched me lock the door.

I ran down the porch stairs. "Did investigators find any other arsenic in the lodge last night?"

Brent followed me. "The air in the lodge was fine, and guests were allowed to return to their rooms before the sun was up. There were a few grains of arsenic on your table around the saucer, and quite a bit more on one of those fancy three-layered plates in front of your donut wall, as if contaminated crullers had been on the plate. It's a good thing you noticed that saucer underneath your hat. There was enough in it to kill a few more people."

We started down the driveway. I asked, "Have investigators checked our Deputy Donut car yet?"

"No, and not your and Scott's clothes. I wanted to get your shop ready so you could open tomorrow. I'll let you know how your car and clothes test."

"Thank you. I made lasagna. Are we still on for dinner?"

He stared toward the end of the driveway where cars were driving up and down Wisconsin Street. "That's really tempting, and I wish I could, but I'll need to work most of the night. The chief's away for the weekend. I'd like to have all of my leads organized before morning when he gets back." He frowned down at me as if I might not remember what a detective's life could be like—the sudden need to work even longer hours than usual, the determination to solve a crime and bring a criminal to justice, the devotion to the citizens he was sworn to serve and protect.

"And calls in the DCI," I commented in a dry voice.

"Which would give me some time off."

"I made lots of lasagna. How about tomorrow night? You do have to eat once in a while."

"Okay, if you'll understand if I have to cancel at the last minute."

"I will. And then we can aim for Tuesday or Wednesday, or . . ."

With a tired smile, he placed one arm around my shoulders and briefly squeezed me to his side. "Thanks, Em. You're the best." I responded with a quick and awkward one-armed hug around his waist before we let each other go and continued walking down the driveway. At the street, he said, "Let me know if you think of anything else, no matter how insignificant it might seem." He turned left, toward the police department and a night of piecing clues together.

I turned right, toward my sweet Victorian neighborhood, my house, a lonely dinner, and the cat who made a house a home.

"Meow!" she said the minute I walked inside.

"Sorry, Dep, I couldn't bring your friend back for lasagna tonight. He has to work. Maybe tomorrow."

Dep stood up on her hind legs. With her claws withdrawn, she boxed the shin of my jeans. "Me*ow!*" She sat down again and stared up at my face.

"I gave you food and water before I left." I went into the kitchen. Both bowls were full.

From the living room, Dep meowed again. She was sitting facing the front door. Her tail swished back and forth across the pine plank floor.

"I know you missed out on your trip to the office today," I told her. "We'll go tomorrow."

I returned to the kitchen and put the lasagna into one of the ovens. When I closed the door, Dep was right behind me. She looked pointedly at the oven door. "Yeow!"

"Lasagna?" I asked. "It's not good for you. And you probably wouldn't like it, anyway."

She trotted to the front door and meowed at it again. I followed her and peered out through the peephole. No one was there. Had someone left something on the porch? I picked Dep up and opened the door.

Nothing.

Dep purred loudly. I closed the door. "Is this what you wanted, a cuddle?" I carried her to the comfy carved mahogany and red velvet couch I'd inherited from my grand-mother. With Dep in my arms, I plunked down and set my phone on the coffee table. Keeping her back legs on my lap, Dep stretched until her front legs were on the table. She nosed the phone.

"You want me to invite someone over so you'll get more at-tention than you get from only one person? Okay, I do have more than one friend who's willing to cater to your royal wishes."

I tried Samantha first. "I just put lasagna in the oven. Want to come over to dinner?"

"Love to! I wondered what I was going to eat."

I wasn't as lucky with Misty. She didn't answer. I left a message.

Dep jumped down onto the Oriental-patterned red, cobalt, navy, and ivory rug and strode toward the kitchen. "Are you happy now?" I called after her.

"Mmp." She sounded a lot like Brent when he didn't quite want to answer a question.

"Would you stop it with the *mmp*s, Dep?" I followed her into the kitchen and started washing romaine lettuce. Dep swaggered into the sunroom and curled up on a radiator cover. "Mission accomplished, huh?" I asked.

But she only opened one eye and closed it again. Naptime.

I arranged frozen homemade croutons on a cookie sheet and slid the cookie sheet into the second oven. Then I made Caesar salad dressing and used a grater to turn a chunk of Romano cheese into thick, yummy slivers. Knowing that Samantha didn't like anchovies, I didn't open any.

Although I had four stools at the island counter in the kitchen, I decided to be more formal for Samantha's visit. I set the table in the dining room. As in the rest of the house except the kitchen and bathroom, the floors were stripped-down pine and the walls were white. The dining room win-dows were high and made of jewel-toned stained glass, which meant that natural light had to filter in from the living room and kitchen. To brighten the dining room, Alec and I had bought a simple white table and white chairs.

Cindy had made our plates, bowls, cups, and serving dishes. They were the same chocolatey brown as Dep's, but ours were plain, without cute white kitty paw prints. Cindy hadn't written our names on ours, either. I used handwoven place mats in deep red and added stainless cutlery.

The top of the lasagna was bubbling in the oven when the doorbell rang. Dep jumped off the radiator cover. Her feet pounding the floors, she beat me to the door.

After working the late shift the night before, Samantha must have gotten some sleep during the day. Her dark eyes gleamed with humor and intelligence. She thrust a bottle of Chianti at me and picked up Dep, who purred her approval. "That lasagna must be delicious," Samantha said. "I can smell the oregano and cheese from here."

In the kitchen, I opened the Chianti. "How are you doing after last night?" I asked Samantha.

"It's always hard to lose a patient. We knew when we wheeled him out of the lodge that there wasn't much hope, so when we heard he didn't make it we weren't surprised. It must have been hard for you, though, finding that powder and guessing that it might be poison." Dep squirmed. Samantha set her down. "And then hearing that the powder was arsenic."

I poured wine into goblets made of clear bubbled glass with dark red rims. "Seeing that powder was shocking and a little frightening, but before I saw it, I guessed that he'd passed out because of drinking too much. He'd been rude to me and belligerent to at least one of his guests. From what I saw of him, he wasn't a very nice person. Before the reception, presumably before he started on the alcohol, he was mean to his new bride."

Samantha clinked her glass against mine. "Really? His bride seemed very upset. She was like a zombie by the time we got her out of the ambulance and into a wheelchair at Emerge. She was sobbing and crying, and it was hard to tell what she was saying, but I'm almost certain she said, 'I shouldn't have done it.' "

Chapter 11

Without taking a sip, I set my glass down on the granite countertop. "Jenn said *what?* She 'shouldn't have done it'? Done what? Poisoned her new husband?"

Samantha also set her glass down. "I'm not positive she said she shouldn't have done 'it' whatever 'it' might have meant, but she quickly added, 'I should never have agreed to marry him, should never have had a reception, certainly not *there.*' And I'm sure about that last phrase, because my partner heard the same thing."

"Jenn seems too sweet to harm anyone." Biting my lip because people didn't always act the way I expected them to, based on first or even hundredth impressions, I turned away and peered through the oven door. The lasagna was browning and bubbling. I put on oven mitts, removed the heavy casserole from the oven, and set it on the counter. I took the croutons out of the other oven and then flung the oven mitts down and asked Samantha, "Did you tell Brent what Jenn said?"

"No. I was almost certain she didn't mean that she'd harmed her new groom. I thought she was just talking about regretting marrying him, or maybe she was sorry she held the reception in a place that, it turned out, killed him."

"It wasn't the *place.* But it might have been the crullers Tom and I made." I mimed a Very Sad Face.

"If so, someone else poisoned them, not you."

"Thanks." I took a larger gulp of the Chianti than I meant to. "Do you know how Jenn is today?"

"She's fine, last I knew. There were no signs that she'd been poisoned. She was released from the hospital this morning."

"Still in her wedding gown?" I drizzled homemade Caesar dressing over the salad.

"You almost made me spew my wine! In Emerge they made her change into a hospital gown."

"Not by herself, I hope. Her wedding dress had about a million tiny and unreachable buttons in back."

Samantha peered at me over her glass. "Her sister was there."

"Suzanne." I sprinkled the croutons and slivers of Romano over the salad.

"Yeah, Suzanne. She didn't say a lot on the way to the hospital, other than urging me to drive faster, but she did mention that she'd have to bring Jenn something to wear home besides that wedding gown."

I carried the salad to the dining room. "How did Suzanne seem, besides planning what her sister might wear next?"

Carrying our goblets of wine, Samantha followed me. "She was clenching her teeth most of the way into town, probably to keep them from chattering. I turned up the heat to the passenger seat as high as it would go, and she had a blanket, but her dress was more suited to a summer day, and shock gets to people that way sometimes. They can't seem to warm up."

I set the salad on the table and gestured for Samantha to take a seat. "So, as far as we know, Roger was the only person who ingested a killing dose of arsenic. If Jenn came in contact with the poison, it didn't affect her too badly."

Samantha pulled out her chair and sat down. "She passed out."

I sat, too. "That was understandable. We'd just told her that the ambulance had come for Roger. Did anyone else

complain of symptoms last night? You'd think that if someone dipped crullers in arsenic, he or she might have gotten at
least a little sick."

"We didn't respond to any other calls last night that could
have been due to poisoning, but when we were driving from
Fallingbrook to the lodge, we saw a small red car stopped beside the road. The car was fogged up inside, but I slowed and
turned a spotlight on it, and my partner and I could make out
someone in the driver's seat. He was hunched over with his
face in his hands."

"A man."

"I could tell *that* much. I'm good at things like that."

I gave her an affronted side-eye.

"He was wearing a suit. We were about to radio for someone to check on him, but he drove away, and we never saw
him again."

"What color was his hair?"

"I couldn't tell, but it was neither very light nor very
dark."

"Which direction did he go?"

"East, but the next right turn would have taken him to
Fallingbrook."

"Did you get his license number?"

"My partner might have."

"If he did, he should give it to Brent. Maybe the man was
feeling guilty for poisoning Roger."

Samantha nodded. "I'll tell him. We didn't think of that,
even though Brent had warned us to suit up for possible airborne poisons. We're programmed to look for illness and injuries, not killers. As far as I know, no one else from the
lodge reported being sick last night or today."

"Was your ambulance thoroughly cleaned after Roger
rode in it?"

It was her turn to look insulted. "Of course. The lodge, too,
apparently, except maybe the banquet hall. Last I knew, it was
still closed, but maybe that's only because of the decorations.

Do you think they keep that room decorated like that all the time? It was a little over the top."

"The gold and periwinkle touches must have been Jenn's, but I don't know about all those white curtains."

She frowned. "Not the best setup for getting rid of airborne contaminants." Then a grin lit her mischievous face. "Sorry for sounding like a textbook." She became serious again. "As far as I know, no one has come down with symptoms of arsenic poisoning from being near all that drapery."

By the time we finished our salad, the lasagna was firm enough to cut.

Samantha tasted it. Her eyes closed. "This is even better than last time."

After we ate seconds, I apologized, "I'm afraid I have no donuts for dessert."

"Uh-oh. Did last night put you off donuts?"

"Deputy Donut was closed today, and I never seem to make them at home anymore."

"Why was your shop closed?"

"Brent had it searched for arsenic. They didn't find any, but the Jolly Cops Cleaning Crew had already cleaned, so today's search by the hazmat guys probably won't be considered conclusive. However, Brent impounded our Deputy Donut car and will have it checked also."

"Brent suspects you?"

"Standard protocol. Clearing Tom and me, if he can, allows him to investigate more likely suspects."

Samantha steepled her hands near her heart and made a swoony cross-eyed face. "Brent would do anything for you."

"He's all yours."

"Don't think so."

I held both hands up, palms toward Samantha. "He's certainly not mine, no matter what you and Misty like to pretend. Besides, you know what he's like—he always has a girlfriend."

"A new one every few weeks." She had to know she was

exaggerating. "He never stays with any of them very long." She swirled the wine in her glass and looked down into it. "But come to think of it, I haven't seen him with anyone since . . . I'm not sure when. Probably over a year."

Brent and I had regained our friendship over a year ago, but I wasn't about to dwell on that coincidence or think about the fact that he and I—and Dep—occasionally got together for quick dinners before Brent had to go back to work. "Go for him, Samantha." They'd be cute together.

"He belongs to you."

"Does not!" Sometimes Samantha, Misty, and I sounded exactly like we had when we first met, back in junior high. Too bad Misty wasn't here to join the conversation. Where was Misty? She hadn't returned my call. "Besides . . ." I drained my glass. "He's not Alec, and I'm never falling for another man who works in a dangerous profession. And in addition to all of that, Brent prefers tall women."

Samantha looked down at Dep, sitting patiently on the floor beside Samantha's chair. "Too many excuses for any of them to be believable."

I stood. "Ha. Would you like some ice cream? I got it from that new shop where they make it themselves."

"Yum! Yes!"

"Vanilla, cappuccino, or some of each?"

She didn't hesitate. "All of them."

I gave us each two scoops, and a shot of coffee liqueur, which we both poured over the ice cream and ate with a spoon. It was scrumptious.

I told Samantha, "Misty came to the lodge last night after you left. Brent asked her to take Scott's statement."

Between the spot of ice cream on Samantha's cheek and the pink streaks in her hair, she resembled a happy elf, possibly one with a secret.

"Samantha! Do you know where Misty is tonight? Is she with Scott? I invited her to join us and she never answered my call."

"I don't know where she is or who she's with."

My phone rang. It wasn't Misty. It was Brent, calling from his personal cell phone, not the police department's number. "I have your car," he growled in a dramatically dangerous voice, "and your clothes. I'll bring them back for a ransom in donuts."

I growled back in an equally dangerous voice, "I wasn't able to make donuts today."

"Slacker. I'll be there in ten minutes, okay?"

"Sure." *Not really, if Samantha's going to pretend it means that Brent and I are in some sort of pre-romance.* I disconnected.

Samantha stared wide-eyed at me. "What's with the sexy voice?"

"It wasn't sexy. It was *threatening*."

"Right. Who were you"—she made air quotes with her fingers—"*threatening?*"

"Only Brent," I said in a totally businesslike voice. "He was growling."

"What? *Brent?* Growling at *you?*"

"Pretend growling. He was telling me that the Deputy Donut car and my clothes tested negative for arsenic. He's bringing them over."

"Right. Anyone would growl about that." She scraped her spoon through the last remnants of her ice cream. "Wait a sec, Emily. Brent has your *clothes?*"

"It was all perfectly innocent." But my face heated as if it hadn't been. "He was outside with Dep while I showered and changed out of my possibly poisoned clothes."

"Dep's an excellent chaperone, of course," she said sarcastically.

"She is."

"And you were the one who immediately started talking about innocence. I never said anything about it one way or another."

"Except in your tone."

She jumped to her feet. "Is Brent coming over now?"

"In a few minutes."

"I should go."

"No, you shouldn't. He's also bringing the blanket that Scott commandeered for me out of your ambulance. You can have it back. Besides, Tom and I don't keep that car here. How about, after Brent gives us the clothes and the blanket, you follow him? He can park the car in the garage behind Deputy Donut, and you can drive him back to his car or wherever he needs to go, and bring me the keys when you get a chance."

She shook her head so decisively that the pink streaks became pink blurs. "Oh no, you don't. Matchmake all you want between Scott and Misty, but leave me out of your plans and plots. When did you start coming up with such ridiculously convoluted schemes, anyway?"

I pretended to be hurt. "Just now." She was right. The needless complications made my matchmaking much too obvious.

"I'm sure you can find another way of ending up with your Deputy Donut car in your Deputy Donut garage and your keys in your pocket. And I really do need to get up early in the morning. You can return the blanket to me another time." She gave me a sly smile. "It's fascinating that a *detective* is bringing your car and clothes back. Don't they usually assign jobs like that to rookies?"

"Not when the detective has been itching to drive that car."

Conceding that I might have a point, she left.

Brent showed up minutes later, still in the black outfit. Reaching across the cat rubbing against his ankles, he handed me a bag labeled with my name. "I'll take your car over to Deputy Donut," he offered, "and bring the keys in a few minutes. Want me to park it in the garage?"

"Yes, please. The garage door remote is clipped to the sun visor, and the button to close the door is outside on the right. Have you eaten?"

"I'm going home soon. I'll grab something. Don't you have to get up early?"

"Yes, but how about while you're delivering my car and bringing back my keys, I'll package some leftover lasagna for you?" *There, Samantha,* I thought, *a nice, uncomplicated plan, with no matchmaking involved.*

And Brent agreed to it, besides.

A few minutes later, he was back. Dep invited him to come in and stay, but he told her he had to walk back to work. I traded the lasagna for my keys.

He sniffed. "Thank you. You might have prevented a cop from starving. And you don't owe me any donuts, either."

"But come for dinner tomorrow night. I'll cook."

"If I can, which probably means if the chief gets the DCI to take over the investigation."

I made a face.

He squeezed my shoulder with his free hand. "Take care, Em." He let himself out.

I locked the door, put the clothes and blanket he'd brought into the laundry, and went to bed.

Around three, Misty texted me. She apologized for not answering sooner. She'd been working and hadn't been able to check her phone.

I woke again to subtle tapping. On the table beside my bed, Dep was inserting her claws underneath my phone, lifting it slightly, and letting it drop. Again and again.

It was five to five.

"Aw, Dep," I complained sleepily, "couldn't you have given me that last five minutes?"

She jumped to the floor. "Meow."

Grumbling, I turned off the alarm. I showered, put on my robe, and fed Dep, who was wide awake and ready for more mischief. I'd have coffee at work. Until then, the jalapeños in the Monterey Jack cheese in my omelet would have to jolt me out of my early-morning desire to doze. I put on my work uniform of clean black jeans and white shirt. I loved sweater weather, and the morning definitely called for a cozy sweater. I chose one that Jenn had knit from heavy teal yarn with wildly entangled cables wandering over it. Finally, I leashed Dep and we headed outside.

Dep pranced down the sidewalk ahead of me, stopping every so often when she was apparently pressured, by a force I couldn't see, to pounce on mysterious objects that I also couldn't see.

Tom's SUV was in the parking lot behind Deputy Donut. I took Dep into the office, released her from her halter and leash, and flicked on the gas fireplace. Leaving Dep in her fun playground, I went into the dining area.

As far as I could tell, the hazmat guys had not undone any of the Jolly Cops' meticulous cleaning. I walked behind the marble-topped sales and serving counter and into the kitchen. Tom waved his enormous marble rolling pin. "Morning, Emily! Happy Columbus Day!"

I returned his greeting without resorting to endangering anyone with rolling pins. Usually we made dough the evening before, but we hadn't done that either of the past two evenings. I washed my hands and put on a clean apron and my spare Deputy Donut hat, and then while Tom cut donuts from plain dough, I made cruller and fritter batter. By the time that Tom mixed yeast dough and put it into the proofing cabinet to rise, the fresh oil that the Jolly Cops had put in the fryers had reached the right temperature, and Tom started frying the crullers, fritters, and unraised donuts.

Like all of our crockery at Deputy Donut, our creamers were off-white ironstone with our logo printed in black on them. I filled some with cream and others with milk and set them and the sugar bowls on tables. Then I hurried back to the kitchen and dipped warm fritters and crullers in glazes and sugar. As the donuts cooled, I frosted and decorated them.

By the time our first customers arrived, trays of pretty and delicious fried foods were in our glass-fronted display cabinet, and both the medium roast Colombian that we served every day and the day's featured coffee, a fruity and aromatic Burundian medium-dark roast, were dripping into pots.

All morning, customers asked why we'd been closed the day before.

At first, I wasn't sure what to say. Words like "arsenic" and "poison" were guaranteed to scare people. Besides, Brent had told me not to mention the white powder to anyone besides Scott and Tom. If Samantha hadn't already heard about it from Brent and the hospital, I wouldn't have discussed it with her.

I answered that something had come up. Then I had to assure everyone that neither Tom nor I had been ill.

As always, policemen came in for their breaks, and many of them bought donuts and coffee to carry back to the station. I eavesdropped when I could, but none of them seemed to be talking about the investigation into Roger's death.

Halfway through the afternoon, I was pulling shots of espresso for a couple of honeymooning tourists. The front door opened. I turned my head toward it and nearly dropped a cup.

Two women were coming into Deputy Donut. They were the women who had asked Saturday night's security guard how to reach the Happy Hopers Conference.

Chapter 12

I wondered if the two women had consulted each other before choosing their outfits Saturday night and this morning or if they always dressed in skinny pants or leggings, super-high heels, and frilly tunics. The blonde appeared to be in her mid-forties. She was taller and wore her hair in long, relaxed curls similar to the way Jenn had worn hers underneath her veil, but while Jenn's face was slender and animated, this woman's face was round and calm. Her friend had lively brown eyes, a pointy nose and chin, a deep tan, and a short, tapered cap of dark hair. She was probably in her mid-thirties. Both women were slim. Maybe their goal achievement through shopping had brought them to Deputy Donut to gain a few ounces.

The blonde was carrying her Happy Hopers Conference tote bag. Had she hidden arsenic in it on Saturday night, and was she bringing arsenic to Deputy Donut, perhaps to plant it for the police to find? Or did she have an enemy in our crowded café?

I wanted to run into the office and call Brent, or into the kitchen to tell Tom that possible poisoners were in our shop and that one of them had a large bag like the one she'd carried Saturday night.

First, I needed to deliver the espressos to the honeymooners.

They asked for directions to Fallingbrook Falls. Keeping my eye on the Happy Hopers, I described the route.

The Happy Hopers settled themselves at a table near the office. *Great.* Whether I wanted to shut myself into the office and call Brent or go into the kitchen and tell Tom about the two women, I'd have to pass their table.

Maybe they wouldn't notice me inching toward the office.

Unfortunately, becoming invisible was not among my skills. The blonde beckoned to me.

Dep sat up on the windowsill facing the dining area. She was not quite giving the Happy Hopers the evil eye through the glass.

Mentally rehearsing hollering evacuation instructions to Tom and our customers and then grabbing Dep and escaping, I put on a fake friendly smile and stopped at the women's table. I thought I caught a whiff of that nostalgia-inducing potpourri. "What can I get you?" I asked. And then I wondered if I'd imagined the potpourri or if the aromas of coffee, spices, and donuts had overwhelmed it.

The brunette gazed toward the display case. From this angle, she couldn't get a good look at many of the donuts, but she would be able to see enough to tempt anyone. Her mouth opened. Slowly, she raised one finger, tentatively aiming it toward the display case.

"Certified organic green tea," the blonde answered firmly, "if you have it."

"We do," I said.

The brunette slumped a little and dropped her hand into her lap. "Same for me."

"What can I get you to eat?" I asked.

"Nothing," the blonde said.

"Nothing," her companion repeated, not sounding entirely happy.

I brought the women a pot of just-boiled water, mugs, and loose tea in infusers. The blonde put her infuser in the cup and poured water over it. She stared over rising steam toward the top of my head. "Wherever did you get your hats?"

Hats, plural? Last I knew, I was wearing only one.

The wall separating the kitchen from the dining area was only shoulder height—my shoulder, not Tom's—so she could have seen Tom's head when she came in.

However, if she was the person who had covered the saucer of arsenic with my hat, she could have guessed that the hat would have been taken into police custody, and that I had to be wearing a spare.

I kept my face as neutral as possible. "We order blank ones from a uniform supply company, and artisans at The Craft Croft make faux-fur donuts to glue on them."

The brunette spoke up. "Does some of the artwork on your walls come from The Craft Croft? I go in there often, and I think I recognize some of the artists."

"All of it comes from The Craft Croft, and it's for sale."

The blonde nodded approvingly. "When we saw your car and your hat, we knew you had good marketing ideas. And we remembered the name of your shop from that antique police car. It was easy to track you down."

Track me down? Not sure how to respond, I smiled.

The blonde asked me, "Do you own your own business?"

"It's a partnership with Tom Westhill. He and I designed our logo and planned the car's and the hats' whimsical decorations together, so I can't take all of the credit. Or the blame. He used to be police chief here in Fallingbrook." There. Maybe the two women would realize that flinging arsenic around Deputy Donut might not go unnoticed.

The brunette stirred her tea with the infuser. "That name does sound familiar."

I was always a little surprised when people didn't recognize Tom's name. He'd been a very popular police chief. I reminded myself that people in the area who had never been in trouble with the law might not know who he was.

The blonde scooted forward. "Here's why we wanted to talk to you. Once a month, I sponsor a program featuring a female entrepreneur. The women tell us how they got started and, you know, give out tips, things like that. You have such clever ideas—the hats and the car and your logo—that I'm sure everyone could learn a lot from you, and with your apparent sense of humor, you'd probably keep the audience's interest, too. You wouldn't be paid, but you'd get lots of exposure for your business. And you would be our guest at dinner. We serve health food." Maybe I'd mistaken a practiced lack of expression for serenity. Her round face and smooth complexion gave an impression of calm, but she'd become very intense, and I suspected that those brown eyes didn't miss much.

I wasn't sure I wanted to eat anything those two women might have a part in preparing, however. "That sounds like fun," I said, not quite truthfully. "I get up at five in the morning, though, and I seldom stay up late."

The blonde shook her head. "We never go on very long. You'd hardly be out later than when we saw you Saturday night."

I'd last seen them when I arrived at Little Lake Lodge with the donuts, just before ten on Saturday night, but maybe they'd seen me after that. Hoping they'd tell me how long they'd stayed at Little Lake Lodge, I said, "That was pretty late."

The blonde lifted the infuser from her cup and clinked it down on her saucer. "Was it? We left around . . ." She turned to her companion. "When was it, about ten thirty?"

The other woman tilted her head as if trying to remember. "Ten thirty, quarter to eleven, something like that."

If they were telling the truth, they left the lodge long before someone hid arsenic underneath my hat. Maybe I'd be able to figure out if they were lying if I wheedled more information from them. "You asked the security guard how to get to your conference from the delivery entrance, and he told you to go around to the front. I discovered later that the lodge has a peculiar floor plan. Did you ever find your way to your meeting?"

The brunette said, "We knew the long way around, but we wondered if there was a shortcut. We were wearing heels and had been on our feet a lot."

But after you asked him about the possible shortcut, you stood around outside in those heels while I went to my car and gathered more things, and it wasn't until you saw me coming back that you headed toward the lobby. And it appeared to me that you left the delivery entrance because you spotted me returning to it. . . .

The blonde added, "We discussed our options and decided not to go back to the conference." Okay, maybe that explained why they'd hung around the delivery entrance longer than seemed necessary.

However, the first time I'd encountered them, they were walking down the driveway from the staff parking lot. But when they left the delivery entrance, they'd gone toward the front of the lodge. Had they been heading toward the conference that they'd just decided to avoid? Or toward their cars in the main lot? But if they'd parked in the main lot, where most of the lodge guests and other conference attendees supposedly parked, what had they been doing in the staff parking lot just before ten? I tried to keep my doubts and questions from showing on my face.

The blonde explained, "That conference wasn't meeting our expectations."

Her friend nodded vigorously. "They promised we could achieve goals through shopping, and if anyone likes retail therapy, it's me. But it turned out that what the conference organizers meant was that we could buy stuff from them, and it was horrible stuff! Just cheap gewgaws that no one would want."

The blonde scowled. "It was one of those multilevel marketing schemes. We were supposed to buy merchandise from them and sell it to other people, and everyone above us on the pyramid would take a cut. Great if you're at the top of the pyramid, but crushing if you're at the bottom."

The brunette tasted her tea. "Bleah." Obviously flustered, she backpedaled. "I didn't mean 'bleah' about the tea. It's good. I meant 'bleah' about the multilevel marketing scheme and the stuff that no one would want. I said it was cheap, but I didn't mean that the prices were low. Far from it."

The blonde said to me, "You were bringing donuts to the inn. Were you taking them to the wedding reception Saturday night?"

"Yes. People like letting their guests choose their own desserts. We made a wall with dowels sticking out of it, and we hung the donuts on the wall. It makes a decorating statement and it's also cute and fun."

"I knew it." The blonde's serene expression didn't alter much. She tilted her chin down and raised her eyes to my face in a way that made me feel like I was being judged. "Your marketing ideas are creative."

"We didn't invent donut walls. The bride knew about them and asked if we could provide one. We painted it in her theme colors, and it turned out really well." *Until it didn't . . .*

The brunette dropped a bombshell. "We both know the groom."

Know, not knew? Had they not heard of his death? Or were they pretending they hadn't? I tried not to look like I was about to race away, slam myself into the office, and phone a detective.

The blonde's serenity cracked again, but only for a second. She darted a quick sideways glance at her friend and then returned her almost-unreadable attention to me. "It was a total coincidence that we were attending a conference in the hotel where he was having his wedding reception."

The brunette shook her head sadly. "Not a nice man," she said.

The blonde folded her hands on the table like someone who was completely relaxed. "True." She leaned forward slightly, toward me. "I've been a life coach in Fallingbrook for years. That man came into town, claimed he'd lived here before, and offered to work as my intern for free. He said he had lots of connections here and he would help me build my client list. We'd work together to coach all the people he would bring to my practice. He really turned on the charm, and I accepted his offer. It worked for a while. He was nice as pie, and my clients began to trust him."

"I did, at first," the brunette admitted. "He talked the talk."

The blonde went on as if her friend hadn't spoken. "But after a few months, he hadn't brought in any new clients. And then one day, he didn't come into the office he and I shared. He just disappeared. It turned out that he'd set himself up as a life coach, taking my client list, and most of the people on it, with him."

The brunette tsked. "Not only that. He told us that *she*"—the brunette pointed her spoon at the blonde—"had been imprisoned in Utah for cheating her clients, and that she was a fraud and we shouldn't trust her."

Although she hadn't added anything to her tea, the blonde stirred it. "That wasn't true. He totally made that up." Her hand shook a little. "I've never even been to Utah."

The brunette added, "I shouldn't have believed him, but I went ahead and met with him to let him coach me. Twice. And then I decided *never again*. When he was the only one coaching, his personality totally changed. How can someone call himself a life coach when all he can do is snarl and sneer at his clients? Not helpful at all. Plus, he was charging twice as much as she'd been. I quit him. Fortunately, *she* . . ." The brunette pointed her spoon again. Wasn't either of them ever going to divulge the other's name? "*She* called and asked why I'd missed two appointments, and that's when I found out that Roger had lied about her and stolen her clients. So, I went back to her right away, and now we're dear friends."

"Trust is crucial to good coaching." The blonde's words came out like a well-practiced lecture.

The brunette sent her a triumphant smile. "And I convinced quite a few of her clients that Roger was a fraud and they should return to her."

The blonde became solemn. "But some of my clients didn't come back to me. They believed Roger's lies."

The corners of the brunette's mouth drooped. "One of the things Roger said he would do probably wasn't a lie. He threatened me, and I bet he threatened them, too, so they were too terrified to switch back to you from him."

I'd been listening, my focus ping-ponging between the two women, but I had to break my silence. "Threatened you?" I repeated. "Terrified his clients?"

The brunette gazed toward the donut display. "The threats weren't specific, which was probably scarier than if they were. He said he didn't get mad—he got even."

My phone was in my apron pocket, but I couldn't pull it out to record the conversation without being totally obvious, and fumbling my fingers inside that large front pocket would have come across as, at the very least, peculiar. Maybe Tom and I needed to install spy cameras in our hats, with the lenses and microphones hidden in the holes of the furry donuts.

And maybe, just maybe, my imagination was spinning out of control.

I glanced toward the privacy of the office. Dep was still glaring at the Happy Hopers.

I needed to call Brent and tell him that the two mystery women were in Deputy Donut and that they'd known and disliked Roger. However, other customers kept me busy, and when there was finally a lull, the Happy Hopers were going outside. The blonde still had her tote. They started up the alley between Dressed to Kill and Deputy Donut.

They'd left cash on the table, giving me no chance to learn their names from a credit card.

Quickly, I shut myself into the office with Dep. I wasn't tall, but the office windows were big, and the sills, padded for Dep's comfort, were low. I sat on the couch where I could look out with only my hat and the top of my face, from about the nose up, showing.

Fortunately, the women didn't turn their heads in my direction. They got into a small white car and started down the alley. The blonde was driving.

I jumped to my feet. Dep decided that the pad of paper on my desk was a perfect, although rather small, bed. I pushed a cute little tortoiseshell paw aside and jotted down the license number.

I tapped my phone's screen. So did Dep. Despite her attempts to call nearly everyone else on my contact list, I managed to ring Brent's personal cell phone.

Usually Brent answered my calls with a friendly, "Hi, Em." This time, he merely barked, "Fyne."

"You're in a meeting," I said.

"Yes." Still formal.

"I'll be quick. The two women who were hanging around the delivery entrance at the lodge on Saturday night just left Deputy Donut. I need to tell you what they said. Also, I got the license number of the car they were driving."

"What was it?"

I told him.

"Can you give me a statement later? I should be done here about seven."

"Sure. Want me to come to your office?"

"No." Decisive.

"My house, then. For dinner."

"Good." He disconnected.

I wondered who was chairing the meeting Brent was in. It could have been Brent or the chief of police or perhaps a DCI agent the chief had brought in to take over Roger's murder case.

Across the driveway, a woman was looking out a window near the back of Dressed to Kill. She turned her head toward the front of the store, though, as if someone had called her, and then she went away from the window. Because of the reflections on the glass, I hadn't been certain who she was. Not Jenn, unless she'd dyed her hair brown since early Sunday morning. Jenn had told me that Suzanne did the books at Dressed to Kill late at night, long after Deputy Donut closed. The woman I saw must have been Suzanne, working during the day.

Where was Jenn, and how was she coping with her grief? I'd been widowed after four years of marriage. Although four more years had passed, I knew I would never completely get over the pain. Jenn had been married about seven hours, but from what I'd seen of her marriage, she hadn't enjoyed all of those seven hours.

Meowing, Dep jumped off the desk and clawed her way up the carpeted tree leading to her catwalk. I left the office before she could bombard me with toys.

At four thirty, I set the lock on the front door so that the few customers remaining in Deputy Donut could leave, but no one could open the door from outside. I switched the sign on the door from WELCOME to OPEN AT 7:00 A.M.

The last customers said their goodbyes. Tom and I started tidying the kitchen.

Someone pounded on the front door.

Tom looked up. "Look who's here, Emily."

Brent?

I turned around.

I should have known from the dry way Tom clipped his words that it wasn't Brent. Tom liked Brent.

Tom did not particularly care for DCI detective Yvonne Passenmath, however.

Wearing her usual rumpled brown pantsuit, clunky black shoes, and angry expression, Yvonne Passenmath was using a fist to thump repeatedly on the metal frame around our glass door.

Chapter 13

"Great," I complained to Tom. "I'll go let her in."

I unlocked the door and opened it. Detective Passenmath trudged inside. Was she sniffing the air because delicious coffee and donut aromas lingered, or was she attempting to intimidate me with her keen observation skills?

From the kitchen, Tom said, just loudly enough, "Hey, Yvonne."

She nodded in his general direction. "Westhill." She turned to me. "I need to talk to you. Alone."

I couldn't help asking, "Without an attorney?"

"Get one if you want. I can wait. I have the statement you gave Detective Fyne, but I have questions."

"Come into the office. I hope you don't mind cats."

"I can take 'em or leave 'em." She called toward the kitchen, "Don't go anywhere, Westhill. You can witness her signature when I'm done with her, and then I want to talk to you, too!"

I opened the office door and let Yvonne Passenmath precede me inside. Dep took one look at the frowning DCI detective and bounded up the narrow staircase to the catwalk. I hoped Dep didn't have any soggy toys up there to drop on Passenmath's head. Passenmath's curly brown hair was frizzy enough thanks to the day's apparent humidity. Underneath my Deputy Donut hat, my own curls were undoubtedly tightening.

Passenmath handed me several sheets of paper. "Your statement. Go over it and see if it's what you meant to say."

I pointed to the couch. "Have a seat."

She glanced down at the cushions as if checking for excessive amounts of cat hair, but the Jolly Cops kept the office clean, and she must have decided it was okay to sit.

I swiveled the desk chair to face Passenmath across the coffee table and then spent about five minutes reading the statement while Passenmath alternately sighed and yawned. I finished reading and told her, "It's fine."

"Don't sign it until we get Westhill in here."

I started to go get Tom, but she flapped her hand at me. "Stay here. You need to answer some questions."

Trying to keep apprehension from showing on my face, I sat again.

Passenmath took out a small black notebook and pen. "There were names painted on the wall you hung donuts on, right?"

Somewhere above our heads, Dep was ominously quiet.

Without glancing up toward my mischievous cat, I answered, "Yes. The bride's and the groom's."

"Whose idea was that?"

"The bride's. She'd seen it in a wedding magazine. She wanted her favorite donuts to go on the dowels beneath her name and the groom's favorites to go on the dowels beneath his name."

"And you were the one who hung the donuts beneath their names?"

"Yes."

"Every single one of them?"

"After midnight, other people might have hung up some of the donuts. I don't know. I was dancing."

"Dancing." She said it like it was an alien activity. I felt sorry for the hard-to-like detective. She demanded, "Weren't you supposed to be working?"

"The bride said beforehand that I should join the party after midnight. She owns the clothing store across the alley." I pointed. "I've gotten to know her by shopping in her store."

"What kind of donuts did you hang on the dowels underneath the bride's name?"

"Her favorites, honey-glazed crullers."

"Dipped in powdered sugar?"

"No, but we make the glaze by dissolving powdered sugar in honey."

"So, what did you hang on the dowels underneath the groom's name?"

"His favorites, raised donuts coated in confectioners' sugar."

"Powdered sugar."

"Yes, but as far as I could tell, Roger didn't eat his favorites. He seemed to prefer the bride's."

Her eyes, which already seemed too small for her wide face, became even smaller. "What makes you think that?"

"When I saw that powder in the saucer, the pattern in it looked like the hills and valleys in a cruller."

"In criminal investigations, we don't jump to conclusions."

One of my eyebrows began quirking upward. I quickly lowered it and tried not to show my skepticism. The last time I'd been around Yvonne Passenmath, she'd seemed very willing to jump to conclusions, especially if her conclusions might implicate me in a murder. "I saw Roger eating one also, but that was before midnight, and the one he ate had not been coated in confectioners' sugar."

"As far as you know."

"I'm pretty sure."

"If a cruller dipped in honey glaze was dipped in white powder and then hung on a wall for a couple of hours, wouldn't the white powder melt until it could barely be seen?"

"I suppose so, especially if the glaze wasn't thick and crusty, and ours wasn't. But the white powder didn't appear until after midnight, at most a half hour before Roger collapsed."

"How do you know when it appeared?"

"To be specific, it didn't appear in the saucer underneath my hat behind the donut wall until after midnight. I don't know where the powder was before that. But when I set my hat on that table, there was no saucer and no white powder." Brent had included that information in the statement I'd just read. However, I didn't blame her for asking the same question in a variety of ways as she tried to get to the truth. Or to get someone to change her story in a way that would show she was lying . . .

"No one else has corroborated when that white powder appeared behind that donut wall." Her squinty dark eyes gleamed.

"Not many people ventured behind those curtains, but at least one person knows when he or she put that saucer of powder down on that table and covered it with my hat."

"Precisely."

I retorted, "Not me."

As if I hadn't said anything, she asked, "What donuts did you hang on the columns of dowels between the ones marked for the groom and the ones marked for the bride?"

"Raised and unraised, decorated to go with the colors the bride chose as her wedding's theme colors. I varied how I hung them, arranging them to look pretty."

"I'm not interested in *pretty*." She said the word disparagingly. "Only in donuts that could have been poisoned."

"A picture I took of the donut wall when I first stocked it

shows what was hanging on it better than my verbal description."

She handed me a business card with her e-mail address on it. "E-mail it to us."

I hid a smile. She was going to see *pretty* whether she was interested in it or not.

She paged back in her notebook. "You said that the groom's favorite donuts were raised donuts coated with confectioners' sugar. Did the deceased personally tell you that those were his favorites?"

"No, Jenn did. His bride."

Passenmath's eyelids nearly shut over those lizard-like eyes, and then she looked down and wrote in her notebook. "During the evening, did you get the bride's and groom's favorites mixed up and placed on the wrong hooks?"

"No, but other people might have rearranged the donuts and crullers while I was dancing." I reminded her of what I'd said in my statement about the five crullers missing from one of the two bakery boxes that had been on the table before I started dancing.

"Are you certain that the missing objects were crullers?"

"Tom and I didn't mix the types of donuts in the boxes. But again, someone might have rearranged them while I was dancing."

"You said there were two bakery boxes on the table when you went off to dance, and when you came back, one box had crullers in it. What was in the other box?"

"I don't know. I didn't open it."

"You brought it."

"I didn't keep a mental inventory of what might have been in the unopened boxes. Anyway, I'm sure investigators took that box. They can tell you."

"They did." Her mouth twitched like she enjoyed demonstrating that she knew more than I did. She asked, "Did the bride spend time around that donut wall?"

"Not at all. As I said in my statement to Detective Fyne, the bride left the banquet hall while I was dancing, and I didn't see her again until right before her husband was wheeled out to the ambulance."

"I've seen the setup in that banquet hall," Passenmath said. "Tell me about the lighting in the minutes leading up to when the deceased collapsed. Were the lights brighter where the dancers and reception guests were, or were they brighter behind the curtains in that narrow space next to the log walls?"

"Where the reception guests were, but even there, the lighting was low."

"So, anyone who was on the more brightly lit side of those curtains, where the dancing was going on, wouldn't have seen who was on the darker side of the curtains or what they were doing. Anyone could have been back there, poisoning donuts."

I agreed. "When I was between the curtains and the room's walls, I was able to see people who were very close to the reception's side of the curtains. And there was a spot just to the left of the donut wall where the edges of two curtains met. Those edges could have been parted slightly if someone wanted to peek out, or pushed aside whenever anyone wanted to come and go between the reception and the space behind the curtains." I moved my hands apart as if opening curtains. "I'd been going back and forth all evening. I think that someone planned ahead and brought arsenic to the reception. And I think he or she arrived in the space behind the curtains by coming in from the service corridor. When I left the back of the donut wall to dance, the door from the corridor to the banquet hall was closed, but after Roger collapsed, that door was unlatched. The culprit could have been alone back there, and could have dipped those five crullers in arsenic. Maybe he or she had seen Roger hanging around taking crullers. The

poisoner could have reached around the edge of the curtain"—I demonstrated pinching an imaginary cruller between
my thumb and forefinger and reaching around a curtain—"and
placed the poisoned crullers on one of the tiered cake stands on
the table in front of the donut wall, and then Roger could have
stuffed them into his mouth."

I wondered if he had crushed them and gobbled them
whole as he'd done with the one he'd eaten after he'd told
Chad to leave. I also wondered if he'd filled his pockets with
crullers before or after he ate the poisoned ones.

I could have told Passenmath that I was *not* the one poisoning the donuts, but knowing her, she would suspect that
my repeated denials were a sign that I was guilty. Maybe my
guesses about how someone poisoned Roger without harming anyone else were already making her suspect me.

She paged back in her notebook, paged forward, wrote a
sentence or two, and clapped the notebook shut as if she'd
just closed her case. "You can leave," she snapped. "Get
Westhill in here."

I hesitated, wondering if I should tell her about the Happy
Hopers. If Brent had told her that I'd called him about them,
she'd be expecting me to mention them.

Her face reddened. "I said you can go now."

"I . . . um . . . I hope the cat doesn't drop anything on you
while I'm out."

"I hope so, too, for its sake. Get Westhill in here so he can
witness your signature."

I sent a warning glare up toward Dep. Hunched over her
front paws with her pupils enlarged as if she were contem-
plating all sorts of diabolical activities, she stared down at
Passenmath.

I hurried to the kitchen.

Tom followed me to the office and witnessed my signature.

"You can go now," Yvonne Passenmath told me. "I've got questions for Mr. Westhill."

Mr. Westhill. People usually called him Chief Westhill or, if they knew him well like I did, by his first name.

Frowning, I left the office and closed the door behind me.

Chapter 14

Tom had tidied the kitchen. In the dining room, I turned chairs upside down on tables. If Alec, Brent, or Tom had been questioning me and I had hesitated like I had around Passenmath just now, Alec, Brent, or Tom would have quietly waited to hear what I wanted to say. They would not have dismissed me as Passenmath had.

I wasn't about to run into the office to tell her to watch witnesses for cues that they might have more to say, however. I was itching to leave so I could shop for ingredients for Brent's and my dinner, but I couldn't go until I collected Dep, and she was in the office.

I glanced through the office window. A red plastic ball with a jingly bell inside it rolled off the catwalk, missed Passenmath by inches, and bounced out of sight, probably ending up underneath the desk.

Maybe flying kitty toys prevented Passenmath from staying. She returned to the dining room. Tom followed her and carefully shut the office door. Passenmath looked annoyed. Tom's annoyance appeared to be tempered with amusement. Passenmath refused his offer of donuts, and he let her out the front.

I told Tom, "She's looking for evidence against Jenn."

"The spouse. That's common."

"And Passenmath likes the easy path to a quick arrest."

"Lucky thing for the bride that Fyne's on the case," he said. "He'll take a broader view. Did she ask you about the bag they found in your wastebasket at the reception?"

"No. What bag?"

"Someone tossed a plastic sandwich bag into your wastebasket. There were grains of white arsenic inside it. I told her there was no way you had taken a bag of arsenic to the reception along with our donuts."

I grinned. "Thanks, Tom, but she knows that you and I would stand up for each other."

Tom folded his arms and frowned toward our front walk, where we'd last seen Yvonne Passenmath. "They found no arsenic in our Deputy Donut police car or in here, though by the time they searched this place, the Jolly Cops could have inadvertently cleaned it up."

"And they didn't find any in my clothes. I don't know about the jacket that I had to leave there, on the floor underneath the table. And I hope she doesn't get a search warrant for my house. Not that she'd find arsenic, but she'd say that was because I'd had time to discard it."

"I'm sure that the killer, whoever it was, did his or her best to get rid of any traces of arsenic, possibly before taking a plastic bag of it to the lodge Saturday night. Are we done here for the night?"

"Almost." I e-mailed a photo of Jenn and Roger's donut wall to the address on Yvonne Passenmath's business card and then boxed half a dozen donuts. Tom, Dep, and I went out the back and locked up. Waving, Tom drove away.

Dep and I walked home. In the living room, I let her out of her halter. She scampered toward the back of the house. I followed, washed her dishes, refilled them, and put a couple of baking potatoes into one of the ovens.

Heading toward the front door, I called out to Dep, "See you later!" She didn't pause her energetic grooming of one hind leg.

I drove my own car, a fast but safe one like the sports cars that Alec had driven, to a block of specialty food stores near Fallingbrook's central square where I quickly purchased what I needed for dinner.

Back at home, I sliced a baguette most of the way through, slathered garlic butter on it, wrapped it in foil, and put it in the other oven. I cut broccoli, chopped veggies for salad, and whisked balsamic vinegar, extra-extra-virgin olive oil, and salt and pepper together for dressing.

The doorbell rang. Dep raced to the living room and waited, nose against the door.

Brent always stood far enough back for me to see him through the peephole. Either he was still on duty or he'd come straight from work. He was wearing gray slacks, a pale blue shirt, a tweed blazer, and a dark blue tie.

Smiling, I opened the door. "Come in."

He handed me a bottle of Merlot. Thanking him, I closed the door. Dep meowed. He picked her up. "Thanks for calling today, Em. Sorry I couldn't talk." He looked tired.

"It's okay. I knew you'd be busy. So . . . let me guess. Yvonne Passenmath was holding the meeting?"

He opened his eyes wide in pretend amazement. "You detected that from my one-syllable comments?"

I laughed. "They were very expressive. Besides, Yvonne showed up at Deputy Donut after work."

Brent frowned. "I told her that we tested your shop, your car, and your clothing and found no arsenic on them, and she read the forensics report, besides. I hope she's not focusing on your shop having been cleaned before we sealed its doors early Sunday morning."

"She'd probably like to decide that Tom and I are responsible for Roger's death, but she said she visited Deputy Donut for me to sign the statement I gave you."

"I could have brought it to you."

"She had other questions for me, about who decided which donuts went where. Apparently, she's searching for evidence against Jenn. But she hasn't ruled me out." I described thinking aloud to Yvonne Passenmath about how the killer might have managed to single out Roger. "Yvonne seemed to take it as a confession."

"She's not the best one at brainstorming theories."

"I should brainstorm my theories only with you."

"As long as you don't *act* on any of your theories."

When Alec was alive, we never ate in the dining room when Brent visited except when he brought a date. Now I wanted to keep my relationship with Brent casual, so I set places for us at the kitchen island, and we started on the Merlot and munched crackers covered in Gorgonzola.

Brent got out his notebook. "I ran the license number you gave me. The car belongs to Vanessa Legghaupt. Does that name ring a bell?"

"No, and although I paid attention, neither of the two women mentioned the other one by name. It was a little odd, actually, the way they only referred to each other as 'she.'"

I gave him a plate with two thick steaks on it, and the three of us, Dep leading the way, went outside to the barbecue. While Dep stayed with Brent and the steaks, I returned to the kitchen, microwaved the broccoli until it was just tender, drizzled it with butter and fresh lemon juice, dressed the salad, put the hot potatoes on plates, cut them open, and garnished them with sour cream and chopped chives.

With Dep meowing behind him, Brent brought the steaks inside. As always, he'd grilled them with neat crisscrosses. We sat beside each other at the kitchen island and cut into the steaks. They were perfect, medium-rare, the way we both liked them.

I asked Brent if he had wanted me to tell Yvonne Passenmath about the Happy Hopers' visit to Deputy Donut.

"Did you?"

"No. She didn't ask."

"That's not surprising. I didn't tell her they'd been at your shop."

"She seems to like to control the direction of the conversation. Good detectives don't do that."

"Mmp."

"You're welcome."

Grinning, he cut off another bite of steak.

I told him everything that Vanessa Legghaupt and her friend had said to me that afternoon.

He summarized, "So, this Vanessa Legghaupt claims that Roger Banchen ruined or tried to ruin both her business and her reputation, and that he told people she'd been imprisoned in Utah."

"Can you check to see if she has a criminal record?"

"I did. She doesn't, but I remembered her name from a case here in Fallingbrook a year and a half ago. She was questioned about a skirmish over a shopping cart in the supermarket parking lot, but witnesses came forward saying that the other woman had attacked Legghaupt, and that Legghaupt had willingly relinquished the shopping cart without laying a finger on the other woman. Legghaupt wasn't charged. The other woman was."

"So, Roger made up that she'd been in prison? That should be enough to anger anyone. And her friend said that she, the friend, not Vanessa, paid Roger double what she'd been paying Vanessa, and then all that Roger did, as she put it, was 'snarl and sneer' at her. Both Vanessa and her friend have grudges. Are you going to go talk to them now? I mean, after dessert?"

"I'll talk to them in the morning. I have a list of the registrants at the Happy Hopers Conference, but now I know where to start, with this life coach. And I'll make certain to mention that I'm talking to all of the conference attendees. They shouldn't be able to connect my questions to you."

I hadn't worried about it. Brent was always circumspect. Besides, if the two women talked as much as they had around me, he would barely have to ask anything. However, if one or both of them had killed Roger, they might clam up around a detective. I added, "I couldn't figure out whether or not they knew he was dead, and I was careful not to ask."

"Word seems to have gotten around."

"So, if someone is avoiding talking about it, they might be pretending they don't know, and you might view them with suspicion?"

He gave me a sly grin. "At this point, we suspect everyone."

"I know, including me." With my own sly grin, I asked, "Do you mind donuts for dessert?"

He made a pretend and very exaggerated scowl. "Of course not."

I glanced toward the coffeemaker. "Coffee?"

"Not tonight, thanks. With Yvonne on the case, I don't have to be on duty all night. I can go home and catch at least a few hours of sleep."

Someone pounded on the front door.

Chapter 15

Brent stood up and asked quietly, "Are you expecting anyone?"

"No, but Yvonne Passenmath knocked like that this evening at Deputy Donut."

Brent started out of the kitchen. "I'll get the door."

Dep and I followed him through the dining room. I stopped at the edge of the living room. Tail straight up, Dep trotted behind Brent.

He peered through the peephole, turned around, gave me a grim nod, and opened the door.

Yvonne Passenmath strode in. "What are you doing here?" she asked Brent. "Business or pleasure?"

Ears back, Dep scooted away, toward the kitchen and sunroom.

Brent shut the door. "I'm off duty, but Emily had some information that I was about to bring you."

"What information?" Why did Passenmath think she had to bark at Brent?

"She gave me the license number of one of the two women who were hanging around Little Lake Lodge Saturday night."

"They were attending a conference, and we already have the list of attendees. You got anything else?" Passenmath had barely moved away from the front door, effectively blockading Brent from coming back into the living room. I hung back in the dining room.

"The woman's ID," Brent answered.

"Bring it to work in the morning. You were going to question all of the conference attendees, weren't you?"

"I'll start with that woman."

"If you have time. We have a lot of ground to cover. Meanwhile, I've got questions for Ms. Westhill."

Brent edged around Passenmath, placing himself between her and me. "Need an attorney, Emily?"

Now that I was part of the conversation, I took a few steps into the living room. I smiled, not very naturally. "No. I want this murderer to be caught." If Yvonne Passenmath asked me something I didn't want to answer, I supposed I would have to dredge up a lawyer. The only one I knew was the woman who had helped with the purchase of this house and of Deputy Donut. Her specialty was real estate.

Yvonne stared at Brent as if hoping he'd leave.

"I'd like to hear her answers, Yvonne, if you don't mind." He said it politely.

She shrugged. "Suit yourself."

I gestured toward the couch, its matching armchair, and the wing chair. "Come in."

Passenmath sat in the armchair and pulled a notebook out of a sagging jacket pocket.

Brent sat in the wing chair and removed a notebook from his shirt pocket.

Wondering how Passenmath would react if I also opened a notebook, I plunked myself into the middle of the couch.

Passenmath gave me the old fisheye. "We picked up a wastebasket at the site, a metal one, kind of purplish. Do you know anything about it?"

"If it's a step-on can trimmed in white lace and gold ribbons, it's mine. I took it there. It should have my fingerprints all over it, and you should be able to find my prints from when I worked at 911. They were still on file during last year's murder investigation."

"Can you tell me why that trash can was full of plastic gloves?" Pointing her pen at me, she looked about to shout, *Gotcha!*

Sitting up straight on that comfy couch seemed all wrong, but I did my best to appear professional and helpful. And innocent. "I took an entire box of them to the reception. The investigators probably have the box containing the ones I didn't use. It's normal food-handling procedure. We wear sterile gloves when we're touching food. We throw them out and then put on a new pair when we need to touch food again."

Like a trial attorney trying to trip up a witness, she demanded, "How many pairs were in that wastebasket?"

"I didn't count, but probably at least a dozen. Subtract the number that are still in the box from the number it was supposed to contain before I opened it, and that's how many should be in the wastebasket."

Passenmath glared.

Oops. I was getting bratty. Careful not to look at Brent, who was probably trying not to smile, I added seriously, "Tom said you also found a plastic bag in that wastebasket, and the bag had arsenic in it."

Scowling did not improve her appearance. "He had no business telling you that."

"Maybe it's good that he did, so I can tell you directly." I raised my chin and gazed right into her eyes. "I did not throw any plastic bags into that can."

'Brent shifted in the wing chair, but he didn't say anything.

Passenmath flapped her hand as if trying to shoo a pesky mosquito. "We have no way of proving that. Any fingerprints on that bag were wiped off."

That gave me an idea. I glanced toward Brent. He was wearing his impenetrable poker face. I turned back to Passenmath. "Can you get prints from the insides of plastic gloves? You should be able to get most of a handprint."

She moved her head slightly as if she wanted to shake it, but she pinched her lips together instead.

"We can check," Brent said.

I leaned forward. "Because most of the handprints inside those gloves should be mine, but at least one glove might have another handprint inside it."

Brent asked me, "Usually, when you remove those gloves, do they end up right side out?"

Picturing myself stripping off gloves, I realized my mistake. "No, actually. It's fastest, most hygienic, and least messy and sticky to turn them inside out as I take them off. But probably not all the way inside out. Most of them end up in sort of a ball."

He nodded. "That's the way we do it, too. We don't let the possibly contaminated surface of a glove come into contact with our skin."

I added, "In any case, handprints inside gloves probably get smeared."

Passenmath seemed to make no attempt to hide her dislike of both Brent and me. "Forensics will look into prints everywhere on those gloves, and on everything else."

"Hold up your hand, Emily," Brent said, "palm toward us."

"Hands up," I joked, but I showed them my palms.

"Her hands are small for an adult," Brent pointed out. "You can put your hands down now, Emily." He said it sternly, but there was a twinkle in those gray eyes.

Like the well-mannered lady I pretended to be, I folded my hands in my lap and said politely, "As I mentioned this afternoon, Detective Passenmath, whoever dipped a cruller or crullers into arsenic and left a saucer of it underneath my hat might have come into the banquet hall by the back door, the one leading to the service corridor, and I suspect that he or she must have also left that way. Before I started dancing, that door was shut. After Roger fell, but before I knew about the white powder, that door was open. I went out into the corridor to see if anyone was there. One meeting room smelled strongly of the fragrance that the two women from the conference were wearing, so your search for disposable gloves with handprints other than mine should take you to the overflowing wastebasket inside that meeting room, near the door to the service corridor."

Passenmath informed me, "All of the trash from every waste container in the lodge was picked up for analysis."

"If it's all been tossed into one big bin, look carefully at anything near a lot of packaging materials from things like souvenirs or, as one of the women described them, 'cheap gewgaws.' And at anything that smells like potpourri."

She printed in her notebook and then shoved it into her jacket pocket. "We don't toss evidence into bins. It's all bagged and labeled, complete with location."

"Sorry, I should know that." Wrong thing to say. Reminding Passenmath that I'd been married to the detective she'd wanted for herself was probably not a good idea. And it probably didn't help that she'd found Brent visiting me, and it wasn't the first time. She'd run into him at my place just over a year before when she was in Fallingbrook investigating a different case. Obviously, someone needed to change the subject. I asked, "Would either of you like a donut?"

Passenmath stood. "We're finished here. For now."

"I would," Brent said. "I'll see you out, Yvonne."

As she left, she told him, "I expect you in the office first thing in the morning."

"I'll be there." He closed and dead-bolted the door.

Dep trotted into the living room and meowed at us.

I informed her, "If you've been lacking attention during the past ten minutes, it's your own fault. You could have stayed in here with us."

Brent picked up the demanding cat and cuddled her while I went to the kitchen for donuts. Back in the living room, I put a plate of them on the table. Dep and I settled on the couch. She purred.

Brent helped himself to a raised lemon donut with lemon icing. "I'm sure that the forensics team would look at the insides of those gloves as a matter of course, without direction from her, but she thought she had you for wearing gloves on Saturday night. Good for you for pointing out that the murderer might have borrowed a pair of those gloves and worn them. Judging by the look on her face, she hadn't thought of it."

"Had you?"

He grinned. "Of course. The murderer might not have put on any of *your* gloves, however."

"*I* would have worn gloves if I were playing with arsenic. To be on the safe side, though, I would have brought my own. And a mask."

"And you would also be a better detective than Yvonne Passenmath."

"I hope she's willing to consider someone other than Jenn as the culprit."

"She is. You."

"I'm trying to ignore that."

He bit into the donut. "Mmmm. Every time I taste one of your donuts, I think it's my favorite."

I thanked him and then remembered to ask, "Did you figure out who owned the black sports car that was steamed up in the staff parking lot early Sunday morning?"

He eyed me like he was about to warn me to stay out of police investigations. Then he relented. "I guess it's not exactly classified information. It belonged to the deceased."

I sputtered, "But it wasn't . . . he couldn't have . . . he'd collapsed about an hour before we saw that car. It probably couldn't have stayed so steamed up that long." A thought struck me. "We didn't check if it was locked."

"We didn't touch any of the cars."

"Who else might have a key? Did he have any family at that reception? They hired all of the attendants besides Jenn's half-sister."

"Most of the people at the reception were Jenn's guests. No one seemed close enough to Roger to be entrusted with car keys."

"And even the best man was one of the hired teens," I said. "Didn't Roger get along with his family?"

"He didn't have close relatives. His parents died when he was a kid."

"How did they die?"

"Car crash. His father was intoxicated. Roger survived with minor injuries."

"Does he have sisters or brothers?"

"No."

"Who raised him?"

"He was sixteen, just barely. He inherited everything and lived on his own in his parents' home, finished school, finished college."

I added, "Drank heavily as an adult."

Brent thinned his lips. "It can affect people that way."

"Did he have a roommate?"

"The bride. No one else."

"So, Jenn might have had a key. I don't know where she kept it, though. I didn't see her carrying a bag."

"That wedding gown had pockets."

I stared at him. "You're telling me that you checked her gown for arsenic. Let me guess. It came out negative. And when Passenmath read those results she was disappointed."

Brent's smile was so quick and slight that I almost missed it.

I accused in a teasing tone, "I can tell by the look on your face that my guesses are right."

He didn't confirm it except by telling me, for about the millionth time, that I should consider becoming a police officer. "But I have to admit that everyone would miss your donuts." That was quite a concession, coming from the man who had, after Alec was killed and I quit working at 911, tried to get me to stop making donuts and go back to 911. He ate another donut, thanked me for dinner and the information, and stood up to leave.

Dep lifted her head and stared at Brent. "Meow!"

He plucked her off my lap and held her up, her nose to his. "I'll be back another time." He hugged her to his chest and turned to me. "In case you didn't pick up on it, Yvonne is very interested that you and Tom made the donuts for the reception."

"I'm glad you had our car and our shop tested for arsenic. My clothes, too."

"It's too bad that the Jolly Cops made it into your shop and cleaned it before we sealed the doors. Yvonne also zeroed in that you were present when the mysterious powder appeared."

"I was dancing."

"But you're the only one who has told us the time it appeared, so . . ."

"That's because I'm the only one who saw it, besides the person who put it there, who probably isn't about to call Yvonne Passenmath and tell her the exact time he did it." I added crossly, "Don't they have serious crimes in other corners of Wisconsin that Yvonne Passenmath could investigate?"

He laughed. "Don't worry. I won't let her charge you."

"Poisoning someone with food that everyone knows I made doesn't make sense."

"Exactly."

"Someone that Tom put behind bars could be trying to frame Tom, I suppose. That's more likely than some random person trying to get revenge on me." I scrunched my mouth to one side. "On the other hand, Yvonne Passenmath doesn't always make sense. She goes for the easy answer, like Jenn, or people she doesn't think much of, like Tom and me."

"We have other leads."

"Vanessa Legghaupt and her friend."

He handed Dep to me and took out his notebook. "Describe that security guard again?"

I cradled the warm, purring cat in my arms. "That means you haven't contacted him yet."

"Mmp." Brent silently read his notes while I again described the man. "You have a good memory," he said when I was done. He put his notebook away, slung an arm around my shoulders, and pulled me close to his side. "Take care of yourself, Em." He released me and left.

I shot the dead bolt and then peeked out.

Brent trotted down the stairs. At the sidewalk, he turned toward downtown Fallingbrook.

The next day at Deputy Donut, I almost expected Yvonne Passenmath to show up again. She didn't, but midway through the afternoon, Misty did, with the officer who'd been her partner on Saturday night. In daylight, I could read the name tag on his uniform. Houlihan.

Life became even more interesting when Scott came in for his break and sat with them. "What's your special coffee today, Emily?" he asked.

"A medium roast, full-bodied Rwandan that some folks say has a high level of caffeine and requires extra cream or milk."

He turned the cream pitcher until the hatted-cat silhouette faced him. "I'll have that."

I grinned. "And to eat? Would you like to try our black-and-white?"

He laughed. "I'm a fireman, not a policeman. Do you have anything in red?"

"Unraised cinnamon donuts with red sprinkles."

"Bring me two."

Misty lifted a finger. "What's the black-and-white?"

"An unraised dark chocolate donut, sliced in half and stuffed with a sweet vanilla filling."

"I'll try one," she said.

"We have a black and white coffee, too—espresso with a dollop of whipped cream."

She made a face. "I'll make do with an espresso, and no dollops."

Houlihan wanted two black-and-whites and a mug of drip Colombian.

I brought them their order and asked Scott how he knew Jenn and Roger.

"I never met Roger before Saturday. I knew Jenn in college, and met her again after she opened her shop."

I feigned a worried face. "Uh-oh."

"What?" Scott asked.

I teased, "The DCI agent in charge of the case is going to think you're a jealous boyfriend."

Scott blushed. "I was never Jenn's boyfriend. Don't tell me they brought in Yvonne Passenmath again."

Misty said, "Okay, I won't tell you that. You'll find out."

Scott's blush receded a little. "I'll never understand how that woman became a detective at the DCI. Or anywhere else."

Both Misty and Houlihan managed straight faces.

I told Scott, "Jenn did invite an old boyfriend to the wedding and reception, the guy I was dancing with when you cut in. Do you know Chad?"

The blush returned. "I never saw him before Saturday."

I prodded, "I guess you don't know his last name."

Scott laughed. "I'm sure that Yvonne Passenmath can learn that from Jenn or from Jenn's guest list."

Misty twisted her black-and-white donut sandwich apart as if she planned to eat the filling first. "Leave it to Yvonne and Brent, Emily. Or else join the police department."

Houlihan didn't say a thing, but he grinned at me. He was cute, with freckles, reddish hair, and greenish eyes. I couldn't help smiling back. He was not, I noticed, wearing a wedding ring.

Later, the three of them left together and sauntered toward the police and fire stations. *Yessssss,* I thought. *Scott and Misty.* And maybe Misty and I could introduce Samantha to Houlihan.

As if they'd been watching for a break when no police officers were inside Deputy Donut, the two Happy Hopers returned and sat at the table they'd used the day before, in the glare of Dep's watchful eye.

I asked the two women what I could bring them. They ordered only organic green tea. A wistful expression flickered across the brunette's face.

When I delivered their tea, the blonde pulled a business card from her Happy Hopers tote. "I forgot to give you my contact information," she said, "in case you're in the market for a life coach. I'm Vanessa."

I glanced at the card. Her last name was Legghaupt, just as Brent had told me. I thrust the card into my apron pocket.

The brunette piped up. "And I'm April."

"I'm Emily Westhill." I gestured at the brochures on the table. "You can find my contact info in there." Not that they seemed to have had any trouble contacting me.

"Guess what?" April said. "A handsome detective interviewed us this morning. Both of us!" She opened a newspaper.

"Remember Roger, the groom we were talking about yesterday, the one from the reception Saturday night?"

I nodded.

She stabbed a finger down onto the newspaper. "It says here that he died—early the next morning after becoming unconscious at Little Lake Lodge. Were you still at the lodge when he collapsed and was taken away? It says here that an ambulance was called after midnight. They say that police are looking into the matter, and that it's a suspicious death." She seemed excited by having known a murder victim. "We left before that, around ten thirty or quarter to eleven."

I was careful not to give much away. "I was there. They evacuated the lodge."

The two women exchanged glances. Vanessa stirred her tea. "You know, you shouldn't be surprised if someone wants to question you." She seemed to be choosing her words carefully. She also wasn't meeting my gaze.

"I wouldn't be," I told her.

"That detective's *hot*," April chirped, as if committing crimes in order to attract the attention of a hot detective might not be a terrible idea. "He asked us who we saw at that lodge on Saturday, so of course we mentioned you. No harm intended."

I managed a poker face almost worthy of Brent. "It's okay. The police know I was there. I gave them a statement that night." I didn't feel that I needed to tell the women that the police had followed up several times. Or that I knew the detective.

Vanessa flashed a stern look at April. "We told him about *everyone* we'd seen. But he already had a list of the people who had attended that multilevel marketing conference. That's why he contacted us." She seemed to be watching me carefully. Maybe she'd guessed that I'd told the *hot* detective about her and April. Did it really matter? Perhaps it did, if she was a murderer.

They didn't stay long. I wondered if Vanessa still wanted

me to give a presentation about being a female entrepreneur, or if she ever had. Maybe she and April had come to Deputy Donut only to learn as much as they could about me. Maybe they had murdered Roger and were trying to figure out how to pin the blame on someone else who'd been at Little Lake Lodge on Saturday night.

Chapter 16

Misty phoned shortly before we closed. "You and Tom can pick up your donut wall now. And I think you have a stainless-steel cart there, too. They've been photographed, and the few grains of poison that were on the table have been thoroughly removed."

"Where can we pick them up?"

"At Little Lake Lodge. The proprietor would like to start using the banquet room again. I'm not on duty tonight, so if you can't pick them up, I could get them for you."

"Thanks, but I can go, unless Scott can take you in a fire truck."

"As if. How come we never noticed Scott in high school?"

"He was older, quiet, and studious. We noticed the jocks."

"We were stupid."

"We were young."

She laughed. "And some of those jocks who still live around here have beer bellies. Scott doesn't."

"And he's probably a lot more fit than they are now, and maybe more fit than they were back then. Go for him, Misty. You two would be perfect together."

"You wouldn't mind?"

"Mind, are you kidding? I've been trying to throw you two together."

"He really likes you," she said slowly.

"Likes. He likes *donuts*. We like each other. As friends. Go for him."

"Maybe I will."

"He comes in most days around three."

I heard a breath of a laugh. "Sometimes I think we never got over being young."

"Who would want to? I'll see if Tom's available tonight. If not, I might get you to help me pick up our things. Good luck with Scott."

"You wish." She disconnected.

I told Tom that we could pick up the cart and the donut wall.

"I was afraid we might have to build another donut wall."

"We might," I suggested, "but maybe bigger, for next time. Except I wonder how many, if any, of the people who said they'd like one at their own events might have changed their minds."

He raised an index finger in an *aha* gesture. "Maybe having a mystery around our first donut wall will make our next ones even more popular."

"You have a very warped sense of humor."

"Huh. No one's ever accused me of *that* before."

"Right." I'd heard Cindy say it many times.

He offered, "If you're busy tonight, I can get a buddy to go out there with me."

"I'm not busy."

"Take Dep home, and I'll finish here and be ready to go when you return."

"But I keep leaving you with the cleanups."

"I don't mind." I knew he didn't. Both of us needed to throw ourselves into working at Deputy Donut, and not only to make it succeed. Working hard was how we coped with missing Alec. Cindy devoted herself to her students at Fallingbrook High, where she taught art. When she wasn't teaching or preparing to teach, she was working in the pottery studio in the basement of Tom's and her house or attending meetings of various community groups, the kind that tried to make the world a better place.

The afternoon was unseasonably warm, making the stroll home with Dep a cheery occasion. Walking back to Deputy Donut without the curious cat was faster, but less entertaining.

Tom had locked Deputy Donut and was listening to the radio in his SUV. I climbed into the passenger seat, and he took off. We did not actually become airborne.

Again, the setting sun blazed across Little Lake. Tom backed the SUV to the lodge's delivery entrance. The door was locked.

Tom peered up toward the wide eaves. "If they have security cameras up there between the logs, they're well hidden." I didn't see any, either.

We walked around to the front of the lodge. In the sunset's pinkish glow, everything looked different. Early Sunday morning, there had been harsh lighting that knifed through the darkness, police cruisers, and an ambulance rushing off carrying a man who wouldn't survive the night.

And Jenn, crumpling to the ground in her white froth of wedding gown . . . I couldn't quite suppress a shiver.

Now the parking lot was only about a quarter full, and no emergency vehicles, school buses, or Red Cross vans were pulled up to the entrance. Beyond the parking lot, a green lawn rose in a gentle slope toward the road. When we'd arrived at sunset on Saturday, I hadn't appreciated how pretty the grounds were, with clumps of white-barked birch trees and gardens of blooming sedum, mums, and decorative kale. Scattered over the grass, yellow leaves glowed like glitter.

We didn't see surveillance cameras near the main entrance, either.

No one was at the reception desk in the lobby, but voices

came from the banquet hall. We walked down the hallway. The banquet hall's double doors were standing open.

White drapes still hung from the ceiling, but the swags of periwinkle tulle, the gold bows with their trailing ribbons, the temporary bar, and the gold-backed chairs were gone.

Dressed in black, three men and a woman were arranging ladder-back chairs around bare tables. The trio didn't seem to notice us. They were repeating the highlights, sound effects and all, of a movie that apparently featured multiple collisions and explosions.

The curtains next to our donut wall had been pushed apart. Someone had removed the tablecloth, vases, and tiered plates from our periwinkle-painted table. They had also detached the donut wall from the table. Dowels sticking straight up, the wall itself was lying on the table. The masking tape square, my down-filled jacket, and my wastebasket had been taken away, but our cart was next to the log wall beside the back door. All of the bakery boxes I'd flattened and stacked on the cart for recycling were gone, probably hauled off to be examined for traces of arsenic.

Above the sputtering of a chair mover's vocal version of something resembling artillery fire, a man called, "What can I do ya for?" The sound effects stopped mid-sputter.

I turned toward the room's main entrance. A man in low-slung jeans and a gray turtleneck ambled toward Tom and me. The man was wearing a dark wool billed hat that I'd once heard described as a Greek fisherman's cap. When he was close, I realized he was actually in his sixties or seventies. His hair was gray, and his neck was crepey and wattled. From a distance, his rangy figure and the slouchy way he walked had made him appear younger.

I waved my hand in the general direction of our disassembled donut wall. "We're from Deputy Donut. We were told we could pick up our cart and donut wall."

The man moved a toothpick from one corner of his mouth

to the other. "Better late than never." His light blue eyes were bloodshot. He had hardly any eyelashes.

I tried a smile. "Are you the one who removed the wall from the table for us? Thanks. You saved us some time."

"I didn't touch any of it. Those CSI guys wouldn't let me in here until this afternoon. My own hotel."

"We'll get the things out of your way," Tom promised. "Mind if we take them out through the delivery entrance, or should I move my vehicle around to the front?"

The man pointed at the room's back door. "Go through that way. The delivery door is never locked from the inside, but you'll have to prop the door open or you'll lock yourself out. We've always been able to keep it unlocked from the outside until now. Over a hundred years, this lodge has been in the family, and never a speck of trouble, not until that woman decided she had to rent this room, gussy it up in all sorts of outlandish ways, and then off her groom."

Tom turned around and strolled toward the table holding the prone donut wall.

"The bride did it?" I asked, my voice squeaking with amazement. Doubt, too, maybe.

"Stands to reason. Marries the guy, he's rich, then bam! She inherits. Besides, don't they say poison is a woman's weapon?"

"He's rich?" I asked. How many people believed that, and where had they gotten the idea? Brent had said that Roger had inherited from his parents when he was sixteen and had been able to finish his schooling. Jenn had told me that Roger had inherited from a distant relative. Maybe Jenn had told that to other people. Maybe the two inheritances had made Roger wealthy.

"Had to be rich. I figured that out, easy-peasy. The bride was the one who ordered all the frou-fra-las, but the groom was the one who signed the checks, every single one of them. And there were a lot of 'em. Usually the bride and her family pitch in. Some pay for it all."

Tom had returned and was standing beside me. "Did you personally witness the bride harming anyone or did you see her acting suspiciously on the video files from your surveillance cameras from Saturday night?"

The man stared at Tom for a few seconds as if wondering if Tom was an undercover cop and, if so, how he should word his answers. But he didn't seem able to resist talking about his lodge. He raised his chin a notch. "I wasn't here Saturday night. And video files? Are you kidding? Surveillance cameras? Over a hundred years we've run this lodge, and never a problem. People come here for the feel of a luxury lodge from a century ago. This place is the real deal. You start installing spy cameras and the like, and bam! You lose that authentic feel. You lose paying guests. No." He shoved his hands into his front pockets and hitched his jeans up to a less precarious position. "None of that modern stuff belongs at Little Lake Lodge."

I nodded. "Besides, you have a security guard posted at the delivery entrance."

The man in the Greek fisherman's cap was shaking his head before I got the word "guard" out. "No, we don't. We've never needed a security guard. I patrol this place day and night. Nothing gets by me. Except Saturday night. As I already told you, I wasn't here." He dislodged the toothpick again. "And I proved it to those nosy CSI guys. People, I should say, since some of them were gals. The daughter had a baby up in Minneapolis. The wife and I have pictures of ourselves in the hospital with the baby late Saturday evening and early Sunday morning, time-stamped pictures, and plenty of witnesses— nurses and even the doctor who delivered the baby. We were in Minneapolis all weekend. That woman detective checked and double-checked."

Tom had already gone back to the donut wall. I persisted. "I saw a security guard at the delivery entrance on Saturday night."

"We don't stop people who rent the meeting rooms and banquet hall from hiring their own security. If it makes them feel safer, so be it. Wedding couples usually do, you know, because of the wedding gifts. Well, carry on."

He turned and shouted at his staff, "Hey! Don't drag tables across the dance floor. Pick them up and carry them."

I joined Tom. He pulled a package of sterile wipes out of his jacket pocket. Together, we thoroughly cleaned the table, the donut wall, and the cart. We balanced the donut wall on the cart and wheeled the cart down the corridor. The chair that the security guard had used was gone. We went back for the table, each took a side, and carried it out. We slid the table into the back of the SUV, wrapped it in blankets, wrapped the donut wall also, and packed it beside the table. The cart went, upside down, into the back seat.

Driving away from Little Lake Lodge, Tom said, "Pity."

"That they have to start locking doors?"

"That they didn't start long ago, and install cameras. Makes the investigation that much more difficult. Not to mention that if there'd been locked doors and cameras, no one might have died."

"There really was a security guard here around ten. I don't know about after that, and he was gone by about twelve thirty."

"I believe you. Too bad no one got his picture."

"And too bad no one got photos or videos of the two women who've been coming into Deputy Donut. It would be nice to know what they were doing that night besides hanging around watching who all came and went." I told Tom everything I'd seen and heard Saturday night and everything the two women had told me since. Outside the passenger window, the forest seemed to stream past us, as if we were standing still and it was moving. But when I looked straight ahead, it was obvious that we were the ones racing along the pavement. "Brent interviewed both of those women today," I said.

"He's a good detective, that Brent Fyne. A *Fyne* man."

"Ha ha."

"And then they had to go and bring in that Yvonne Passenmath again." Reciting a string of choice words, he pulled into the lot behind Deputy Donut and parked beside our loading dock.

We wheeled the cart into its usual spot in the combination pantry and storage room. We stowed the donut wall and its table in the basement, which we kept mostly empty. The tables, chairs, and umbrellas from our patios were already down there, some of them upside down and sprouting appendages like the arms and legs of ghostly cast aluminum skeletons. Every month or so, the Jolly Cops Cleaning Crew gave the basement a good cleaning.

Tom ran up the stairs. Unwilling to let the older person put me to shame, I ran, too. Neither of us ended up out of breath. Telling Tom to say hello to Cindy, I left for home.

Dep was a little indignant about being left during what she thought of as our dinner hour, but after a few minutes of cuddles in the wing chair, she hopped off my lap and asked to be let out into the backyard. She didn't stay long.

Under her watchful eye, I ate leftover lasagna at the kitchen island.

"What do you think, Dep, should I call Brent?"

"Mmp."

"He probably knew from the beginning of the investigation that Little Lake Lodge doesn't have surveillance cameras."

"Mmp." Helpful cat.

"And he probably knows by now that the lodge doesn't have its own security guards, and that the one I'd seen had probably been hired by Jenn or the Happy Hopers Conference."

Dep gave me a cross-eyed look. "Mmp."

"Yes, there was another meeting room, but I don't know whether it was used that evening." When I'd peeked into it after twelve thirty, it had been neat and tidy. "Besides, Tom might have called Brent while I was eating dinner."

Dep galloped toward the living room. I followed her. She stood beside the front door. "Meow."

"Dep, are you telling me that Brent would be bothered less by hearing information that he already knows than by missing out on it entirely?"

"Meow."

"You're right. We don't want Yvonne to learn something before Brent does. Thanks for your input, Dep."

"Meow."

I plunked down on the couch and called Brent's personal number.

"Hi, Em," he answered.

"You're not in a meeting."

"I'm at home."

I told him about the lack of surveillance cameras at Little Lake Lodge and that the lodge's owner hadn't hired a security guard Saturday night. I added, "The owner says he can prove he wasn't at his lodge on Saturday night."

"Yvonne checked. Both the owner and his wife were visiting the maternity ward at a hospital in Minneapolis. Did the lodge owner tell you who hired the guard you saw?"

"No. He said that wedding couples often hire them during receptions, because of the gifts. Or the conference organizers might have hired him, to protect the cheap gewgaws, no doubt."

"Mmp."

"Did you ask Jenn if she hired the guard?"

"Yes, and she regretted that she hadn't thought of hiring one. Or a bodyguard for Roger."

"Why would she have thought that Roger needed a body-guard?"

"I asked the same thing. She said, 'Because of the way things turned out.'"

I could tell from his tone that he didn't quite understand Jenn's reasoning. I didn't, either. "So Jenn didn't go on her honeymoon by herself?"

"She said the idea didn't appeal."

"Or you told her not to leave town."

"After everything that went on, she would have missed her plane, anyway."

"Is she a suspect?"

"Everyone who went near that lodge Saturday night before midnight is."

"And spouses always get close scrutiny."

He quoted in a very dry voice, "'The course of true love never did run smooth.'"

I couldn't help bursting out laughing. "I should let you go. You're suffering from sleep deprivation."

"Thanks for calling, Em. Don't be afraid to call, even if you think we already know what you're going to tell us. And let me know if you think of anything else or remember anything else, especially about that security guard."

"Have you located him yet?"

"Mmp." I interpreted that as a no.

I prodded, "No one admits to hiring him?"

"Strange, isn't it?" It wasn't an answer, exactly, but I understood, as I was sure he meant me to, that he hadn't figured out who had hired that security guard and he still didn't know the guard's identity. "Give Dep a hug for me," he said.

I realized that my cat had been loudly meowing on the couch beside me during the entire conversation. Brent and I said our good nights and disconnected.

Dep got the hug she'd obviously been demanding all along,

and then she levitated onto my shoulders and draped herself around my neck like a warm and rumbling scarf.

I didn't think I'd have much more to tell Brent about that security guard. I'd already given Brent the best description I could.

The next morning, the security guard showed up at Deputy Donut.

Chapter 17

What was it, a conspiracy? Three people had hung around the delivery entrance at Little Lake Lodge on Saturday night. And here it was, only Wednesday. The two women had visited Deputy Donut twice, and the security guard had just walked in.

He wasn't in his uniform, but as far as I could tell, his shoes were the ones he'd worn on Saturday night, complete with the broken and knotted-up shoelace. The industrial-strength shoes didn't quite go with his white socks, faded jeans, plaid shirt, and gray hoody. His ruddy face was heavy around the jowls.

He sat by himself near a table where a bunch of retired men met nearly every weekday morning for coffee, donuts, and a lot of laughing. The security guard had his back to them, and he appeared to be reading our Deputy Donut brochure, but a slight smile tugged at his lips when the men behind him burst into guffaws.

I went to his table and asked what he'd like. He didn't appear to recognize me, possibly because I was wearing my Deputy Donut hat. When I'd worn it near him at Little Lake Lodge, he'd been dozing.

I told him we were brewing a fresh pot of the day's featured coffee, a full-bodied dark roast blend from several African countries. His voice as raw as it had been Saturday night, he ordered a mug of the coffee along with an unraised dark chocolate donut with hints of ancho chilis.

I went into the kitchen and told Tom that I had to call Brent and why.

Tom glanced into the dining area and immediately turned his head away. "Tell Brent that the man is Gerald Stone. He can look him up in the police files if the name doesn't ring a bell."

"Would you like to be the one to call Brent?"

"No. I want to keep an eye on Stone."

I said in a menacing tone, "I'm going to have a lot of questions for you later."

He grinned. "And I'll have answers. Meanwhile, don't let Stone sell you any drugs."

Mouthing, *Oh,* I backed away from him.

I served Gerald Stone, who didn't appear the least bit stoned, and then I had to attend to other customers before I could take a break and shut myself inside the office with Dep. Turning my back to the dining room, I admired the morning sun glinting on trees behind our parking lot while I called Brent's personal line.

"Hi, Em," he answered.

Obviously, he wasn't in a meeting with Yvonne, but I didn't waste time. I blurted, "That security guard is in Deputy Donut. Tom says to tell you he's Gerald Stone, and to look him up in the police files."

"Thank you. Thank Tom, too. That case was before my time on the job, but I heard about it. I'll find out where he lives, and I won't show up at your donut shop with sirens blasting. But take care, okay?"

"You and Tom have sooooo many questions to answer."

"Can I bring pizza and beer over tonight?" I heard the hint of a smile in his voice.

"To my place? Sure!" Dep was head-butting my arm. She meowed.

Brent must have heard her. He laughed. "See you around six thirty?"

Leaving Dep to mutter about being shut inside the office where she could look at but not climb around on us, I went out to the dining area.

Gerald Stone didn't stay long. He also paid cash and left me a big tip, but no drugs, poisons, or other toxic substances that I could detect. I cleaned his table very well. But then, I always cleaned the tables very well.

In the afternoon, Scott came in for his break and sat with police officers and other firefighters. Misty didn't show up. I hoped Scott was as disappointed as I was.

After we closed, Tom and I tidied the kitchen. I asked him who Gerald Stone was.

"About fifteen years ago, when I was police chief, and you were in kindergarten—"

"Nice try. Fifteen years ago, I was in high school." Well, nearly.

"Uh-huh. Stone ran a pharmacy out on Packers Road."

"I remember that. We always thought Stone Drugs was a funny name. But I never went there, so I never saw the guy before Saturday night."

"Now it's Fallingbrook Pharmacy. Fifteen years ago, though, Stone was a successful pharmacist, maybe a little too ostentatiously successful, judging by his large house and luxury car. He spent a lot more for them and for vacations than we'd have expected from his pharmacy's income, and there were rumors about how he managed to afford everything. We were certain he was selling prescription drugs illegally. We were about to nab him, but the flow of drugs stopped suddenly, and we never did find conclusive evidence. Soon after we ended our investigation, he sold Stone Drugs, his large house, and his expensive car. He moved into a small apartment and became a part-time security guard."

"Maybe he was in over his head, and financial institutions caught up with him, and he had to sell."

"Could be, but if he had mortgages and loans, we never found out who the lenders were. He'd paid off the mortgage on his store a year or so earlier, and he didn't appear to have borrowed to buy the mansion and the car."

"And now he's switched from dealing drugs to delivering poison?"

"There's not a whole lot of difference. Let me know if he comes in again. I'll keep an eye on him."

"And so will the cops in here, no doubt."

"Most of them won't remember him. Very few of us worked on the case, and we've all retired."

Tom left for home.

Although Dressed to Kill was supposed to be closed, a small bright red hatchback was parked behind it.

Dep and I walked down the driveway between Deputy Donut and Dressed to Kill and turned south on Wisconsin Street.

The sign in the door of Dressed to Kill announcing that the store would be closed for two weeks was gone, and the door was unlocked. I poked my head inside.

Wearing black cords and a black turtleneck, Jenn was near the front, folding sweaters. Her long blond hair was tied back in a low ponytail. "Hi, Emily." She looked surprisingly in control of herself.

"I won't come in," I said. "I have the cat with me, on her leash."

"That's okay. We don't have to worry about a food license."

I ushered Dep in and gave Jenn a hug. "How are you doing?"

"Still in shock. I can't believe what happened." Her lips trembling, she turned away and wiped her eyes.

I picked Dep up before she could wind her leash completely around a rotating display rack and start it spinning. "It's horrible," I agreed.

Jenn turned toward me and managed a weak smile. "I didn't like being home alone, so I came here to distract myself. But while I was sitting at home, I did create a couple of sweaters with my knitting machine." She pointed. I admired the sweaters, one black and one gray, probably colors that matched Jenn's feelings. She turned her head toward the back of the store and called, "Suzanne, come meet Emily!"

Looking almost gaunt, and bent slightly as if in pain, Suzanne came from near the change rooms and joined us. She was wearing tight blue jeans tucked into gray leather boots—zipped up, I noticed—and a bulky blue-gray sweater.

We shook hands and exchanged pleasantries and sympathy, and then a customer came in. Jenn greeted the customer. Suzanne strode away down the aisle between the change rooms and disappeared behind them. A door clunked shut. I told Jenn goodbye and took Dep home.

Touring our backyard, I discovered one partially opened pale pink rose. It smelled like my grandmother's favorite roses had, and also like the fragrance surrounding Jenn on Saturday night. At first, I'd attributed the fragrance to her bouquet, but it had still been strong later, when Jenn was outside without her bouquet. She must have dabbed a lot of floral perfume on herself that day. Maybe she'd left the banquet hall around midnight to refresh her perfume.

I cut the rose, put it and some water into a small emerald green glass vase, and set the vase on the coffee table in the living room. Outside the back door, Dep meowed pitifully. I opened the door. She ran inside with her tail puffed up as if she'd decided that gusts of wind were pursuing her.

A few minutes later, Brent showed up at the front door with my favorite pizza and beer. He was in a blazer, slacks, tie, and button-down shirt. The evening was chilling rapidly and the sun would soon set, so we ate at the island in the kitchen.

Dep hung around trying to make Brent believe that no one

ever fed her. We finished all but one chunk of crust. I gave it to her. The cat who had been trying to convince us that she was starving batted the crust around, leaped up into the air, pounced, caught the crust on a claw, tossed it, and started the chase again.

In the living room, Brent and I settled into comfy seats, the wing chair for me and the armchair for him. Brent refused my offer of coffee, but he liked the dark chocolate ancho chili donuts.

I picked up the small vase with the even smaller and slightly droopy rose in it. "The last rose of summer," I said.

"Does that make you sad?"

"I like all of the seasons. But the poor thing does look pathetic." I sniffed it. "Smells good, though." I stared up at the ceiling, but I wasn't seeing the ceiling. I was seeing the darkened meeting room with the Happy Hopers banner, I was seeing myself as a child in Williamsburg, and I was smelling the rose overtones in the potpourri, both in that shop in Williamsburg and at Little Lake Lodge late Saturday and early Sunday. I lowered my head and stared straight at Brent again.

"What?" he asked.

"You know I told you that Vanessa Legghaupt and her friend April, the two women who had been attending the conference advertising 'goal achievement through shopping,' smelled like potpourri, and so did the meeting room that their conference had been held in?"

He nodded.

"I assumed that meant that Vanessa and April had recently been in that room. I also guessed that whoever coated crullers with arsenic might have fled from the lodge through the service corridor and then through that room, which kind of points to one of those two women as the culprit. Or both of them. However, the wastebasket near the door was overflowing with packaging materials. Maybe someone had unwrapped containers of potpourri or had spilled potpourri-scented cologne and Vanessa and April smelled like the room, not the other way around. Potpourri smells like lots of spices and flowers all mixed together, but that night, roses were one of the more prominent fragrances in it, and I was sure I smelled roses." I took a deep breath. Brent was watching me intently, with no sign of judgment on his face. "I don't want to tell you what I'm thinking."

"Then don't." He said it mildly.

There was no way I would withhold information from this man. Alec had trusted him. They'd been best friends. I trusted him, too.

And Brent and I were friends.

I took another deep breath. "I have to. Jenn was wearing a very strong perfume that night. It smelled like roses, specifically like old-fashioned roses similar to this one. The overwhelming smell of potpourri in that room could have masked other perfumes that someone hiding in that room could have been wearing."

"That makes sense."

"But Jenn murdering her newlywed husband *doesn't*."

"Follow the money," he reminded me. "Roger had a lot of it. And his will was written in a generic way, several years ago, probably before he met Jenn. If he was married, everything was to go to his wife. If he wasn't, his fortune was to be divided among about thirty different charities, equally, and they were major charities, mostly international, so the amounts each would receive would have been a mere drop in the bucket. Not enough to risk their reputations for."

"But you're keeping an open mind about it."

"I haven't ruled out anything."

"But Jenn's so nice! Sweet."

Brent raised an eyebrow.

"I talked to her in her store briefly this evening. She was trying not to cry about Roger's death, and not succeeding."

"Mm-hmm." It wasn't an agreement.

Dejected, I slumped down on the sofa. "Early Sunday morning, someone else was wearing a fragrance that the potpourri could have masked. Jenn's ex-boyfriend Chad was wearing a spicy aftershave."

"Strong?"

"Not particularly. I noticed it when I was dancing with him."

Brent looked down at his notebook.

Brent and I were both loyal to Alec, so I wasn't sure why I had to defend myself to Brent. "I didn't dance with Chad very long. Scott cut in. But my impression was that Chad was a good man." The sudden closeness I'd felt with Chad during that short dance and the way that closeness had made me uncomfortable didn't seem to have any bearing on whether or not Chad might have poisoned Roger. I didn't try to explain to Brent how dancing with and talking to Chad for only a few minutes had convinced me that Chad could not be a killer, but I did tell Brent about the deft way Chad had stopped the boys from racing around in the banquet hall and how he'd refused to get them beer from the bar.

"He's a high school teacher," Brent explained.

"At Fallingbrook High?" If so, Cindy would know him.

"Up in Gooseleg." That was the next big town north of Fallingbrook, and the closest one that also had a high school. The two schools were football rivals.

"Does Chad live up there?"

"On the way. In a cabin in the woods."

"Not far from Little Lake Lodge?"

"Fifteen or twenty minutes east of it."

"You've questioned him about Saturday night."

"Yes, and Yvonne has, also. He said he left Little Lake Lodge and went home shortly after midnight."

"He certainly left the banquet hall then."

"You know, if the potpourri didn't originate from those two women, but came from something in the meeting room, and either Chad or Jenn fled there after poisoning Roger, the potpourri would have masked their scents, as you just said.

But if the killer *wasn't* wearing a strong scent, all you'd have smelled was potpourri. And anyway, if the potpourri fragrance was coming from the stuff in the wastebasket, it doesn't mean that Roger's murderer ever went into that room."

"Too bad. I'd have liked to say I sniffed out a clue."

Brent gave me a sour grin. "You might have, but don't count on it."

"And the killer went *somewhere,* probably into the service corridor."

"Probably. And as you pointed out, that hallway leads to many possible escape routes."

I found it hard to believe that either Jenn or Chad could have murdered anyone. I didn't know about Vanessa or April. And Gerald Stone was even more of an enigma. "Did you talk to Gerald Stone?"

"I did. He confirmed that he was at Little Lake Lodge Saturday night."

I kicked off my flats and tucked my legs underneath me. "Does Stone know I sent you?"

"Maybe, but he does have a valid Private Security Permit, which allows him to work as a security guard in Wisconsin, and I'm sure he thinks I found him through the registry. I would have, eventually, but you saved me some time."

"Who needs surveillance cameras when we have people?"

"Right. Except that not everyone's as good as you are at both observing and describing. And the video from his apartment building shows him returning. He said he didn't remember when he left Little Lake Lodge, but if he went straight home, as he said he did, he would have left there about ten after twelve Sunday morning."

"That puts him at the lodge right about when the crullers were being dipped into the arsenic." Dep jumped into my lap. I stroked her. "Did he see anyone in the service corridor?"

"No, but he said he might have dozed off. He wasn't sure if he heard people walking around in that corridor or only dreamed it."

"Unless he was pretending, he was sleeping, and snoring, shortly before ten that evening when I came in carrying that metal wastebasket. It rattled each time I took a step. But there was music going on then, and except for one or two short breaks, the band played until Scott ordered the evacuation. Except during those breaks, I'm not sure how much Stone could have heard of people walking around the service corridor even if he was awake. He could be making up hearing someone else to cover for his own sneaking around." I leaned forward. "Did you arrest him for poisoning Roger?"

"Just being at the site at the right time isn't enough, even though no one admits to hiring him."

"So, he had no reason to be there?"

"I didn't say that."

I retorted, "Not exactly."

He glanced at me. "You're not hearing this from me."

I grinned. "Or anyone."

"Okay, here's the story you didn't hear. Stone had a reason, of sorts, to be there. He'd been hired at another resort, but he went to the wrong place. When he realized his mistake shortly after midnight, he left."

I furrowed my brow in mock confusion. "Shortly after midnight! I saw him at Little Lake Lodge before ten. Wouldn't the place where he was supposed to be have contacted him?"

"You'd think so."

"I know what he must have told you. He forgot his phone or the battery had gone dead."

"Have you planted listening devices in our interview rooms at headquarters?"

"Yeah, sure. *Not.* It's easy to guess what excuses Stone would give for staying at the wrong place for so long. Maybe the dog ate his phone."

Brent laughed. "He didn't try that one."

"Did he give you the name of the other resort?"

Dep hopped off my lap and onto Brent's. Brent smoothed the stripy orange patch on Dep's forehead. "Good questions,

Em. Stone said he'd forgotten the name of the resort, so he went home, and then he discovered that he hadn't made a note of where he was supposed to be, and he wasn't sure he had the right date, either."

"That sounds concocted. Stone did it! He put the poison on that saucer, dipped crullers in it, and gave them to Roger!"

"Not so fast, Em. We might know more after we have his briefcase tested."

I tilted my head. "Did you get a search warrant for his briefcase?"

"He volunteered it."

"Maybe it's not the same briefcase."

Brent reached into his blazer's inner pocket. "That's why I brought this." Holding Dep in one arm, he stood and handed me a photo of a black briefcase that bulged as if something was in it, even though the top was open and no contents were visible.

"I . . . it could be the same one. The one he had Saturday night was also black, and I don't think it was leather."

Brent sat down, on the other end of the couch from me. "You can't definitely say that it's not the same briefcase?" Dep took a flying leap off his lap, skidded across the coffee table, and landed softly on the floor.

"No, or that it is." I returned the photo to Brent.

"Fair enough." He stowed the photo in his pocket. Dep apparently thought that was an invitation. She jumped into his lap again. Then she gently pulled his jacket away from his shirt. He was wearing a shoulder holster.

I grabbed her away from Brent.

"It's late," he said. "I'd better go."

I cuddled Dep against me. "Thanks for the pizza and beer."

"Thanks for the donuts. And you'll be careful around Gerald Stone if he returns to Deputy Donut?"

"I'm always careful. Tom's the reckless one."

Brent could tell I was joking. "Yeah, Chief Westhill never pays attention to what's going on around him." Brent smiled at Dep and gave her head a knuckle-rub. "Good night, Dep."

She batted at his hand.

We laughed and I opened the front door. As Brent went out, he gave my head a knuckle-rub.

Being generally better behaved than my cat, I didn't bat at his hand. I closed the door. And locked it.

Chapter 18

The next morning, I was behind the counter at Deputy Donut when another unexpected visitor arrived. Grasping the neck edges of the long beige sweater coat she wore over brown cords and a crisp white blouse, Jenn opened our front door only enough to edge in sideways. She was pale, her hair was hanging down limply, and her eyes were wide with something like fear. She came straight to the counter, leaned toward me, and whispered, "I need your help."

My heart went out to my bereaved friend. "What would you like me to do?"

"I need your advice. Can you come over for tea with Suzanne and me after you're done here tonight?" I could barely hear her.

"Five thirty?" I asked.

She nodded.

"Can I bring donuts?" Maybe mentioning donuts was not a good idea. . . .

She gave me a half smile. "Sure. No one seems to be keeling over in here." Her smile awry, like she didn't know whether to laugh or cry, she hurried out.

About a half hour later, Misty and Houlihan came in. They sat near the office again, causing Dep to go through about a million of her come-hither gyrations, seemingly meant to make Misty spend her coffee break in the office snuggling the cat. It didn't work.

To my surprise, Gerald Stone returned and sat by himself near the retired men. I wanted to believe that he was visiting Deputy Donut two days in a row because he really liked our coffee, donuts, and friendly atmosphere. But my years around police officers had taught me to be alert for signs of danger.

Stone could have returned because he'd guessed that I had told Brent his identity.

Stone could have returned because he wanted to silence me. Or Tom. Or both of us.

Tom seemed to have difficulty keeping an eye on Stone without letting Stone see his face.

Handing Misty a cruller on a plate, I whispered to her, "See that older guy by himself near the front?"

"The guy in the torn sweatshirt?"

"Yes. Watch him, okay? In case he starts dipping other people's food in arsenic?"

She raised her eyebrows. "You serve *that* now?"

I did my best to look insulted.

She asked me, "Is he the security guard Brent questioned yesterday?"

"Yes, and he would recognize Tom, so Tom's trying to watch him while keeping a low profile."

"Peeking over the half wall, you mean?"

"So that only the fuzzy donut shows."

Knowing I was joking, she laughed.

I headed for Stone's table. Maybe he did recognize me from Saturday night and had returned to Deputy Donut to try to figure out if I remembered seeing him at Little Lake Lodge. What would he do to me if he was certain I could report him? Or if he guessed that I already had? I was glad he hadn't brought a briefcase, but that didn't mean he didn't have a stash of poison in a pocket. I pasted on a welcoming smile and asked him what he'd like.

He ordered our featured coffee of the day, a Jamaican blend containing a hint of Jamaica's renowned Blue Mountain beans. He also ordered one of the lemon and green tea donuts that I'd concocted specifically for Vanessa and April if they showed up.

They didn't, not in the morning, not at lunchtime, and not before we closed at four thirty, without Stone or anyone else filling saucers with strange white powder.

I had a feeling that Tom would not approve of my spending time with Jenn and Suzanne, who might, to his retired-police-chief way of thinking, be murder suspects, so I didn't tell him where I was going. I merely said that I would lock up. Promising to say hello to Cindy for me, he left.

I suspected that crullers were no longer Jenn's favorites. I packed a box of lemon and green tea donuts. Leaving Dep to entertain herself in the office a little while longer, I went out onto the back porch and locked the door.

The small red hatchback was again parked behind Dressed to Kill, but there were other cars in the lot, too. I carried the donuts down the driveway and opened the front door of Dressed to Kill.

Bells jingled. Jenn glanced up from the sweater she was showing a customer. She looked less panicky than she had in the morning, maybe because she loved talking about sweaters and knitting. "Where's your cat?" she asked me.

"I left her in the office in the back of our shop. She spends her days there. She likes it. She won't mind playing or snoozing in there a little longer."

"Go right through to our office. It's beyond the dressing rooms. Suzanne's there."

Admiring gorgeous sweaters, dresses, skirts, and jackets, I made it through the store to the back. Although I knew, from looking out our office windows, where their office was, I'd never before been inside it.

In addition to two desks at windows overlooking the parking lot, there was a kitchenette, complete with a double-burner hot plate, a coffeemaker, a microwave oven, a double sink, a half-size fridge, and a round table and four matching chairs, white like most of the room, including the shiny tile floor. The table was set with three lime green place mats and three dessert plates, three cups, and three saucers, all of the dishes dark blue. With a sparkly light fixture over the table and late-afternoon sunshine slanting in through the back windows, the office was bright and inviting.

Suzanne was hunched over a computer at one of the desks. Her back was to me, so she probably hadn't heard me come in.

"Hi, Suzanne," I said, "what an office!"

Suzanne pushed her chair back, stood up, and turned to face me. Apparently, it was dress-in-shades-of-brown day at Dressed to Kill. Suzanne was wearing a chocolate brown sweater, matching cords, and brown shoes or boots with white and yellow daisies printed on them.

For Tom and me, every day at Deputy Donut was dress-in-black-and-white day. I was in my usual Deputy Donut uniform of black jeans and white shirt. I'd removed the cute apron and funny hat and put on a warm red cardigan that I'd bought at Dressed to Kill.

A pencil was poking out of Suzanne's hair above her ear. She pulled the pencil out. "We had a kitchen built in here so we wouldn't have to leave for meals." She set the pencil on the desk, carefully, like she was afraid of breaking the lead.

She and Jenn could have bought quick but not particularly well-balanced meals at Deputy Donut, like deep-fried jalapeño cheese nuggets with crullers for dessert, but except for Jenn's brief foray earlier that morning, neither Suzanne nor Jenn had ever been inside Deputy Donut. But then, Dressed to Kill opened later in the mornings than we did and stayed open later in the evenings. Plus, according to Jenn, Suzanne worked nights, long after Deputy Donut closed. Jenn was by herself in their store most of the time and wouldn't be able to leave.

Suzanne plugged in an electric teakettle.

"Here." I set the box of donuts in the center of the table. "Maybe I should have brought them on a plate."

"We can take them straight out of the box." She opened it and looked inside.

I told her, "They're green tea with lemon."

"I'll make green tea."

"Yum."

Maybe Suzanne had a tendency to smother Jenn, but she knew how to make tea. She poured hot water into a white teapot decorated with cobalt blue flowers, loaded a large infuser with green tea leaves, dumped the hot water out of the teapot, inserted the infuser, and poured freshly boiling water over it. She didn't talk. She seemed to be concentrating on the steeping tea, but I was certain that something was bothering her, probably whatever had brought Jenn running into Deputy Donut that morning to ask for my help.

The bells at the front door jingled, and then Jenn breezed into the office. "Perfect timing!" She sounded perkier than she looked. "Thanks, Suzanne."

Some women could flush prettily. Suzanne's thin face became blotchy. "Emily brought donuts."

Jenn gestured for me to take a seat at the table. "Thanks, Emily. And for coming over."

I sat where I could see through the window above the sink and across the driveway to Deputy Donut. Seeing Tom's and my shop from another perspective, even though it was only a brick wall and a sliver of office window, was kind of fun. I was proud of Deputy Donut and the satisfaction it gave us and our customers.

Suzanne poured tea into our cups and handed around a

bowl of sugar and a plate of sliced lemon. She sat down with her back to the desks.

Jenn squeezed lemon into her tea. "We asked you over, Emily, because things have gone from horrible to even more horrible. That detective said Roger was poisoned. She seems to believe that I gave Roger crullers that were coated with arsenic instead of sugar." Tears welled in her eyes. "But I didn't!"

"I know," I said. Jenn had been nervous about her wedding and about marrying Roger, but I could never imagine her killing him to end the marriage just hours after it began. I couldn't imagine her killing anyone, period.

Follow the money, Brent had said. I hoped that my tinge of skepticism wasn't showing on my face.

Suzanne spooned sugar out of the bowl and stirred it into her tea. "Of course you didn't." She set the spoon on her saucer. "Someone else did, and if the police have any sense, they'll figure that out." She turned to me. "But here's what scares me even more than Jenn being falsely accused—whoever killed Roger might have been trying to kill Jenn. The doctors at the hospital said that Jenn fainted due to stress and shock, but what do they know? She could have been poisoned. And since someone didn't succeed in killing Jenn then, he or she might try again."

"Why would someone kill me?" Jenn wiped her eyes. "I don't have enemies."

Suzanne corrected her. "That you know of. Maybe someone didn't like the sweater you sold her or hates this store for some reason. Maybe someone doesn't like brides, or brides wearing strapless gowns, and you were their first attempted victim."

Her theories sounded farfetched to me. However . . . "The crullers," I said slowly. "They were on the dowels marked 'Jenn.' "

Jenn sniffled. "And Roger's favorites, plain raised donuts

coated with confectioners' sugar, were on the dowels on his side of the donut wall. So why was he eating crullers? Someone made him do it?"

I had difficulty picturing anyone *making* Roger do anything, but Jenn had a theory. "Maybe he was trying to keep me from eating them. Maybe he tried one and it seemed off, so to protect me, he ate more of them."

After the way that Roger had talked to Tom and me, I could more easily imagine the disagreeable groom tossing the crullers out and then going to the microphone and announcing to everyone that our donuts were terrible. Brent had told me that white arsenic was tasteless, so I doubted that it would have noticeably changed the flavor of the crullers.

I knew one thing for sure. Those crullers had been delicious when I took them to Little Lake Lodge.

I didn't tell the two women that Brent had told me that crullers had also been stuffed into Roger's pockets. Why would Roger have done that? He'd talked to Jenn in an insulting and demeaning way. Was gobbling and hiding her favorite crullers, effectively keeping her from eating them, a way of controlling his bride? I asked, "What makes you believe the police think you killed Roger, Jenn?"

"The questions the detective asked, about Roger's money and his will and what I plan to do with the money I'm supposedly going to inherit from him. Insinuations. And she outright said that in her experience, murderers were often spouses."

I bit into my donut. Inside, its color outdid the lime green place mats. It tasted exactly the way I'd intended, green tea with a hint of lemon in the glaze. "That detective, was she Yvonne Passenmath?"

"Yes," Jenn said. "A stubby, mean-looking woman with beady eyes."

I tried not to laugh. "She's taller than I am."

Jenn smiled. "Nearly everyone is, Emily." She took a bite of donut. "This is very green. Are these made with matcha?"

"Yes."

Jenn stared at her donut. "Why is the powder from green tea leaves so much greener than the leaves themselves?"

"Focus," Suzanne reminded us. She looked at me with, I thought, hope. "You solved one of that detective's cases about a year ago."

I didn't like thinking about it and repressed a shudder. "Sort of."

"You can help us solve this one, and save Jenn from whoever might have tried to kill her and might attempt it again." Suzanne leaned back. "I've already figured out some clues." She tapped one index finger on the other. "One—there were people hanging around the lodge Saturday night who didn't seem to belong there, two women and a man dressed up like a security guard, but I wasn't sure he was one. All three of them were outside the lodge's delivery entrance."

So . . . I hadn't been the only one to notice them. "What time?" I asked.

"About nine. I had to go back out to my car to get Dressed to Kill business cards for aunts and cousins."

I ran a finger along one side of the lime green place mat. "Were the two women and the security guard together?"

"The security guard was outside the door when I went to get the cards, and when I came back, he was gone, but the women were still there. I don't know whether or not the three of them spent time together."

I pointed out, "You said they were all outside the delivery entrance. Were they together then?"

Suzanne shook her head. "Not close together, and the women were talking to each other. The security guard didn't seem to be part of the conversation, but I couldn't be sure." Her descriptions of the two women and the security guard weren't very detailed, but they didn't rule out Vanessa, April, and Gerald. She added, "A couple of days ago, I saw those two women get into a car behind Deputy Donut and drive away. And yesterday, I saw that security guard leave your shop, Emily. Do you know those people? Are they regulars?"

"None of them showed up in Deputy Donut until after the . . . tragedy." I cast an apologetic look at Jenn. "On Saturday night before ten, I saw all three of them near the delivery entrance. I was driving my Deputy Donut car and wearing my Deputy Donut hat, and I told the guard I was from Deputy Donut, so they all knew where to find me."

"Why would they want to do that?" Jenn demanded.

Her voice caustic, Suzanne answered, "To spy on you, Jenn. In case you've forgotten, our shop is next door to that donut shop."

In case you've forgotten. Maybe Jenn hadn't noticed Roger's verbal abuse. Maybe she expected everyone who cared about her to make little digs like the one her half-sister made. But I didn't have firsthand experience with siblings, let alone half-siblings. I asked Suzanne, "Do you think that the two women and the security guard might have acted together?" If they did, the police might be able to encourage one of them to confess and implicate the others.

Suzanne shrugged. "That's what we need to find out."

Jenn wrapped a hand around her cup. "But if three of them are after me, they could have three times as many chances to . . ." She looked about to cry. "To attack me?"

I offered, "This might help. I saw the two women together, both at Little Lake Lodge and at Deputy Donut, but the security guard seemed to be at Little Lake Lodge on his own. And he comes to Deputy Donut by himself, too." I sipped my tea. It was delicious, made of high-quality tea leaves, and perfectly steeped.

Jenn's lips twisted into something resembling a smile. "Three people might be after me, or two." Her shoulders slumped. "Or maybe only one. Great."

I set my cup into its saucer. "All three of them could be innocent, and coming to Deputy Donut to try to figure out who killed Roger. They all knew that I was there that night. And I brought the donuts. Maybe they suspect me."

"Well, *I* don't!" Jenn stated firmly.

I thanked her.

"One of those three people must have poisoned the donuts," Suzanne concluded. "None of your wedding guests would have, Jenn."

I immediately pictured the slightly amused Chad. At first, he'd seemed unconcerned about having broken up with Jenn, but a few minutes later, I'd gotten the impression that losing her to Roger was painful. Maybe he had planned that Roger wouldn't survive the evening.

But Jenn had said he was a good friend, and I wasn't about to say anything accusing about him in her presence. I was certain that Brent had not ruled out reception guests, and I knew he was scrutinizing every possible suspect, including Chad. And Jenn and Suzanne. And although Brent knew me well enough to be certain that I wasn't a killer, Yvonne Passenmath would not fail to add me to her list of suspects, for all the good that would do her.

Maybe I was being foolishly optimistic.

Suzanne tapped one index finger down on the other again. "Two—we can try to figure out what combination of those two women and the security guard committed the crime, or if it was only one of them." Tap. "Three—we need to find out a few things, like what they say on those TV shows. Who had the motive, the means, and the opportunity?"

I imagined Brent's face if he heard this. Or what Alec might have said—*they watch a crime show, and suddenly they're experts.* He might say it about me, also, I reminded myself, if he were alive and knew I was meeting with neighbors to try to solve a crime. I had not been and would not be interfering with the police investigation, however. Brent had asked me to relay any new information, and in the office of

Dressed to Kill, I was merely being receptive to any new information that might come along.

I knew what April's and Vanessa's motives were, but unless Brent gave me permission, I wasn't telling anyone besides Tom about those motives. But I had no idea what Gerald Stone's motive might have been. There were a few things that I could tell Suzanne and Jenn, however, things that anyone could have observed on Saturday night. "All three of those people were carrying bags that could have concealed poison," I said.

"I noticed that," Suzanne said. "The guard had a briefcase, and the women had bags from some conference."

I added, "Yesterday at Deputy Donut, the blond woman gave me her business card."

"Can I see it?" Suzanne asked.

"I don't have it with me. Her name's Vanessa Legghaupt. She works as a life coach."

In one smooth motion, Suzanne snapped her fingers and then pointed her index finger like a revolver at me. "Aha! Roger was a life coach. This Vanessa person was probably jealous of him, afraid he'd take business away from her, or something."

According to Vanessa, Roger *had* stolen clients. I didn't say it, though. For all I knew, Vanessa and April had made it all up or had reversed the story, making Roger look like the client-thieving culprit, when Vanessa was the actual thief. I leaned toward believing Vanessa's and April's stories about Roger, however. I'd seen Roger's sneering and snarling personality. And although it was hard to picture, I had to believe that Roger could have acted as charming at first as Vanessa and April had claimed. If he hadn't been able to turn on the charm, Jenn would probably never have gone out with him, let alone agreed to marry him.

Suzanne topped up my teacup. "Can you come over and tell us if those two women visit Deputy Donut again?"

"We usually have a shop full of customers, so I need to be there during business hours. Tom does most of the work in the kitchen while I'm usually the waitstaff, but we both pitch in where we're needed. But Vanessa's friend said she loved to shop. If I see them heading toward Dressed to Kill, I'll phone to warn you."

Suzanne asked, "Do you have our number?"

"Give it to me?" She did, and I programmed it into my phone.

Jenn polished off a donut and wiped her fingers on her napkin.

Suzanne lifted the lid of the teapot and peeked inside. "What time of day do those two women usually come in, Emily?"

"They've come in twice, around mid-afternoon. The security guard came in about ten thirty, both this morning and yesterday. But, you know, people who aren't in law enforcement can't interfere with a police investigation."

Suzanne lowered the lid of the teapot. "I'm not going to interfere, but I can't just sit here and let the police build a case against my sister. Or let a killer remain free to poison her."

Jenn drained her cup. "It won't come to that, Suzanne." She said it soothingly.

"Always the idealist." Clearing the table, Suzanne whisked my full cup away. Maybe she thought I didn't like it, when I'd actually been waiting for it to cool a little.

I stood, too. "I'd better go rescue my cat. Thanks for inviting me over."

Suzanne started running water in the sink. "Come back tomorrow after you close, and I'll let you know what else I find out."

"Okay." I started toward the front of the store.

Jenn leaped up from her chair. "Wouldn't the back way be faster?" She opened a windowless steel-clad door at the rear of the hallway next to the office wall.

I thanked her. "It would."

She smiled, but I could see the sadness lurking in her eyes. "Any time. And come to the back door again tomorrow. It seems more neighborly, somehow." Her smile became more genuine.

I smiled back. "I'll bring donuts, but I don't promise not to wander around among your wonderful merchandise."

"You've already been doing a good job of keeping us in business, almost by yourself."

"Your sweaters," I said, "are to die for." My cheeks heated. "Oh, sorry."

"That reminds me," she said. "I *never* should have called the shop Dressed to Kill. I'm thinking of changing the name. If you come up with any ideas, I'd be glad to hear them."

I loved Jenn's sweaters. The first name that popped into my mind was Dressed to Sweat.

I managed not to say it.

I went back to Deputy Donut and retrieved Dep. We walked home in the warm light of the setting sun. I fed Dep and made myself a delicious salad of Boston lettuce, dried cranberries, crumbled feta, and walnuts. I started a load of laundry and then sat down in my comfy wing chair. I thought I would read, and I thought Dep would join me.

Dep, however, kept going to the front door and pawing at it. I asked her, "Are you in a snit because I left you in your fun playground for an extra hour this evening?"

She turned her back on me.

I reminded her, "We don't invite company over every night."

The baleful look she gave me over her shoulder said that seeing Misty in the donut shop had made Dep miss her more than ever.

"And I didn't learn anything new to tell Brent," I informed the impertinent cat. "We need him to solve a murder, and not waste time with us."

Dep stomped away.

I called after her, "Not that being with you is a waste of anyone's time!"

Dep did not reply.

"Maybe tomorrow," I muttered under my breath. "Maybe Yvonne Passenmath will arrest Gerald Stone and we'll all be back to normal."

Chapter 19

At Deputy Donut shortly before ten the next morning, I peered into the office window to check on Dep and make faces back at her. Unlike her, I did not meow.

A small red car pulled into the parking lot behind Dressed to Kill. I was fairly certain it was the one I'd seen there after work the past couple of days, and I watched absently to see who got out of it.

No one did. From behind, I couldn't tell who the two people in the front seat were. They closed the distance between them until their heads resembled one. After about a minute, the pair separated. The passenger door opened. Jenn got out, blew a kiss at the driver, and headed toward Dressed to Kill's back door. She disappeared from view, and the car turned around. I was able to read the first part of the license number.

Chad was behind the wheel.

He went down the driveway toward Wisconsin Street.

Questions and surmises swirled in my brain, and the one that seemed to lodge itself in the most prominent position was the least important one. If Chad taught high school in Gooseleg, what was he doing in Fallingbrook at ten on a Friday morning in October? I shook off that question and let myself into the office.

Dep wanted to be cuddled. Instead, I picked up the phone and called Samantha's work number.

She was there, ready to rush away to emergencies. I told her about the red hatchback and rattled off the partial license number. She repeated the numbers to someone in her office and told me that her partner hadn't written it down, but he thought the numbers I'd given Samantha were similar to the license plate of the fogged-up red car he and Samantha had seen parked by the side of the road early Sunday morning. I hung up and stared down at my meowing cat. "Samantha told me that the man, who must have been Chad, was sitting with his face in his hands. Does that sound like a man who might be upset?"

"Meow."

"And maybe regretting having done something drastic and deadly?"

"Meow."

"Did Chad dip the crullers in arsenic, and then simply drive away, not knowing for sure who would eat them?"

"Mew."

"Was Roger his target, or could it have been Jenn?" The thought gave me the shivers, but Dep only curved a dainty front paw and brushed at it with her tongue. "Surely, Chad wasn't trying to poison *me*." He'd only just met me. I added, for Dep's benefit, "Chad probably doesn't take arsenic everywhere he goes in case he decides to poison someone. Besides, he seemed to like me."

Dep lifted her head and stared at me. The tip of her cute little pink tongue stuck out of her mouth.

"Thanks for your help, Dep." I went back into the dining area and closed the office door behind me.

The group of women who called themselves the Knitpickers were wrestling with the front door. As usual, their hands were full of bags and baskets of yarn, needles, and projects, and the front door appeared to be winning the battle. I held it open and welcomed the women, who were some of my favorite customers, to Deputy Donut.

South of Dressed to Kill, Suzanne was striding north in one of Jenn's long sweater coats worn open over a very short skirt and very tall boots. The boots were zipped all the way up, which was good because their tops were above her knees. Unzipped, they would have dragged behind her and flopped dangerously around the extremely high heels. I waved, but she didn't seem to see me. She disappeared into Dressed to Kill.

I helped the Knitpickers settle at their usual table beside a front window, near the table where the retired men sat, and brought them their hot beverages and sweet treats. They always ate first and then washed their hands before they settled into the morning's business of knitting, chatting, laughing, and sometimes poking good-natured fun at the retired men, who were skilled at returning the teasing.

My wish that Passenmath would arrest Gerald Stone and let everything go back to normal had not come true. Around ten thirty, Gerald Stone showed up at Deputy Donut and sat near the chortling group of retired men as if he hoped to be invited to join them.

Again, he wanted to try the day's featured coffee. "It's from Haiti," I told him. "The beans are Blue Mountain, like the Blue Mountain beans from Jamaica, and grown under similar conditions. It has a lot of the same smoothness."

"I'll try it," he said in that voice that sounded both porous and hard-edged. He nodded at the chalkboard where I'd listed some of the day's more unusual donuts. "And bring me a couple of those unraised dark chocolate and bacon donuts."

At the serving counter, I plated his donuts and poured his coffee.

Suzanne came in, the first time ever. Maybe she'd thought I was beckoning to her when I waved. She caught me staring at her and shook her head slightly. Then she glanced toward Gerald Stone for a second before darting another swift look at me. She started past his table. Suddenly it appeared that those high heels tripped her. She toppled toward Gerald Stone. He jumped up, grasped her elbow, and steadied her.

She went pale.

I hurried to her. "Are you okay?"

"I just twisted my ankle," she said. "No big deal."

"Sit down," Stone said. "I'll buy you a coffee. That'll make you feel better."

"I couldn't." She sat down, anyway, in the chair next to his.

I suspected she'd seen him come into Deputy Donut, followed him, and pretended to stumble. I was afraid the twisted ankle was real, however. "The coffee's on the house," I told Stone, "hers so she'll rest her ankle, and yours for saving her from falling."

Suzanne gave me a stern look. "Thanks." She held her right hand out toward Gerald Stone. "Call me Vinnie."

I hoped I managed to keep the surprise off my face. *Vinnie?*

Gerald shook Suzanne's hand. "You don't look like a Vinnie."

She plunked her purse on the spare chair next to her as if she planned to spend the rest of the morning at that table.

Back in the kitchen, Tom was obviously trying not to gawk. He mumbled to me, "Did I see that woman on Saturday night? Was she the bridal attendant who was trying to keep those boys from sliding across the dance floor?"

"Yep. She's Jenn's half-sister."

"Think she knows Stone?"

"She does now."

"Just stumbled upon him?"

I made the appropriate groan. "I think she saw him come inside and followed him."

"Keep an eye on them."

"Yes, sir."

Gerald Stone and Suzanne stayed, nursing their coffees and then spending another hour sipping second mugs of coffee that Stone insisted on buying. They seemed to have a lot to say to each other.

I'd barely seen Suzanne—or Vinnie as she was calling herself—talk much or act very animated, and I didn't know she was capable of flirting, but she obviously was. When they left together around eleven thirty, she was limping only slightly. Stone offered her an arm, and she took it. They walked slowly toward Dressed to Kill.

The evening before, as I'd left the tea party at Dressed to Kill, Suzanne had told me to return to find out what she'd learned. I hadn't expected her to come up with much during twenty-four hours.

Apparently, I had underestimated her.

It was worrisome, though. If Stone had killed Roger and his next intended victim was Jenn, Suzanne might accidentally tell him too much, giving him a better chance to harm Jenn.

Halfway through the afternoon, Misty and Houlihan came in, laughing and talking. Scott joined them a few minutes later. Dep took one look at Misty and started meowing loudly enough to be heard through her window.

I took Misty's, Houlihan's, and Scott's orders. Misty asked if she could go into the office to give Dep the attention she obviously required.

I went with Misty and asked her how she and Scott were getting along. She hugged Dep and peeked around the cat's whiskers at me. "Exactly the same as ever. I don't think he even notices me."

"Except to come in during your break and sit with you."

"And with a bunch of his firefighters. And Hooligan Houlihan."

"Is that his name?"

"No, but he prefers it to his real name."

"Which is . . ."

"He won't say."

"Does Samantha know him?"

Misty grinned. "Not yet."

"We'll have to find a way."

"Does she ever come in here?"

"Too tempting, she says."

Misty laughed. "Wait until she sees Hooligan. She'll forget to be tempted by *donuts*."

"Does he have a girlfriend?"

"He doesn't talk about that, either."

I asked her how the investigation into Roger's murder was going.

She scratched Dep's chin. "Not well, I suspect, but Brent would know more."

"Is Passenmath annoying everyone?"

"Probably. That woman is close to unbearable. Brent needs a break. He'd probably like to spend more time with you and Dep."

I backed toward the office door. "I'd better get your donuts before Scott and Hooligan Houlihan starve out there."

She cocked her head in a superior way, one eyebrow up. "You don't think that someone who has known you since we were fourteen and has since become a super-observant police officer doesn't notice when you change the subject?"

I opened the office door. "Did I?"

"Ha!" She set my purring cat gently on the couch and then followed me into the dining area.

Scott and Hooligan Houlihan both smiled at us, probably because we were giggling almost like we had when we were fourteen and, along with Samantha, had spent most of our time discussing which boys we liked best, and which of those boys might like us back.

Misty sat down with Scott, Hooligan Houlihan, and the other police officers and firefighters at their table. I took them their coffee and donuts, and then refilled trays with donuts that Tom had frosted and decorated.

A tall man entered our cozy café. His eyebrows angled downward at their outer edges, and he was smiling.

Chad. If he taught school up at Gooseleg High, he had started work late that day and ended early.

His smile warming, he sat on a stool at the counter. "Hey, Emily, I told you I'd find you again."

And later, when he'd been conspicuously absent from the reception, someone had gone into the back of the banquet hall and had dipped crullers in arsenic and put them where Roger was likely to find them before anyone else did. And Roger had been Chad's ex-girlfriend's husband.

Even worse, only this morning I'd seen Chad departing rather fondly from that same ex-girlfriend.

This was Friday. Jenn had been widowed almost six days.

Despite his flirtatiousness, Chad had made a good first impression, but I didn't dare trust him.

I tried not to glance toward the table of police officers and firefighters. From the corner of my eye, I could tell that Misty had lifted her head and was staring at me, but I couldn't see which direction Scott was looking. "Hi, Chad. Welcome to Deputy Donut." I knew I was being ridiculously formal. "What can I get for you? We have a bigger selection than we did Saturday night, plus coffee and tea."

He sauntered to the display case and pointed at raised donuts with fudge icing—always a favorite. "Two of those, please, and a latte."

He sat on the stool again and watched me prepare his coffee. I set it and a plate of donuts in front of him. He pointed with a thumb over his shoulder. "Hey, is that guy over there the one who stole you from me on Saturday night?"

"He's one of our regulars."

"What's with the matching blue pants and shirt? Is he a cable repairman?"

"Fireman, along with the other people at the table who are dressed the same way. The red and white badges on their shirt pockets are shaped like Wisconsin, with the firefighters' emblem embroidered on them."

"I mistook the shape for a box cutter." *Right, an insignia that every well-dressed cable repairman would wear.* "How do you know him? Did your house burn down? Or is it because he's a regular here?"

"I've known him since high school."

"I can't catch a break."

"I told you about Alec," I reminded him.

"I know, but there's always hope, or there should be, anyway, or where's the fun?"

"Um . . ." *That was a long clinch you and Jenn were in this morning.*

Chad rescued me from my sudden speechlessness. "Did you go to school around here?"

"I've lived in Fallingbrook all my life, except for college."

"Do you have family here?"

What was with all the questions? I told myself that Chad was only being friendly, but the personal questions were making me uneasy. "My parents." I didn't have to tell him that they went to Florida every winter and had already left Fallingbrook. To them, "winter" in northern Wisconsin was the entire year except for June, July, and August, and they often decided that winter included the first half of June and the last half of August.

Chad nodded toward Tom. "Is that your dad?"

"My father-in-law."

"You said you were widowed." He started on the first of his donuts. "Mmmm."

"My in-laws are as close as parents." Closer, actually, except during parts of June, July, and August, and if I were to be completely honest, maybe I felt closer to my in-laws even when my folks were in town.

It wasn't that my parents and I didn't love each other. We did, and we would fly to each other's aid if necessary. But they'd had me when they were in their early forties, and by then they'd made being laid-back into an art form. Even though I was their first and only child, they were relaxed about raising me. Unless they thought I was heading for real danger, they had let me make mistakes and learn from them. After I reached adulthood, they didn't interfere in my life and

I didn't interfere in theirs. We weren't exactly aloof, but at a young age, I'd learned to be, or at least to act, emotionally independent.

My parents had grieved when Alec was shot, but they were proud of me and of the parenting style that had helped me become, they thought, strong and self-sufficient. Maybe my own pride had made me hide that I was sometimes anything but strong and self-sufficient. After our initial mutual condolences, we had mostly avoided talking about Alec's death, and my parents had gone on believing that I could cope with anything. Or I hoped they had.

Tom, Cindy, and I didn't discuss our shared grief much, but it had forged a bond between us. When I was around them, I never had to pretend I wasn't hurting. If any of us needed to talk about Alec, we could, with very little awkwardness. Besides, Tom and Cindy were younger than my parents and lived in Fallingbrook year-round. I felt at home around them. And Tom was the best business partner anyone could have.

Chad smiled at me over the top of his mug. "You make really good coffee," he said.

Misty, Scott, Hooligan Houlihan, and the other police officers and firefighters got up to leave. Misty must have noticed that I wasn't entirely comfortable around Chad. She looked straight at me and raised a questioning eyebrow. To show that I was fine, I smiled and waved.

Scott hesitated as if wondering if he should come over and intervene. I smiled as reassuringly as I could at him also, and he hurried to catch up with Misty.

I was almost positive that Scott would tell Misty that the man who was talking to me had attended Saturday night's reception. And when Misty got back to the police station, she'd tell Brent or, if she had to, Yvonne Passenmath. *Great.* Yvonne would come stomping in to talk to me. And to Chad.

But Yvonne didn't come in, and neither did Brent.

Chad left. Still on foot, he turned toward the driveway between Deputy Donut and Dressed to Kill. I hurried to join Dep in the office where, like Dep, I could spy on the great outdoors, otherwise known as the driveway and parking lot.

Chad walked up the driveway and got into the red car he'd driven earlier. Cuddling Dep, I watched. Chad didn't drive away, and I needed to get back to our customers. The next time I looked out, after serving dozens of donuts and mugs of coffee, Chad's car was gone.

People seemed reluctant to leave Deputy Donut at four thirty. Tom and I closed the shop late and tidied as quickly as we could, and then he went home to dinner with Cindy. Telling Dep that I'd see her soon, I took a box of donuts outside and across the driveway to Dressed to Kill.

I knocked on the taupe-painted steel door at the rear of Jenn and Suzanne's shop. No one answered. The knob wouldn't turn. I knocked again. I was about to go around to the front when I heard a bolt slide with a stiff, grating sound. I didn't remember hearing that sound the night before when Jenn let me out.

The door opened. Suzanne stood back and waved me in. I heard Jenn and another woman chatting enthusiastically in the front of the store.

Again, the table in Jenn and Suzanne's comfy office had three place settings, with purple place mats this time. Putting the box of donuts on the table, I asked Suzanne, "How's your ankle?"

"It's okay." She started the electric kettle. "Go on out into the store and hurry Jenn along."

Although I had no plans to rush Jenn's customers out of her store, I browsed, admiring pretty clothes until Jenn's customer paid for dressy slacks and a gossamer knit shawl. Wearing gray jeans and a shell pink sweater, Jenn gave me a hug. I followed her to the office.

"Tea's ready," Suzanne said. "Have a seat."

I again sat facing the window above the sink. Jenn was to my right, where she'd been the evening before. Standing, Suzanne poured tea into our deep blue cups.

Jenn opened the box of donuts. "C'mon, Suzanne, I've been dying to hear what you found out today."

Suzanne eased into the chair with its back to the desks. "Poor choice of words, Jenn."

Jenn flushed.

The room became silent as if we were all waiting for another customer to enter the front door and set the bells jingling. I couldn't merely sit there admiring the box of donuts. I turned to Suzanne. "How did you end up with Vinnie as a nickname?"

Jenn sat up straighter and stared at Suzanne. "What? Vinnie? Since when?"

"My middle name's Lavinia, Jenn, as you should know."

"I do, but I've never heard you call yourself Vinnie."

"I like it," I said. "It's cute."

Suzanne looked annoyed. "I wasn't trying to be cute. I didn't want you giving away my real name."

Feeling chastened, I helped myself to a donut.

As if she wanted to inject some neighborliness into our tea party, Jenn asked, "What kind of donut is that, Emily?" She sounded stiff and formal.

"Bacon and sun-dried tomato, made with baking powder, not yeast. I brought three of them and three raised peanut butter donuts filled with grape jelly and coated in sugar. This one's my dinner and the sweeter one will be my dessert." My attempt at a folksy and friendly tone probably came across as overdone.

Jenn selected a bacon and sun-dried tomato donut. "Great idea." She bit into it. "Mmmm! It's good. Try one, Suzanne."

"I can't. I'm going out to dinner."

Jenn beamed. "You have a date?"

Suzanne pooh-poohed it. "No big deal."

I felt like dozens of millipedes were slithering down the back of my neck. If Suzanne's date was with Gerald Stone, it was potentially a *very* big deal.

Not wanting to tell Jenn and Suzanne things that Brent wouldn't want me to, I managed a weak objection. "Not with that security guard, I hope."

Suzanne's face became almost as cold and hard as the last name of the man she'd stumbled into in Deputy Donut that morning. "I can look after myself. It's not like a real date. I need to find out all I can about him so I can protect my sister."

Jenn asked, "Is he the security guard from Saturday night?"

"He told me he works as a security guard part-time, so I asked him if I'd seen him at Little Lake Lodge on Saturday night, and he said he'd been there. Bingo." She said it all, including "bingo," in a dry and unexcited tone.

Jenn asked, "Did you find out his name?"

Suzanne sat up taller. "Unless he's making it up, his name is Gerald Stone."

The uneaten half of Jenn's bacon and sun-dried tomato donut landed on her plate. "The Gerald Stone who used to own Stone Drugs?"

"That's what he said."

Jenn put her palms on the table, levered herself up, and towered over us. "Don't go anywhere near that man, Suzanne."

Chapter 20

Suzanne demanded, "What are you talking about, Jenn? Why should I stay away from Gerald Stone?"

Jenn grasped the back of the chair she'd left. Her knuckles whitened. "Gerald Stone is dangerous."

Suzanne stared up at her half-sister, still looming over us. "We don't know that for certain. That's what I'm trying to find out."

Groaning, Jenn fell into her chair.

I took a deep breath. "We should let the police do the investigating."

Suzanne turned to me. "*We* are not going out with Gerald Stone, and *I* am not going to do anything that will endanger me, or either of you. I'm just going to meet Gerald for dinner, and then I'm going home. By myself. I won't ask leading questions. I'll let him talk, and if I learn anything that the police should know, I'll tell them, okay?"

I suggested, "You might want to ask him why he went from being a successful pharmacist to a part-time security guard."

Suzanne thrust her face forward. "Didn't you just tell us not to interfere with the police investigation? Asking Gerald Stone questions could endanger us. Gerald Stone is going to do the talking."

I quickly apologized. "You're right. But if he mentions why he retired early from being a pharmacist—"

"I'll remember what he says," Suzanne snapped. "Don't worry. It's my own sister's life I'm trying to save."

I apologized again.

Jenn didn't seem to notice that she was tugging at her own hair as if trying to pull out fistfuls. "Years ago, Gerald Stone tried to poison Roger."

I nearly jumped out of my seat. "He *what?*"

As if deflated, Jenn sank lower in her chair. "Roger was just out of college, planning to go on to pharmacy school. He got a summer job at Stone Drugs. He noticed that there was something off about Stone and the way he was doing business. Stone must have guessed that Roger suspected him of fiddling the books or filling prescriptions wrong, or something illegal." Jenn picked up a peanut butter and grape jelly donut. Even though it didn't have a hole, she seemed to be looking through the jelly-filled portion to the cobalt blue plate underneath it. "And the next thing Roger knew, he—Roger, that is—was sick. Roger thought he had stomach flu, but it wouldn't go away, and no one else seemed to catch it. Roger didn't figure out that Stone was poisoning him until he realized that he was the only one eating Stone's homemade cookies and brownies. Roger quit the job and immediately got better. But Stone's treachery changed Roger's life. Roger gave up becoming a pharmacist."

About fifteen years ago, according to Tom, the police were looking into the possibility that Gerald Stone was illegally selling prescription drugs, but the flow of drugs stopped suddenly, and they couldn't find evidence that Stone had broken any laws. Roger could have graduated from college about fifteen years ago. Maybe it was Roger's suspicions that had caused Stone to clean up his act and leave the profession he'd tarnished. I asked Jenn, "Did Roger tell the police about his suspicions?"

She tore her donut in half. Grape jelly oozed onto her plate. "He didn't have proof. He thought it was funny. That's one of the things you didn't appreciate about Roger, Suzanne. He could be easygoing even when other people tried to attack him. He could laugh it off and go on. That's what made him such a good life coach and . . ." Her voice softened. "And such a good person."

I asked Jenn, "Have you told the police about that previous attempt at poisoning?"

"I didn't think of it until now."

I urged, "Call Detective Passenmath and tell her."

Jenn licked jelly off her little finger. "She'll think that I should have told her before. I didn't, so if I tell her at this late date, she'll think I made it up just now to cover myself."

"Maybe not," I pointed out. "You're under a lot of pressure and stress. It shouldn't surprise a detective if it takes you a few extra days to remember something that Roger told you happened a long time ago."

"I suppose." Jenn didn't sound convinced.

I leaned forward. "It all fits." I wasn't going to tell Jenn that the police had investigated Stone, probably around the time that Roger thought he'd been poisoned. "Roger moved away, and after several years, he came back to Fallingbrook. Stone could have heard that Roger was back, and Stone could have felt that Roger was again a threat to him. Then Stone must have learned about your wedding. He wanted to silence Roger, and he knew exactly when and where to find Roger."

Suzanne stared toward the window above the sink. "Now maybe you understand why I need to learn more about Gerald Stone."

Jenn shuddered. "And why he's probably dangerous. Don't go out with him, Suzanne."

Red splotches broke out on Suzanne's face. "And let him get away with murder? And possibly try to kill you, too?"

"Don't you understand?" Jenn was almost shouting. "Gerald Stone killed Roger to keep Roger from telling anyone about whatever illegal thing Stone was doing. Stone had no way of knowing that Roger took it all as a joke and would never have bothered to report him. And Stone has no reason to come after me. He's never met me."

I said calmly, "Jenn, if Stone knew about your wedding, he knew you were Roger's fiancée. Stone could easily have guessed that Roger told you about Stone's possible illegal activities and about Stone trying to poison him."

With her forefinger, Jenn scraped grape jelly from her plate. "That's kind of farfetched."

"It doesn't matter," Suzanne said. "You have to be prepared for anything."

I nodded.

Jenn leaned back and crossed her arms, threatening to smear grape jelly on the pretty pink sweater. "It seems to me that the best way to keep ourselves safe from Gerald Stone is to stay completely away from him, Suzanne. By trying to protect me from him, you're putting yourself in danger. You have to keep *yourself* safe from him also."

Suzanne heaved a huge sigh. "I will."

I warned, "Don't let him put anything into your food or drink."

Suzanne retorted, "Don't you think I know that?"

Feeling guilty for insulting her by stating the obvious, I offered a weak smile.

She explained slowly, as if Jenn and I didn't understand English, "I'm only trying to figure out who killed Roger. It might not be Gerald. It could be those two women who were hanging around the back door at the lodge. Don't be surprised if 'Vinnie' comes into your donut shop to talk to those two women, too."

Jenn suggested, "Instead of going out alone with Gerald

Stone, you could meet him only at Deputy Donut where Emily can help keep an eye on him."

Suzanne glowered at her. "I could, but I'm not." She turned her attention to me, and the glower dwindled to a puzzled frown. "Did I see Chad come out of your shop today?"

"You could have. He was there."

Jenn stared down at torn-up donut bits marooned in a sea of grape jelly on her plate. I suspected that she didn't want her sister to know she'd been with Chad before work that morning. A prolonged goodbye in his car in the parking lot behind the store she owned with Suzanne didn't seem like the best way to keep the relationship a secret, however, even though Jenn probably hadn't expected Suzanne to arrive at work so early.

"What did he want?" Suzanne's question had a sharp edge, as if she suspected Chad of killing Roger, and of possibly having tried to kill Jenn.

"Coffee and donuts." Immediately regretting my snarky response, I added, "And to say hello, I guess. We talked a little Saturday night, and danced together after midnight."

Jenn nodded at me and said softly, "I saw you." I couldn't tell if she was jealous of me for spending time with her ex, who now seemed to be her ex-ex, but I didn't think she was. Maybe Chad had told Jenn that I had suggested he could win her back.

Suzanne asked Jenn, "Are schools off today?"

Jenn lifted one shoulder and let it fall. "I guess they are, up in Gooseleg, anyway."

Suzanne eyed her. "I didn't see kids around here during school hours."

Jenn asked me, "Aren't Fallingbrook and Gooseleg in different school districts?"

"They were when I was growing up."

Suzanne stood and began clearing the table. "Chad had

better not start hanging around you, Jenn. The police will be certain you offed Roger."

Jenn blanched. "I thought you liked Chad. Liked him better than Roger."

"I do like him," Suzanne said. "But I don't want you giving the police fodder in their case against you."

"They don't have one. We—"

Suzanne interrupted her by looking straight at me. "Come back tomorrow night after work and we can share what we learn." I couldn't tell if she suspected Chad of killing Roger, but apparently, she wasn't about to continue discussing Jenn's former boyfriend around me.

"Okay," I said. "You two be careful."

Jenn let me out the back. I stood outside the closed door for a second, but didn't hear that rusty-sounding bolt. Had Suzanne gone to the extra trouble of bolting the back door earlier that evening because she had, only an hour or so before, spotted Chad's car behind Deputy Donut? Unless I was mistaken, Chad's car had been parked behind Dressed to Kill other days. Maybe Suzanne hadn't noticed or didn't know that the car belonged to Chad, if it did.

I crossed the driveway to the back door of Deputy Donut. In our office, Dep actually stood still and let me fasten her halter around her. She didn't attempt to bite the halter until I began attaching the leash.

Outside, I was glad that I owned another warm jacket besides the one the investigators had confiscated. The cool evening seemed to encourage Dep to dawdle more than usual on our walk home.

I let her play in the backyard before we went inside for our dinners. The two donuts I'd eaten had not been quite adequate, after all. I ate a salad and an apple.

Dep again acted like I was supposed to go to the front door, open it, and let her friends in to see her. "There's a problem," I informed her. "I know I should tell Brent that the man Samantha saw parked near the lodge and looking upset, or something, on Saturday night was almost certainly Chad, but if we invite Brent over, I'll feel like I have to tell him what Suzanne and Jenn said, and he's not going to be happy that the three of us are doing anything that might resemble snooping where we shouldn't."

"Meow."

"Thanks for the advice, but calling him would probably be just as problematic."

The phone rang. Brent. "Misty tells me that Scott ID'd the widowed bride's old boyfriend in your shop today. Are you okay?"

"I'm fine. As far as I know, he didn't bring any arsenic."

Brent understood my sometimes-peculiar sense of humor. "Great," he said dryly.

"I'd have called you if I thought it was crucial, but Chad didn't stay long and didn't make any confessions. I still don't know his last name."

"We do."

"I'm almost certain that Samantha and her partner saw him when they were bringing the ambulance to Little Lake Lodge early Sunday morning after Roger collapsed." I described the similarities between the cars and the license numbers, and I gave him what I'd read of the license plate on the car Chad had been driving.

"Thank you. I'll talk to Samantha and her partner. Meanwhile, just a sec. I'll look up Chad's license number."

"Chad seems really nice. When they saw him with his face in his hands early Sunday morning, he could have been sick, he could have been sad that Jenn was married, or he could have been regretting something like leaving arsenic where someone might eat it."

"Witnesses' interpretations of body language don't always hold up in court."

"I suppose you're right. Especially when the car's windows are fogged over."

"Were they?"

"That's what Samantha told me. You and Misty's partner, Houlihan, wrote down the license numbers of the cars in the parking lots at Little Lake Lodge. If Chad's car was there, then maybe he wasn't the man that Samantha and her partner saw. Or he could have come back to the lodge, followed the ambulance, perhaps."

"There, I got Chad's plate number. It includes the numbers you gave me. And his car was definitely not among those at Little Lake Lodge when Houlihan and I checked all of the cars."

I told Brent that I'd seen the red car in Jenn's parking lot at various times during the week and that, after a pair of people in it seemed to have their heads close together for a minute or so, Jenn got out of the car and blew a kiss, and then Chad drove away.

"Very interesting," Brent said. "He's been telling us that they're just friends."

"Maybe that's changing." I was glad I was talking to Brent over the phone and he couldn't see the sudden blush heating my face. Brent and I were just friends, a relationship that was unlikely to become closer. Quickly, I asked, "Were schools in Gooseleg closed today?"

"You picked up on that, too? After Misty told me that Chad was in your shop this afternoon, I checked. Yes, Gooseleg schools had a long weekend, starting today." He was silent for a second. "It's interesting that those two women from the conference, Gerald Stone, *and* the ex-boyfriend have all landed in Deputy Donut since the poisoning. Were any of them customers before?"

"Not unless they came disguised. Are they your prime suspects?"

"Mmp."

"Our donuts were a hit on Saturday night," I informed him haughtily. "No one should be surprised that people who tried them for the first time would want more."

Apparently, my attempt at imitating some of Suzanne's sterner tones didn't frighten Brent. He laughed.

I asked, "Are you making progress?"

"On the case? I wish. Passenmath has us concentrating on collecting and watching surveillance videos from every business south of Little Lake Lodge. We're supposed to view them north to south, in order, to figure out which vehicles were coming from Little Lake Lodge."

"Um, I'm not a detective, but wouldn't questioning reception attendees about where they were and who they saw and when they saw them be more useful? For instance, the teenagers who were groomsmen and bridesmaids left at midnight, and they didn't come back."

"A patrol cop stopped the van those kids were in, because they weren't quite in it. They were hanging heads and arms out windows. The cop pulled them over at twelve twenty-one on Wisconsin Street north of the town square. He kept them there until twelve thirty-four."

"They left the reception at midnight, before I put my hat on the table."

"Because of the timing, we've ruled them out for harming Roger, but the officer gave them a warning. He also gave the father who was driving a ticket. Ironic, isn't it? The kids' foolhardiness could have cost them an arm or worse, but it prevented them from being implicated in a murder."

"I hope no one tells them that. They might continue riding around with their arms and heads out windows."

"The Fallingbrook Police Department school outreach team is about to do their annual safety presentation at the high school. Maybe the message will sink in this year."

"With teens . . ."

"We all think we're invulnerable at that age, don't we?"

"I did."

"And we weren't. And still aren't."

The warning in his voice made me want to say, *Mmp*. I settled for, "Yes, sir."

"And you'll call me if you need me or learn anything else."
It wasn't a question.

"Okay. Oh, wait. I did learn something. Have you talked to Jenn recently? She said Gerald Stone once tried to poison Roger. Years ago, from the sound of things. I . . . she doesn't know that I know you, outside of this case, at least. Her half-sister was there when Jenn told me. She doesn't know that I know you, either."

"I won't let on that you and I are friends." Brent didn't seem to notice the unspoken words echoing through my brain. *Just friends*. He kept talking. "I'll ask Jenn again about any enemies that Roger might have had. Passenmath is about ninety-nine percent convinced that Jenn killed her bridegroom."

"Jenn's afraid of that, and that's why she doesn't want to tell Passenmath about this detail that she just remembered. I told her she should. However, I wouldn't be surprised if Roger made up most of it, although it sounds like he might have suspected some of the same things about Gerald Stone that Tom suspected fifteen or so years ago."

"Take care, Em."

"You, too." But Brent had already disconnected.

The next morning, Gerald Stone returned to Deputy Donut. He ordered the day's special coffee, a medium roast grown in the mountains of Guatemala. He also wanted one of our fig marmalade donuts. I wondered if his willingness to try new things included other sorts of risk taking, like engaging in criminal behaviors. Drugs, for instance. Or poisoning and attempting to poison people.

As the minutes ticked by and Suzanne didn't join Gerald at his table, I became more and more uneasy. The first chance I got, I closed myself into the office with Dep and called Jenn. "Is Suzanne okay?" I asked.

"Yes. She's here."

"How did her date go?"

"She says she'll tell me when you get here. That way, she doesn't have to go over it all twice. Or interrupt me when I'm with customers."

"I'm sorry!"

"It's okay. I'd have told you if I was with a customer. One lady just left, but there are others on the sidewalk outside."

"Suzanne's date is here."

"I'll tell her. Maybe." Over the phone, I could just barely make out the bells at Jenn's front door jingling. "Customers are coming in. Gotta run. See you this evening."

I gave Dep a kiss and went back to work. Either Jenn didn't tell Suzanne that Stone was in Deputy Donut or Suzanne didn't want to or need to talk to him. He left around a quarter to twelve and strolled slowly toward Dressed to Kill.

Misty and Houlihan came in for their afternoon break, but Scott didn't show up. Since it was Saturday and there was definitely no school, I thought Chad might come in, but he didn't.

Misty had only espresso, black. She was cutting back on donuts, she said. Houlihan, who ate two unraised chocolate donuts covered in chocolate frosting and shredded coconut, agreed with me that Misty was missing out on a good thing.

Again, it seemed that Vanessa Legghaupt, the Happy Hoper life coach, must have lurked outside until the police officers left before she ventured in.

"No sidekick, today?" I asked her.

"We don't spend every minute together." It came out as criticism.

"What can I get you?"

"Organic green tea."

"And would you like something to eat?"

"Of course not." I'd been thoroughly corrected. She removed a book from her Happy Hopers tote. The title was *The Spinach Line—Let Greens Help You Win Life's Races*. When I brought her the tea, she didn't look up from her reading.

After a while, she set the book down and beckoned me to her table. "Remember, we talked about you giving a presentation to my women's group?"

"Yes."

"Are you still willing?"

Hadn't I merely commented that I didn't stay up late most nights? However, learning more about Vanessa and her friend could be useful. "Yes."

"I know it's short notice, but we had a cancellation, so can you come tomorrow evening? We eat at six, and the meal doesn't take long. You'd be presenting at about six forty-five."

"I'm not sure how much I have to say."

"You won't have to talk long. We go home at seven. Just tell us how you got started, and describe this place." She waved her hand to encompass the shop. "Tell us the problems you had with start-up and how you overcame them, and any problems you've encountered along the way. And I'm particularly interested in how you incorporated your logo and the police hats and car into a cohesive theme. That's called branding. The ladies will get lots of ideas."

"Can I bring a friend?" With luck, Misty would be available and Vanessa wouldn't realize that Misty was a police officer. Samantha would be supportive, too, and the evening might be fun for all three of us, especially afterward. We could gossip, and they could tease me about my bloopers, real or imagined.

"As long as they're female," Vanessa said firmly. "We find we encourage each other and grow as individuals more when no men are around. But bring as many women as you like. Just let me know so we'll have enough food. Your dinner will be complimentary, but we charge a very small amount for guests. Part of our goal is to show that it's possible to eat well without spending a fortune. Which is another reason we don't welcome men. They'd want meat."

I might miss meat also, and so would Misty and Samantha.... "About how many women do you expect to attend? I could bring donuts."

"Thirty or forty. But no donuts, unless they're made without sugar other than honey, and without fats. We eat only health food. We don't serve wheat, either."

"Okay."

Vanessa stared expectantly at me as if she wanted to see and hear more enthusiasm.

"It sounds like fun," I added.

"It is, but fun is not our primary purpose."

Why wasn't I surprised? She reminded me, not in appearance, of Yvonne Passenmath. Imagining Yvonne Passenmath interviewing Vanessa Legghaupt, I almost laughed aloud. Those interviews had to be somber and earnest affairs, with each woman attempting to outdo the other one in being stern and conscientious.

Vanessa told me that her women's group met in her studio about a mile south of downtown Fallingbrook. "Do I need to pick you up?" *Need?* The offer seemed somehow less than gracious.

"I'll drive," I said. "I'll bring the Deputy Donut delivery car, since I'll be talking about it in my presentation."

I feared she might tell me that she expected everyone to ride unicycles to and from her workshops, but she said, "Perfect." She gave me the address, paid for the tea, stuffed her book into her Happy Hopers tote, and went out.

After Tom left for the evening, I boxed donuts to take to Jenn and Suzanne and carried the box into our office. Dep had been napping on the back of the couch. She stood up, stretched, took one look at the bakery box, turned around, and settled down with her back to me.

Apparently, my clever little cat had figured out the new addition to my schedule and wanted me to understand that she did not approve. Laughing, I told her I'd be back soon.

Chapter 21

✻

Suzanne must have seen me coming. She opened the back door and waved me inside. Again, I heard Jenn's voice in the front of the store. A customer laughed.

I held the box of donuts up for Suzanne to see. "I brought three unraised goji berry donuts with pomegranate glaze, and three raised pumpkin spice donuts."

Suzanne pointed at the table, and I set the box on it. The place mats were bright yellow. Suzanne was good at combining fun colors with the dark blue dishes.

She went to the sink and began filling the teakettle.

Yesterday, she'd waited until both Jenn and I were present to tell us what she'd learned, and she didn't seem about to talk now. "I'll go look through the store," I told her.

If she answered, I didn't hear her above the water gushing into the kettle.

I looked at almost everything in Jenn's store twice before her customers left. "I'm glad to see you, Emily," Jenn said. "Suzanne's not telling me anything."

Jenn and I went into the office and sat in our usual places at the table.

Suzanne warned, "The tea's getting cold."

She poured it for us. I cradled my cup in my hands. The tea was still too hot to drink.

"So, Suzanne," Jenn said. "Tell us about your date with Gerald Stone."

"It wasn't a date. It was an information-gathering session." She slapped her hands down onto her bright yellow place mat. "He's guilty."

Jenn asked, "Did he confess?"

"He didn't have to. I pieced it all together."

I set my cup into its saucer. "Did you tell the police your conclusions?"

"I don't have enough information yet. Almost."

Jenn twisted strands of her long blond hair around a finger. "You're not going out with him again, are you?"

"I told you," Suzanne said. "They aren't real dates. Are you going to let me tell you what I found out, or do you want to be the one doing the talking?"

Jenn let go of her hair and looked down at her plate. "Sorry."

But Suzanne sipped at her tea instead of telling us her news. Jenn and I both bit into pumpkin spice donuts. Jenn gave me a thumbs-up.

Suzanne set her cup down with exaggerated care. "First, I asked him how someone so young could be retired. I pretended he looks too young, which he very definitely does not. But he fell for it. He said he had hobbies he wanted to pursue."

"What hobbies?" I asked.

"I'll *get* to that." Suzanne was obviously annoyed at my interruption. I wasn't sure I blamed her. "I also asked him if he often worked for Little Lake Lodge. He said he sometimes does."

The owner of Little Lake Lodge had told Tom and me that he never hired security guards. But I was learning not to interrupt Suzanne, so I didn't.

She went on. "He said he was working for himself on Saturday night, though."

I sat very still. Gerald Stone had told Brent that he was at the wrong resort, but couldn't remember what the right one was.

Jenn repeated, "Working for himself? What does that mean?"

Suzanne gave her much-younger sister an approving nod. "Excellent question, Jenn. I asked him. He said he wanted to be there for *you.*"

Jenn squeaked around a goji berry donut, "For me? I don't know him. Why would he be there for me?"

"He said he knows you. Knew you '*when.*'" Suzanne closed her mouth and stared at Jenn expectantly.

Jenn started shaking her head, and then her eyes opened wide. "I remember going to a drugstore with Mom when she was still able to get around. Was it Stone's drugstore?"

Suzanne put her cup down. "That's what he said. He claims he remembers you." Suzanne's mouth twisted to one side. She obviously didn't believe Stone.

Jenn shook her head, swishing her hair past her shoulders. "I don't remember him. I had to sit on a chair and not move when we were in there, so I swung my feet, fidgeted with my hands, and sighed a lot."

I smiled at Jenn. I could relate.

Suzanne continued looking grim. "He said she was the bravest, sweetest woman he'd ever met."

Jenn looked down at her plate. "He's not lying about that."

Suzanne said what I was thinking. "He could be, if that's not his real opinion. He could have said it to make himself seem like a good person who would never poison anyone. Maybe he never even met Mom. One of his employees could have told him about her coming in with a little girl."

Jenn argued, "When I went there with Mom, it was years before Roger worked there."

"I didn't say it *wasn't* before then. I didn't mention Roger's name. Gerald had other employees, other years, Jenn. Get with the program."

Jenn mumbled, "Sorry."

I had a sudden urge to swing my legs and sigh. I didn't need to fidget, though. My hands were occupied with my second donut. I wasn't sure about the goji berries, but Tom's pomegranate glaze was delicious.

Suzanne narrowed her eyes for a second, then went on with her story. "He said he knew she was battling cancer. He remembers her courage and her concern about her daughters, especially you, because you were so young. He noticed that she stopped coming in, and eventually he found out that she'd died. After that, even after he retired, he noticed if you were mentioned in the newspaper, like when you graduated from high school and earned those scholarships. He saw your wedding announcement, so he appointed himself to guard the back door of the lodge. He said that wedding gifts often disappear during receptions. That wasn't going to happen to you if he could prevent it."

Jenn made a face. "In other words, he's been stalking you and me for years. That's creepy."

I agreed. Silently.

Suzanne said, "It would be, if it were true. He could have known our mother or, as I said, known *of* her from an employee, and it probably wouldn't have been hard for a pharmacist to guess from prescriptions that she had cancer. He could have made up the rest of it. He was sketchy about details. He claimed he'd seen *Vinnie* mentioned, but that's impossible, since nobody ever called me Vinnie before yesterday when I made up the nickname. Also, he didn't quite remember if you'd won scholarships or not."

"What were his hobbies?" I asked again.

Jenn suggested, "Following women around?"

"That's where I tripped him up," Suzanne said. "He seemed to have trouble remembering what his hobbies were, and I don't think the problem was his memory. Finally, he said gardening, golf, and playing online games like chess against real people, but they're people he doesn't know."

Gardening, I thought. *He sold his house and moved into an apartment to give himself time to garden, but after he moved into an apartment, where did he do his gardening? A community garden?*

Suzanne cast a glance at me. "No wonder he doesn't have much to do besides sit around in your coffee shop."

If Misty or Samantha had said something like that to me, I'd have taken a pretend swipe at them, but I had a feeling that Suzanne wouldn't understand that sort of playfulness. I stayed in my seat and kept a bland expression on my face.

Jenn leaned forward. "Suzanne, if Roger was right that Gerald Stone tried to poison him years ago, we know exactly why Gerald Stone was at Little Lake Lodge." Tears welled in her eyes. "Yes, he read about the wedding in the paper, but he wasn't there to look out for me. He was pretending to be working as a security guard that night, but he was really there to do what he'd tried to do years before, poison Roger." She bowed her head and mumbled, "This time, he succeeded."

Suzanne leaned back and folded her arms. "That's exactly what I was telling you."

I praised Suzanne's information collecting. "Your theory does hang together. I should go so you can call Detective Passenmath and tell her what you've just told us."

"I'm not done gathering evidence, yet," Suzanne told us. "I'm going to keep spending time with Gerald until I get him where he deserves to be. Behind bars."

Jenn and I argued that Suzanne had enough evidence to interest the police and that she should let them take it from there.

She refused to change her plans. "Come back tomorrow after work, and we'll put our heads together with what I'll have discovered by then," she said.

I told her I couldn't. "I'm giving a presentation."

"About what?" Jenn asked.

"Being a female entrepreneur, starting a business, the branding Tom and I've been doing, things like that."

"That sounds interesting," Jenn said. "Where is it?"

I told her and added, "I'm not sure you really want to come, though. The group is sponsored by Vanessa Legghaupt, the life coach who was hanging around Little Lake Lodge during your reception."

"We're going," Suzanne stated.

"But only for Emily's speech," Jenn corrected her. "I'll need to be here until six, and then, if the police still have our cars, we can take a cab."

"See you there," I said. Jenn let me out the back door.

I fetched Dep and took her home. After feeding her a nice, well-balanced meal of cat food, I couldn't convince myself that donuts were sufficient, especially for someone who often grabbed a few fried goodies for lunch and "needed" to do taste tests throughout the day. I made a salad of baby greens with Parmesan and olives. I also made a resolution to get more exercise. I suspected that running around a donut shop all day wasn't going to be enough, unless I stopped eating donuts, but how could I? Tom and I were always concocting new flavors that we had to sample before selling them to customers.

I called Misty and told her I was giving a presentation at a workshop sponsored by one of the suspects in Roger's murder. "I'm coming, too," she said. "Not in uniform. I can't pass up an opportunity to mingle with people who would sign up for a Happy Hopers conference."

I asked if she'd like to come over to my place right then for a drink, but she couldn't. She was heading into work soon.

Samantha was also about to go to work, but she said she would attend the next evening's workshop. "In case these women put poisons in their health food."

"I'm not sure any of us should actually eat at this event."

"I agree, but if you have to go to the dinner, I'd better be there, in case you do eat something."

After we disconnected, I apologized to Dep. "Neither of them can come over right now, I'm afraid."

Dep batted a ball with a bell inside it underneath one of the stools pulled up to the kitchen counter.

I phoned the number that Vanessa had given me and told her that I was bringing two guests to the dinner and that two others planned to come only for the presentation.

"You're doing a fabulous job, Emily," she said in a semi-breathless and encouraging way.

The doorbell rang. I told Vanessa goodbye and then walked quietly through the dining room.

Dep galloped to the front door. Those little kitty feet could make a lot of noise.

I tiptoed through the living room. Dep was facing the door and meowing so loudly she was nearly howling. She turned and stared at me as if wanting to know what was taking me so long.

Cautiously, I looked through the peephole.

Brent was on the porch.

Uh-oh. How was I going to prevent myself from telling him that I'd been meeting with other women—at least one of whom the police suspected of murder—to try to figure out who killed Roger?

I opened the door and tried to appear welcoming as I invited him in. "Have you eaten?" I demanded.

He picked Dep up and gave her a kiss. "Have you?"

"Yes, but I asked you."

"I had enough."

"Whatever that means. Come on." I led him, still carrying Dep, toward the kitchen. "I had a salad and can make you one, too, or if you want to wait, I can cook a frozen lasagna. I didn't bring any donuts home, sorry."

"I grabbed a sandwich, but a salad would be nice, and the donuts can wait." Dep squirmed. He put her down.

I didn't ask him what week or month he'd grabbed the alleged sandwich.

I made a salad for Brent and put it on the island for him, then sat on the stool beside his. Dep jumped onto my lap, stretched, and put her front paws on Brent's leg while her back feet were still on mine. Luckily, Brent and I were both wearing jeans, so the claws Dep inserted to steady herself didn't hurt, much.

I wondered why Brent had dropped in. Maybe he had questions about Roger's murder, but the jeans usually meant he wasn't on duty. Dep scrambled up to his shoulders, rubbed her face against his ear, and purred.

Brent said nothing, as if he was waiting for me to speak, like maybe confess I'd been spending time with potential murder suspects.

I had to break the silence, or I might actually confess it, which could make Brent tell me to quit, which I didn't want to do until I learned more. Besides, I needed to help Jenn convince Suzanne to stop going out with Gerald Stone, even for what she called information-gathering sessions. I asked Brent, "Did you talk to Jenn about her story of Gerald Stone trying to poison Roger years ago?"

"I did. Before that, I talked to one of Stone's employees from when Roger worked there. She remembered Roger, and corroborated that Stone baked cookies and brownies for his staff. She was on a diet, though, and didn't eat any of them, and she didn't know if other employees did. When I told Jenn all of that, she said that Roger had become suspicious of Stone, and was afraid that Stone had caught him sleuthing, and Stone had tried to poison Roger. Then Roger quit his job and fled the area."

" 'Fled'? Did Jenn say that?"

"That was my word, not hers."

"You sound like you think Roger did something criminal."

"Do I?" He finished the salad and thanked me.

Dep slithered off his shoulders. He caught her in his arms.

She lay on her back, tilted her head until it was almost upside down, and blinked up at me as if attempting to inform me that Brent was supposed to visit us every evening.

"Maybe Roger was breaking laws," I suggested. "Maybe Roger, not Gerald, was the one selling prescription drugs illegally. Jenn said that Roger was wealthy because of inheriting from, as she put it, a 'distant relative.' Her lack of detail makes me wonder if the story was true. Maybe Roger didn't inherit except from his parents, and he ran through that money quickly. Maybe he was a drug dealer, stealing painkillers from his boss, Stone, and selling them on the street."

"Mmp."

Interpreting Brent's response as a suggestion to come up with more theories, I stared back into his watchful eyes. Tom had told me that Gerald Stone had been living beyond his apparent means, and therefore Tom had suspected that Gerald was illegally peddling prescription drugs. "Could Roger have become wealthy through blackmail?" I bopped my forehead with a fist. "That could be it! Maybe Roger was blackmailing scads of people. Any one of them might have killed him." I pulled at my curls. "How can you stand being a detective? So many culprits, so many clues, so little time."

"We take it step by step. And don't forget that Yvonne Passenmath is the lead detective on this case. She has other help besides me."

I tapped my fingers on the granite countertop. "Gerald Stone retired, sold his pharmacy, sold his house and his car, downsized to an apartment, and became a part-time security guard. Could he have sold all of those things to meet Roger's blackmail demands?"

"We'd need proof of blackmail."

"You didn't find any evidence of it among Roger's things? Like large deposits to his bank accounts?"

"Did Roger strike you as the type to blackmail someone and deposit the proceeds in a way that left a paper or digital trail?"

"I talked to him only briefly a couple of times on Saturday night, so I'm not sure how well he would cover up any criminal activities. From what I saw of him, he was mean and self-centered, and also verbally abusive, particularly to his new bride."

"Is that all?"

"Probably not. Let me guess. Passenmath thinks that Jenn suddenly snapped on Saturday night and did him in. And Jenn just happened to have a supply of arsenic on hand, maybe tucked into her bouquet or the pockets that you said were in her gown, in case she saw a chance to use it." I folded my arms. "Jenn didn't have to marry him, and she wasn't going to have to stay married to him if she changed her mind. Roger's murder wasn't an impulse. It had to be pre-planned. Jenn didn't need to go to such extremes, especially in a public place. She could have found a much less conspicuous method of doing him in later, in the privacy of their own home."

Brent was grinning.

"What?" I asked. "Don't you agree?"

"I like watching you argue with yourself. You really should join the force, you know. You could be carrying on these arguments with yourself all day every day, and we'd all applaud when you solved the case."

I grabbed Dep out of his arms. "Give me back my cat."

He laughed, stood up, and smiled down at us. "I should go. If you think of anything else, let me know."

"Okay." Carrying Dep, I accompanied him to the door.

He gave my shoulders a quick squeeze. "G'night, Em."

With Dep in my arms, I couldn't hug him back. I let him out and locked the door.

I had managed not to confess to my meetings with Jenn and Suzanne or to the next night's presentation at Vanessa Legghaupt's studio. I told myself the latter was because only females were invited to the presentation.

The truth was that I didn't want him to think I was interfering in his investigation.

Because, maybe, I was.

But I wasn't exactly keeping the presentation a secret. Misty was one of Brent's colleagues in the police department, and I'd invited her to it. Carrying Dep upstairs, I murmured, "I can go to bed with a clear conscience."

"Mmp," Dep said.

Chapter 22

The next morning, Dep allowed me a few extra moments of sleep, but she could have given me more. Our shop didn't open until ten on Sundays.

Shortly before nine, Dep and I walked at Dep's chosen stop-and-go pace toward Deputy Donut. I muttered, "I should have written a speech for tonight."

Tail straight up, my cat pranced as far ahead of me as her leash would allow.

"You're right," I said. "You never prepare speeches ahead of time. Why should I?" Probably because I wasn't a cat. But Dep was too polite, or something, to mention it.

Gerald Stone didn't come in, and neither did Suzanne, which wasn't surprising, since the shop she and Jenn owned wouldn't open until noon.

Shortly after noon, I visited Dep in the office and peeked out the windows. I didn't necessarily expect to see Suzanne, and I didn't. I phoned Jenn. "Did Suzanne go out with Gerald Stone last night?"

"Yes. She called to tell me she got home safely to her apartment. She wouldn't tell me what she learned. She's not coming in until later. She said she'll update us tonight after your presentation."

Maybe I would be able to include Misty in that meeting.

Suzanne was going to have to tell the police what she'd learned about Gerald Stone, preferably sooner rather than later.

That afternoon, when I wasn't serving customers, I joined Tom in the kitchen. Rolling dough and decorating donuts, the two of us brainstormed ideas for my speech. We'd planned Deputy Donut together, and no one could have worked harder to make it succeed than he had.

I told Tom about Vanessa's restrictions on donuts. Tom was always happy to take on challenges. We created and baked gluten- and fat-free mini-donuts sweetened with honey. When they were cool enough, we drizzled carob glaze on some of them and left the others plain. His eyes twinkled. "Tell this life coach woman that you're always thinking of new ways to promote our store and our products, and this is one of them."

The rest of the day, I thought about—and frequently discarded—what I would say.

Misty was apparently on late-night shifts. She and Houlihan didn't come in. Scott did, with other firefighters. They ordered large raised donuts frosted with chocolate fudge.

Scott asked me, "What's today's coffee?"

"It's a light roast from the Andes in Bolivia. It's low acid with fruity and nutty hints."

"I'd like that," Scott said.

Beside him, a firefighter piped up. "Of course he would, if it's nutty."

"And only lightly roasted," I added.

Scott laughed.

I brought them each one of our tiny health-food donuts to try. They said they liked them, but they were too small.

After we closed for the evening, Tom said he didn't mind cleaning up. "You're going to spend your evening promoting our store, Emily."

I quickly took Dep home and left her there with food and water. I drove my own car back to Deputy Donut, parked it in the lot behind the store, and arrived inside in time to help Tom tidy and decide what supplies to order.

We filled a couple of bakery boxes with the health-food donuts. I put the boxes, a stack of brochures, my Deputy Donut cap, and a clean apron inside a cardboard carton and closed the flaps. I would not open the carton until right before my speech.

Tom accompanied me and the carton to the fun 1950 Ford in our garage. "Don't let anyone poison your food or drink, Emily."

"I'll fill up on donuts instead."

"Not if someone dips them in what looks like powdered sugar."

I laughed. "It won't be sugar. These life coach ladies sweeten with honey."

"Don't let them dip them in *anything*." He waved, and I drove off.

Glancing at Fallingbrook's architecture as I drove, I could see how the town had spread since its early days as a mining and timber outpost. Around the time that log buildings were being replaced by larger brick ones, tourists began arriving by rail to visit the waterfall on the Fallingbrook River and the many other falls, streams, creeks, rivers, and lakes in the nearby wilderness. By the middle of the eighteen hundreds, a thriving downtown surrounded Fallingbrook's grassy central square. Deputy Donut and my residential neighborhood were built in the late eighteen hundreds, around the south and west edges of the original center of town.

After that, the village expanded southward. I drove south, down Wisconsin Street, to a section of the street that had been constructed in the 1930s and was wide enough to accommodate the automobiles of that era plus angle parking. Vanessa's studio was in a long row of two-story buildings with big windows in front. I could have walked to her studio from Deputy Donut or my house if I'd wanted to spend a half hour carrying a lightweight but awkward carton.

Since I couldn't take the car inside as an example of Deputy Donut's branding, I parked in front of Vanessa's studio where, I hoped, many of the audience members would notice the car as they arrived.

I got out, grabbed my carton, and shoved the door closed with a hip.

Halfway down the block, Misty and Samantha were walking toward me. Misty was in jeans and a purple sweater. With her blond hair down, she didn't look like a police officer, except for her perfect posture and the way she was obviously aware of her surroundings. Samantha came up almost to Misty's shoulder. A pink jacket over her black slacks and turtleneck went with the streaks in her dark brown curls. All three of us were wearing running shoes. I wasn't sure about the other two, but I was hoping we wouldn't have to run from anything.

We did run, though, *to* each other for hugs, one-armed in my case. They both offered to carry the carton. I refused to hand it over. "It's not heavy."

Misty asked, "What's in it?"

"A surprise."

"A good one, I hope."

I put on a show of great solemnity. "I need props for my presentation."

She looked down at my hatless head. "Let me guess. You're bringing one of your funny hats."

"Funny," I complained, acting wounded. "It's *just like* a police hat."

"Right. Ha."

Samantha scolded, "Be serious for a second, you two. Are we actually going to eat with these ladies? I'd never hear the end of it from my buds at work if they had to bring an ambulance for me."

Misty suddenly became a serious law officer. "Let's pay attention to how the food is served. If someone is bringing us food from who-knows-where, we won't trust it. But if we can see the food being served, and everyone is being served from the same cooking pot, then the only way we're going to be poisoned is if everyone else is."

Samantha nodded slowly. "That's very reassuring, Misty. My buds will need to bring an ambu-bus."

Misty responded, "We could simply not eat anything."

Samantha wrapped her arms around her middle. "I didn't have time for lunch."

I suggested, "How about this? If we decide that the food is okay, we can eat it, but we will not leave our plates or cups unattended. If there's any possibility that someone has added anything to our food or drink, we won't touch it."

Misty looked off into the distance beyond me. "I suppose we can be vigilant enough to be safe."

"Look at it this way," Samantha contributed. "If anyone gets poisoned tonight, the police are going to suspect the women running this thing of poisoning Roger Banchen Sunday morning."

Misty opened her eyes wide in apparent, and obviously fake, astonishment. "Great. That case will be closed, and we'll all be dead."

Samantha retorted, "We'll be revived in the ambu-bus. By hot EMTs."

Misty laughed. "I can hardly wait."

"Let's watch each other," I suggested, "for signals." Alec and I had had one. If one of us brushed hair away from our forehead and then tugged hard at an earlobe, it meant "rescue me." It was handy at parties when one of us was stranded in the corner with someone droning on and on about their great-aunt's shin splints. "How about this?" I suggested. "If for any reason, you think the meal is dangerous, rest a wrist on the top of your head until the other two notice, and then none of us will eat or drink a thing."

Misty protested. "You and your signs and signals, Emily. If

there's obvious danger, I hope that any of us will announce that fact and phone for help."

"Fine," I said. "I'll do that, too, but I'm not going to yell in front of our hostesses, 'Hey, I think the food might be safe!' "

"Just wrinkle your nose like a rabbit if you think it's safe," Misty said.

Samantha laughed.

I agreed, "Okay, if you two promise to do it, too." We'd been standing outside Vanessa's studio long enough that if anyone saw us, they might wonder what was wrong, especially when Samantha and I practiced wiggling our noses. Luckily, no one, not even Vanessa's clients, came along.

Samantha turned and read aloud the sign on Vanessa's door. " 'A Leg Up for Hope—The Legghaupt Life Coach Method.' " She paused and then dropped her punch line. "Is this Legghaupt woman a life coach or a dog trainer?"

Misty and I burst out laughing.

Suddenly I needed to restrain myself.

Vanessa Legghaupt was heading toward the other side of the glass door. I wondered if the smile on her face would disappear if she knew why we had such big ones on ours.

Chapter 23

Vanessa opened the door. "I see you brought your friends, Emily. Excellent. So glad you could join us." She handed Misty and Samantha each a business card. "I'll give you all a tour of the premises." She pointed toward a large room to our left, the room with the wall-to-wall show window next to the sidewalk. "We have this exquisite boutique where people can purchase books, yoga mats, exercise clothes, and items that inspire, like lovely stones with motivating words and messages carved in them. Our large meeting room is in back. We can go down this long hallway . . ." Gracefully, she extended one arm, palm upward and opening like a water lily, toward a narrow corridor sandwiched between the boutique and what appeared to be a closed stairway to the second floor. "Or we can go through the boutique and my office. Come, I'll show you."

She ushered us into the boutique. She was a life coach who owned a boutique. Was that another form of goal achievement through shopping? I had to admit that shopping accomplished a lot of my goals. Whenever I needed a quart of milk or a new chair or a pretty sweater, I went shopping.

The boutique smelled like potpourri. Vanessa led us past a rack of handwoven garments and a display counter filled with jewelry made from chunky metals. Next to a shelf of greeting cards decorated with feathers and dried flowers, we rounded the sales counter. Vanessa opened a door behind it and waved us through.

Her office was decorated like a British men's club from Victorian times, with dark wood paneling and two oak desks. I guessed that one was Vanessa's. Roger had probably used the other one until he absconded—if he did—with Vanessa's client list. The desk chairs, a couch, and two armchairs were all upholstered in green leather. The carpet was a deeper shade of green. "I meet with clients in here." Vanessa pitched her voice low, showing reverence for the elegant space. "Some life coaches might opt for a new-age feel, but I prefer luxury. It's comfy and calming. Besides, many of my clients are determined to increase their wealth. Being in this environment helps them visualize their own eventual financial success."

Misty, Samantha, and I made appreciative murmurs.

"Now, come see our meeting room." Vanessa's tone changed to perky encouragement. "You can leave that box in here if you like, Emily."

I was not about to let the donuts out of my sight. "I'll keep it with me. I'll need it for my presentation."

She glanced at the bulky—and rather unsightly, I realized—carton in my arms. "If you're sure it won't be in your way . . ." She opened the door to a larger room. It was like a small gymnasium, with rock maple on the floor and acoustic tile on the walls and ceiling. There was a small stage to our left. Tables and chairs were lined up so that no one would have their backs to the stage, and no one would be facing it. Audience members would only have to turn sideways to see the speakers.

The far end of the room was an open-concept kitchen that anyone would love in their home and wasn't bad for an institution, either, with multiple ovens and burners, plenty of storage space, a huge fridge-freezer combination, and hard, shiny white counters, one of which, an island, divided the kitchen from the rest of the room. The island was being set up as a buffet. "Wow," I said, about the kitchen.

Vanessa was obviously and justifiably proud of it all. "We can fold up the tables, stack the chairs, and stow them away. We have plenty of room for exercise, yoga, meditation, courses, lectures, sit-down meals, and nearly everything we can think of." She led us to a square table near the stage, with three chairs around it in a U shape, the middle one with its back to the stage. Vanessa placed her hand on that chair. "Emily, I'm putting you at the head table with April and me. Your friends can sit wherever they like."

We thanked her, and she went off to greet newcomers.

Misty and Samantha chose the two seats nearest the head table. They'd be together, and I would be almost within whispering distance of them. I set the box behind my chair, next to the stage. Since I'd be sitting with my back to the box, I went over to Misty and Samantha and asked them to keep an eye on it and let me know if anyone tampered with it.

"Good thing I keep handcuffs in my bag," Misty muttered. I wasn't sure if she was serious.

Samantha raised her gaze to the ceiling and let out a huge sigh. "Show-off."

Almost every woman who entered the room—they all came from the hallway, not from Vanessa's office—laughed and called out, "I can tell our speaker's here!" and then commented on the Deputy Donut car. Everyone seemed to love that car, especially the donut and the sprinkles. I was beginning to like these ladies.

After about two dozen people arrived, we were invited to the buffet table. April told me, "As our guest speaker, Emily, you should serve yourself first. I'll go ahead of you to show you the ropes."

It appeared that everyone would be served from the same kettles and woks.

I turned around, found Misty watching me, and wrinkled

my nose like a bunny. Misty scrunched her mouth to one side, apparently her method of showing she got the message. Samantha smiled and wiggled her nose. She looked about to put her hands, index fingers pointed up like bunny ears, to the sides of her head, but she seemed to think better of it. Still grinning, she lowered her hands to her sides.

Following April's example, I scooped brown rice out of a kettle. Next, five women stood behind five woks. "We take turns serving," April informed me. "My turn was last month." A tented card in front of each wok listed the ingredients in that particular wok. April explained, "Some of our members are allergic to certain veggies and nuts." April selected a mixture featuring baby corn, broccoli, and cashews. It looked good, so I asked for the same meal. At the end of the lineup of woks, we could choose from a variety of sauces. I opted for hot and spicy. The cold beverage was tap water in a punch bowl with ice and lemon and lime slices, while the hot ones were various herbal teas and—surprise, surprise—organic green tea. I ladled cold water for myself.

The meal was delicious. After we finished, we each took our dishes to the buffet table, where this week's servers collected them and packed them into the dishwasher.

Dessert was platters of fruit. We used tongs to pick up melon slices, pineapple wedges, small bunches of grapes, and quartered apples and oranges. I remained quiet about the treats I'd brought.

After we ate the fruit, Vanessa climbed the two steps to the stage and introduced me. I joined her and set my carton on the stage beside the podium.

Suzanne and Jenn slipped into the room from the hallway and sat at the first table they came to.

Vanessa went back down to the head table and sat with April. They tilted their heads back and looked up expectantly at me. I thanked Vanessa and the entire group, and then launched into the talk I'd been thinking about all day. "Thank you for the yummy dinner. I'm a little embarrassed to be speaking to this group, especially after that meal, because I run a donut shop, and donuts are not exactly health food." As I'd hoped they would, women laughed. I bent over, opened the carton, pulled out my Deputy Donut hat, settled it onto my head, and struck a pose, pointing at the donut. Nearly everyone laughed. Maybe my speech wouldn't put very many of them to sleep. I glanced at Samantha, saw the teasing light in her eyes, and remembered how her smile had caused me to giggle back in ninth grade when I was giving a report to the entire class and trying to be serious. Careful not to look at Samantha or Misty again, I told the story of Deputy Donut.

I didn't explain that I'd started making donuts to console myself after my detective husband was killed, didn't mention that my business partner was Fallingbrook's former police chief, and I downplayed my connections with other police officers. Vanessa and April were possibly murderers, and I didn't want them to be careful about telling me things, like potentially important clues. As it was, the name Deputy Donut and the police officers they might have seen in or near our café were probably more than enough to make them super-cautious around me.

I told the women that I had always loved making donuts and had started my business by taking "cakes" made of stuck-together donuts in fun shapes, like princesses and race cars, to kids' birthday parties.

"The next thing I knew," I said, "people were begging me to open a shop where they could buy my donuts and coffee every day. And my cat was already named Deputy Donut, and you all know the stereotype about police officers and donuts." People laughed. "My cat doesn't like donuts," I said, "except as hockey pucks, which is a great game for her except that I don't care for sticky floors." More laughter.

In the back of the room, Jenn held up her phone, probably taking my picture as I spoke. I smiled to show her that I appreciated the thoughtful gesture, and then went on with my lecture. "My father-in-law wanted to join the new venture, and we named the shop after my cat. So, now we had the beginnings of a brand. We would feature cats, cops, and donuts inside our café, on our signs, and in our advertising and promotion. We designed the hats, and our logo." I pulled the apron out of the box and put it on. "Only the people closest to the stage will be able to see the detail, but it's the silhouette of a cat wearing, rather jauntily, a cap like the one on my head. If you look closely, you'll see the donut on the cat's hat."

A woman called out, "I saw that logo on your car outside!"

I smiled. "And using a pretend police car with a donut on top to deliver our donuts fit in with everything else." Women applauded. I told them about the search for the perfect building, the headaches of renovation, and the satisfaction when everything came together. I ended with, "Seeing people close their eyes in bliss when they take a bite of a donut or a sip of coffee or tea makes our hard work worthwhile."

Vanessa joined me at the podium and said into the mic, "Has your venture made you wealthy beyond your wildest dreams?"

I made an exaggerated face of dismay and leaned toward the mic. "I'm not sure about *wildest,* but we have so many customers that we're going to need to hire at least one more employee."

She turned the mic toward her mouth and asked, "Have you thought of changing to all organic, gluten-free, and sugar-free products? The public are becoming more health conscious every day, and you would increase your sales. There's sugar in honey, but honey provides other benefits."

I had just been life-coached.

"It's an idea," I agreed, "and that leads me to my next topic." I smiled, drawing out the moment and enjoying the quiet anticipation in the room. "I have something for you all." Knowing that I had their full attention, I picked up the carton and carried it off the stage. The counter they'd used as a buffet table was now cleared of everything except a replenished bowl of ice water, carafes of hot water, clean mugs and glasses, and pretty wooden boxes of different types of organic teas. I set my cardboard carton on the floor beside the counter. With a dramatic flourish, I removed the bakery boxes and set them on the counter.

I heard a chorus of "ooohs." Some might have been of hunger, but others might have been of concern.

Frowning, Vanessa reached for the microphone.

I quickly said, rather loudly, "My partner and I created vegan mini-donuts for you to sample. They're gluten-free, made from ancient grains, with no added fats, no eggs, no dairy, and the only sweetening is honey. You might think you see chocolate on some of them, but it's a carob glaze. Come help yourselves."

On the stage, Vanessa tapped the microphone and got everyone's attention. "Wait," she ordered.

Uh-oh. Did she object to carob? My hand over one of the bakery boxes, I hesitated for a second, but then I stubbornly continued opening the boxes.

"I have a confession to make," Vanessa said into the mic.

Near the back of the room, Suzanne sat taller. Jenn glanced quickly at her sister, but Suzanne focused on Vanessa. Jenn pointed her phone's camera toward Vanessa.

At the front of the room, Misty was also sitting up straight and watching Vanessa. Samantha winked at me. My answering smile was a little strained. I fanned out our logo-printed paper napkins and put them next to the boxes. I set the Deputy Donut brochures beside the napkins.

Every inch dramatically earnest, Vanessa tossed her blond hair behind her shoulders. "If it weren't for chocolate," she announced, "I might not be here tonight." Members in the audience gasped. She hushed them with a raised hand. "I would be alive, but I might not be here." She pointed down toward the stage floor. "Here as in *here,* in this room."

She took a deep breath. "As you all know, the Legghaupt

Life Coach method promotes healthy eating. We avoid junk foods and empty calories."

Women in the audience nodded, and some cheered and applauded.

When the noise died down, Vanessa continued. "However, we all have cravings sometimes, particularly for foods that might not be good for us, and sometimes we need to listen to our bodies. My weakness is chocolate, and that weakness might have actually saved me from a fate almost as bad as death. Or maybe as bad. Maybe even worse . . ."

She looked out over the audience as if gauging our reaction. No one seemed to be moving. She went on. "Just over a week ago, I took April to a conference. I think we told many of you about our disappointment with that conference. Since it wasn't everything we'd hoped it would be, we left early. However, I had this nearly uncontrollable craving for a chocolate bar, and not an expensive, dark chocolate one with some redeeming features, either. No, I wanted one of those milk chocolate ones with a sweet and gooey center and maybe a few nuts, the sort of chocolate bar that one can buy in vending machines. But it was about eleven at night and there were no vending machines where we were. I didn't want anyone who knows me in Fallingbrook to see me buying chocolate. I didn't want any of you . . ." She waved her hand, palm down, to encompass the entire audience. "To know about my failing. We got into the car and drove, not toward Fallingbrook, but away from it. We drove north for over an hour until we found an all-night convenience store at a gas station, and we not only got our chocolate bars, we ate them. And we kept our shameful secret."

She made an overly sad face. "But about the time we were buying those chocolate bars, a tragedy occurred in the building where the conference we'd left was being held, and a man died." Obviously, Vanessa didn't realize that Roger's widow was in the audience. Jenn stopped taking pictures, laid her phone down on the table in front of her, and sat with her head bowed and her hands clasped on top of her phone. Even from the far side of the room, I saw how white her knuckles became.

"Now, here's the thing," Vanessa said. "The police suspect foul play. All week, the police have harassed April and me, interrogated us about where we were that night, and neither of us wanted to admit that we'd driven for miles hunting for cheap chocolate bars. Finally, we had to confess that we'd been together, which immediately gave both of us an alibi."

The trace of a frown crossed Misty's face, and I knew what she was thinking. Waiting an entire week to tell the police they'd been together somewhere far from the crime did not necessarily exonerate either of the two women.

Vanessa continued her story. "If we hadn't told the police that we'd been together, we might have ended up being arrested for harming that man! So, thanks to giving in to our desire for chocolate, April and I are here tonight." She smiled. "Now go enjoy Emily's carob donuts. I'm sure they're delicious, and better for us than chocolate bars crammed with dangerous chemicals. I'm going to have one!" Still smiling, she ran gracefully down the steps from the stage.

Women scraped their chairs back and headed for the bakery boxes of health-food mini-donuts.

Vanessa shook my hand. "I told you that you could do it, Emily. You did fine. The women all appreciated what you had to tell them. Thank you. And now, the next time someone asks you to give a speech, you won't be worried. You'll know you can do it!"

I hadn't exactly been worried. I'd only told her that I hadn't prepared a speech. Maybe to a life coach, I'd sounded anxious. I thanked her.

Women rushed to the buffet table for donuts.

Jenn and Suzanne each took one. I thought I'd brought enough donuts for everyone to have at least one, but some of the women liked them so much that they kept coming back for more. I didn't eat any.

While I was standing nearby accepting compliments, Jenn put her hand on my arm, bent down, and whispered, "Now we *know* that Gerald Stone . . ." She winced and her eyes reddened. "Did it."

Behind Jenn, Suzanne's eyes seemed to roll back into her head. She turned pale and wavered. I reached around Jenn and attempted, unsuccessfully, to grab one of Suzanne's arms. "Suzanne!"

Jenn whipped around, saw her sister about to fall, and darted a hand out toward her.

Suzanne sagged, touching the back of a woman behind her. The woman turned, looked about to scold whoever had bumped her, and then must have realized what was happening. She caught Suzanne just as Suzanne appeared to lose consciousness.

"Samantha!" I shouted. "Misty!"

Chapter 24

❧

In seconds, Samantha was kneeling beside Suzanne and taking her pulse. Jenn was on Suzanne's other side, holding her hand and talking to her. Samantha looked at Jenn. "Your sister's coming around. Her color's better."

Jenn squeaked, "Should I call 911?" She was nearly as pale as Suzanne.

Samantha answered, "I'm an Emergency Medical Technician. I don't think she needs an ambulance."

Jenn rubbed her hair out of her face. "How did you know she's my . . . oh, you're the one who . . ." Tears brimmed over.

Samantha said gently, "Yes. My partner and I took you to the hospital early last Sunday morning. I heard about your husband. I'm sorry." Except for the pink streaks in her hair, none of Samantha's usual impishness was visible.

Suzanne opened her eyes and struggled to sit up. Jenn and Samantha helped her, and then Suzanne insisted on moving onto a chair. Samantha asked Jenn to get Suzanne water or fruit juice. Jenn jumped up and headed to Vanessa.

Misty took me aside and asked, "Did you see what she ate, if anything?"

"She wasn't here in time for dinner, and I don't think she ate anything besides one of my health-food donuts." I glanced toward the bakery boxes. "They're all gone. I think nearly everyone in here had one."

"I didn't. I was talking to Samantha. We didn't get to the donuts in time. Did you eat one?"

I shook my head. "Not here. I wasn't sure there would be enough. I ate one at Deputy Donut earlier. And I'm sure no one did anything to those donuts after I brought them here."

Misty frowned toward Samantha, who was helping Suzanne hold a glass of water. "Did that woman have anything to drink that you know of, I mean before right now?"

"I didn't see her drink anything, but I wasn't watching everyone the entire time."

"Think she's pregnant?"

"I . . . hadn't thought of that. She's about forty-five."

"Doesn't rule it out. Her sister's, what, ten years younger?"

"Jenn's about that. But she's not . . ." I was going to say that Jenn wasn't pregnant, but I didn't really know. "Wait a second. Jenn fainted Saturday night."

Misty tilted her head.

"I thought she fainted from shock," I said. "Or tight clothing."

"Could be," Misty agreed.

Samantha patted Suzanne's shoulder and joined us. "I don't think it's anything serious. Suzanne said she was too hot."

"Forty-five," Misty concluded.

Samantha asked, "What? Oh, I get it. Yep, I've answered calls after women had their first hot flashes and thought they were dying."

Misty asked us both, "Think we can let everyone go?"

"I don't think it's a matter of letting," I answered. "It's seven. Vanessa told me that's when the meeting ends." At least half of the attendees had already left, and most of the rest of them were chatting while moving toward the hallway leading to the front door. Many of the women had probably been too busy catching up with one another's news to notice Suzanne's collapse.

Samantha said seriously, "You can't let Emily go, Misty. This is the third person in just over a week who has fainted or collapsed after being near her donuts. And Yvonne Passenmath is leading the investigation."

Swearing, Misty hauled out her phone. "Hey, Hooligan, can you swing by here and pick me and some non-evidence up?" She disconnected and grinned. "He's on his way."

"Hooligan?" Samantha asked.

"My new partner."

"Did you give him the address?" I asked Misty.

"I already told him where I was going to be and that I might need him to pick me up if I was going to get to work on time. That's why I wanted to come in your car, Samantha. I left my jacket in it, though. I'll send him to get it from you."

I tried to suppress a giggle.

Samantha looked from one of us to the other. "Are you two trying to set me up with a . . . with a *hooligan?*"

"Wait until you see him," I said.

She raised her nose in the air. "I need to go to work, too."

I pointed at Suzanne. "You *are* working, Samantha." Well, maybe. Suzanne and Jenn stood up and walked carefully toward the exit, which was no longer clogged with chattering women. Samantha started after them.

Misty called, "If you see a uniformed cop out there, bring him in!"

Without turning toward us, Samantha waved in acknowledgment.

A few minutes later, Samantha returned without Misty's jacket, but with Hooligan Houlihan. His freckled face wasn't good at hiding a blush. Samantha didn't have freckles, but she was blushing, too. She told us, "Suzanne walked outside with no problem and got into a cab. Jenn promised to stay with her and call us if necessary. Suzanne said she didn't need help. She was going to go home and relax."

I gave Houlihan a short statement. After he finished writing in his notebook, he put the bakery boxes, leftover napkins, and brochures into the carton, shouldered the carton, and let us lead him out.

Vanessa waylaid us at the door to her boutique. "What's going on? Are you in trouble, Emily?" She was good at sounding both concerned and empathetic. And a bit judgmental.

"I hope not!" I acted like I was joking, but I wasn't. Had someone, while taking a donut, dribbled poison on other donuts?

"She's not," Houlihan concurred.

"He's a friend," Misty explained.

"Okay, kids," Vanessa said. "Have fun!"

I smiled at her. "We always do."

"Good." But her lips thinned, as if she was considering saving us from a life of too much happy hoping and not enough goal achievement. And not enough shopping, either, possibly, although I didn't think her boutique had been open for business that evening. "Thanks again, Emily."

Hooligan Houlihan's squad car was parked next to my "cruiser." Misty and Samantha headed toward Samantha's car. Houlihan put my carton in the back seat of his car, shut the door, and watched Misty return, carrying her jacket. "Misty told me that she, you, and another woman have known each other since junior high. Is Samantha the other woman?" He had a delightfully lopsided grin to go along with the blush. "That doesn't sound right. I mean the third woman."

"Yes."

"You're the one who makes donuts, so Samantha's the EMT?"

"Yes. She drove the ambulance away early Sunday morning, just before you arrived."

Misty opened the passenger door. "Let's go, Hooligan."

He smiled across the top of his cruiser at me. "She's actually letting me drive."

"Only until I'm in uniform again." She slid into the passenger seat and closed the door.

He glanced at Samantha's car and then looked at me again. "See you in your donut shop, Emily."

He threw himself into his cruiser, backed it out of its space, and raced toward downtown and the police station.

Samantha drove past and waved at me.

I got into my donut-topped "police" car. Why were Misty and I matching Samantha with Hooligan Houlihan? I had earmarked Brent for Samantha.

Maybe Hooligan was better for her. Brent's girlfriends were usually taller than Samantha, and he never stuck with any of them for very long. Besides, I'd enjoyed watching the interest spark between Samantha and Hooligan. Even though I didn't know Hooligan well, he and Samantha seemed right for each other.

I followed Samantha most of the way to downtown Fallingbrook, but she drove faster than I was willing to push my vintage car, and she was way ahead when she turned off toward Emergency Medical Services headquarters.

In the deepening dusk, motion detectors lit the lights behind Deputy Donut. I backed the Fordor into its garage and started across the lot to my own car. No one else seemed to be around, but downtown was not exactly quiet at seven thirty. The diner across Wisconsin Street was nearly always busy around suppertime, and despite the calendar saying that it was the middle of October, the evening's warmth must have encouraged the people at the Fireplug Pub, next to the fire station, to open its outdoor patio, complete with live music.

I buckled myself into my car, but instead of starting the engine right away, I sent Jenn a text. She responded that Suzanne was fine, but tired, and they were sorry we couldn't have the meeting we'd planned after the presentation. She attached the photos she'd taken that evening. I sent a message thanking her and then zoomed in on the photos.

There were clear ones of lots of our faces, including Vanessa's and April's.

Vanessa had claimed that the two women could give each other alibis because they'd been together. She'd said they'd driven north of Little Lake Lodge for over an hour until they found a gas station with an all-night convenience store that sold chocolate bars.

Vanessa had also said that she and April had told the police about their chocolate binge, and the police had stopped "harassing" them. Maybe Passenmath had already sent someone to find that gas station and commandeer any surveillance files.

But maybe Passenmath was still systematically reviewing only the videos south of Little Lake Lodge.

I could call Brent and tell him what I'd learned, but if Vanessa had been speaking the truth, she'd already told the police about April's and her so-called alibi. Judging by Misty's face when she listened to Vanessa, the alibi was news to Misty. Maybe when Misty began her shift, she would ask the detectives on the case if Vanessa and April really had told them about their chocolate-craving binge.

I didn't know if the gas station existed, and I was no more eager than Passenmath probably was to send law-enforcement staff up into the north woods on what might be a wild-goose chase.

What had made the owners of Little Lake Lodge name their banquet hall after a cliché describing a fruitless mission? *Fruitless,* I thought. Maybe they didn't plan on serving fruit in their banquet hall.

I slapped at my cheeks to stop my aimlessly wandering mind. Maybe I'd eaten something at Vanessa's studio that was causing me to hallucinate. Or maybe my own bedtime was approaching. Five in the morning was going to be way too soon. I wanted to go home, relax with Dep, catch up on chores, and go to bed.

But would I sleep, or would I wonder about that gas station? Would I regret not chasing after some possibly nonexistent videos?

Most surveillance systems automatically wrote over their files after a certain amount of time.

Dep would be fine at home alone for two or three more hours.

I took a deep breath and started my car. At Wisconsin Street, instead of turning south toward the sweet cottage I shared with my sweet and sometimes bossy cat, I turned north.

I passed the town square, the police department, and the fire station. New subdivisions lined the road for about a mile, and then I was in the woods, and Wisconsin Street became a state highway. I stayed on the highway instead of taking the twisty county road that led to Little Lake Lodge, other resorts, and individual cottages, summer homes, and hunting and fishing camps.

The first gas station I came to was only about a half hour north of the turnoff to Little Lake Lodge, so was probably not the one that Vanessa had told us about earlier that evening. I stopped anyway and pumped a few gallons of gas. I went inside. The attendant seemed jumpy, as if afraid of being robbed. Maybe the small amount of gas I'd bought was a warning signal.

I paid him and then showed him my phone screen displaying Vanessa's and April's faces. He flinched.

I came up with a very lame explanation. "My cousin was in town last week, and she thought she lost her prescription sunglasses here."

"No one left sunglasses here."

"Do you remember if one of these two women bought gas here? Or maybe a chocolate bar?"

"I never saw them."

"Were you at work here last Saturday night? That's when my cousin was around here buying candy."

"I was working, but I didn't see those people or any sunglasses." He backed away.

I returned to my car and sat fiddling with my keys. Vanessa

had said that she and April had driven north for over an hour. Did I want to drive around that long? But maybe they had zigzagged between lakes, while I was on the most direct route heading north. Surely, the next gas station couldn't be an entire half hour away from where I was now.

I reminded myself that I wasn't interfering with Brent's investigation. If I found the gas station, I was merely going to pinpoint where to send him. Or I was going to tell him that Vanessa might have made up a nonexistent gas station as part of her alibi. But he would still want to follow up and see for himself that the gas station was only a fantasy. If it was.

If I was putting the words "gas station" and "fantasy" in the same thought, maybe it really was time for me to go home for some much-needed sleep.

But maybe the gas station with the chocolate bars was close, and I was about to find it.

I eased away from the gas station where the attendant claimed not to have seen Vanessa and April. I turned north.

"A cousin lost her sunglasses," I muttered to myself. "At night in October. Can't you come up with a better story, Emily?"

Remembering Brent's teasing about arguing with myself about clues, evidence, and suspects, I clamped my lips together.

There wasn't much traffic going north, but cars, pickups, and campers streamed south, leaving the warmish weekend in the wilderness and heading back to Fallingbrook and nearby towns.

Every five minutes, I told myself to turn around, but I kept thinking I'd find the gas station just over the next rise or around the next curve. "I'm driving myself around the bend!" Considering that I'd just said it aloud, putting it to music, no less, it was probably true, and maybe it was a sign that I should turn around and go home. I had plenty of gas, but if I thought I might run low, I could stop at the gas station where I'd just bought a few gallons and unnerve that poor attendant more. *Not a good idea, Emily,* I told myself. But I didn't say it aloud.

And I continued driving north.

I almost missed it, on the other side of a brightly lit motel with a flashing neon VACANCY sign and an arrow pointing toward the motel.

Since buying only a few gallons of gas might have been what scared the previous gas station attendant, I parked near the little store where a sign in the window said, among other things, CAMPING SUPPLIES and PAY FOR GAS HERE.

A bell rang when I entered. Two women, one in her thirties and the other in her fifties, were talking and laughing behind the counter. "Can we help you?" the older one asked. They looked almost identical except for their ages. They even had the same purplish red shade of hair.

"I'm looking for a chocolate bar." It was almost as inane as the story about the cousin and the sunglasses. Rows and rows of chocolate bars were right in front of my thighs, on the other side of the counter from the two women.

They were polite. The older woman smiled and pointed a finger toward the counter in front of me. "Help yourself, and if you don't see what you want here, go back there—we have shelves of candy."

I studied the rows of chocolate bars and picked out two different ones, either of which could have been the one Vanessa described, milk chocolate with a gooey center, and some nuts. "You're a lifesaver," I said. "I was craving these."

The younger woman giggled.

I handed her bills. While she jingled through change in her cash drawer, I said, "Friends told me about this place. Just over a week ago, Saturday night, I think it was, they had a huge craving for chocolate bars, and they found your store and were very happy about it. That started me craving chocolate bars, too."

The younger woman said, "I remember one woman coming in here about then, talking about craving chocolate. She bought, like, ten bars, didn't she, Mom?"

That wasn't quite the way that Vanessa had told it. . . .

The mother grinned. "Lots of 'em, anyway."

The daughter laughed. "And she said she felt guilty about it!"

The mother added, "I told her not to, that we all need to do something fun for ourselves once in a while, but that seemed to be the wrong thing to say. She was very serious. I was afraid she was going to change her mind and return the candy bars for a refund."

"Small world." Considering that I'd already said that I came up here on my friends' advice, that was another lame comment. I pulled my phone out and showed them a picture of Vanessa and April. "Was she one of these women?"

They looked at the picture. The daughter pointed at Vanessa. "That's the one!"

I pointed at the tiny image of April. "On Saturday night, the woman who came in here was with this woman. Did she come in, too?" For sure, they were going to think I was a detective. Or nuttier than the candy bars I was melting with my hotly lying little hand.

The mother shook her head. "Just that one woman came in here, by herself."

The younger woman looked at her mother. "Remember her bag, Mom? What did it say? Something about Happy . . . um . . . Hopers, was it?"

"That was it. We read it wrong at first and nearly had hysterics." The mother laughed at the memory.

Her daughter joined in. "Then we saw what it really said, 'Hopers.' And below that was something else funny, something about shopping."

The mother swept her hand across the counter. "And as soon as she was out that door, we were rolling on the floor laughing. Something about it made us think that she believed that by buying a dozen chocolate bars she'd accomplished something important."

"I remember now," the daughter said. "Her bag said: 'Goal Achievement Through Shopping.'"

The mother snapped her fingers. "That was it! Isn't it funny?" she asked me.

I smiled. "It sure is."

The mother swatted at her daughter's arm. "Here we are, poking fun at this nice lady's friend."

"Don't worry," I told them. "I thought the words on her bag were both funny-ha-ha and funny-strange." I told them goodbye and drove to the far side of the motel, out of sight of the two women, and switched off my engine. Maybe Brent already knew that the gas station existed and that Vanessa had been there one night recently, buying chocolate bars.

Then again, maybe he didn't. And I still didn't know if April had actually been with Vanessa. April could have been back at Little Lake Lodge, pressing crullers into a saucer of arsenic.

Before I could speed-dial Brent, my phone rang.

Brent. Calling from his personal phone.

Chapter 25

How did Brent always seem to know when I was about to call him? He couldn't be tapping my phone or reading my mind. It was a coincidence. A weird one, possibly, except that Roger's murder had forced us to get in touch with each other frequently.

"Hi, Brent," I said.

"Are you okay?"

"Sure."

"I'm at your house and your car's not here, and you're not answering the door. Dep is howling at me, though." I heard the smile in his voice.

"I'm at a motel north of Fallingbrook."

"Just checking that you're okay." He seldom sounded that formal. Did he think I was with a date at the motel?

"Don't go," I said. "I parked here to call you. I gave a presentation at Vanessa Legghaupt's studio earlier this evening."

"*What?*"

"Vanessa has programs about female entrepreneurs, and this evening's speaker had canceled. Vanessa asked me to give a last-minute talk on starting up a business."

"Emily, that woman is a, well, not exactly a suspect, but—"

"I was perfectly safe. Misty and Samantha came, too. They weren't on duty. They came as friends. While we were there, Vanessa told us that she and her client April had an alibi for last Saturday night. She said they told the police they were together buying chocolate bars, but I wanted to make certain that you knew about this supposed candy-buying shopping trip."

"They did tell us about it."

"And you don't believe them."

"We need to check it out. They took a long time to tell us their story. You've said they come into Deputy Donut, right? And that they never buy anything besides organic green tea?"

"Right. But Vanessa said that on Saturday night, she had cravings for chocolate. What does Passenmath think of their alibi?"

"I don't think she feels the need to confirm the alibi that the two women provided for each other. It supports her theory that the bride murdered the groom."

I groaned. "I still don't think she—or any bride—would go to such lengths to kill her bridegroom in a public place. Women poison their husbands, but not at resorts."

"It can happen anywhere."

"I suppose. And I suppose I'm not helping Jenn's case by confirming Vanessa's and April's alibi. Well, Vanessa's. I didn't confirm April's. I located the store where Vanessa bought the chocolate bars, and I also found two women who remember Vanessa buying them. They ID'd her by her photo, and they also remembered the wording on the tote bag she was carrying."

"What are you doing—oh, never mind, you'll tell me later."

"That sounds like a threat."

"It is." But his voice was kind, and he wasn't scaring me. He became more serious. "Where are these women who remember Ms. Legghaupt buying the chocolate bars?"

"In a convenience store north on the state highway. There's a gas station with it. And a motel."

"What's the name of the motel?"

I wriggled around in my seat to read the sign. "Believe it or not, it's the Teddy Beddy-Bye-Bye Motel."

"I know it." I reminded myself that he knew the somewhat seedy-looking motel as a detective, not necessarily as a patron. "We haven't yet collected surveillance video files that far north. I'm off duty, but I'll be right up to question the two women and check for videos. You said the women are in the convenience store?"

"And they look like mother and daughter. One's about in her fifties, the other about in her thirties, both with square faces and purplish red hair. I can wait for you, or go ask them to wait for you."

"I'd rather you left the police work to the police." I knew that was an understatement. "Besides, Dep's still howling for you to come home."

We disconnected and I started the engine. "Thanks, Dep," I grumbled as I pulled into the southbound lane of the highway. "But wouldn't it be simpler for Brent if I just stayed here? What if those two women finish their shift and another square-faced mother-daughter pair replace them? Brent's questions will mystify them."

Talking to my cat in her presence was one thing. Talking to her when she was miles away was probably another.

I turned on the radio and sang along.

I was almost halfway back to Fallingbrook when I realized that I hadn't given Brent a chance to explain why he'd dropped by my house at almost eight thirty at night or why he'd gone to the door after noticing that my car wasn't parked in its usual spot.

A sleek dark car zoomed north past me. Brent in an unmarked police cruiser? I hoped that he and Passenmath would soon figure out—correctly—who had murdered Roger and arrest the culprit. I was pretty sure, if Vanessa's and April's

alibi held up, that the culprit was Gerald Stone. He and
Roger had known each other fifteen years ago, and from the
sound of the stories that Roger had told Jenn and that Gerald
had told Suzanne, the relationship between the two men had
been at best uneasy and at worst murderous.

At home, Dep studiously ignored me until after I crawled
under the covers and turned off the light. She was totally silent,
but a warm, slight weight landed on my shins, and then the
purring began.

On Monday morning, I didn't know if Brent had confirmed Vanessa's and April's chocolate-bingeing alibi, but
whatever he had discovered at the gas station and convenience store at Teddy Beddy-Bye-Bye Motel, it apparently
hadn't been enough to narrow in on Gerald Stone and arrest
him. The former pharmacist came into Deputy Donut at
eight thirty, about half an hour before the weekday morning
group of retired men usually arrived

He sat at their table. Again, he wanted the day's featured
coffee, a medium roast from Timor. When I told him about
its full body and slightly spicy overtones, I couldn't help remembering Chad, the aftershave he'd worn on Saturday
night, and the way he seemed to radiate kindness, along with
the flirting.

I still couldn't see Chad as someone who would murder to
get his old girlfriend back. As Suzanne had said, Chad could
have simply asked Jenn to return to him.

Gerald Stone, with his alleged history of selling prescription drugs illegally and attempting to poison Roger, seemed
like a more probable killer.

But I couldn't fault Gerald Stone for his donut choice.
Again, he was adventurous, opting for a raised donut filled
with a sweet yet pungent tamarind sauce. When I brought
him the order, the other men still hadn't arrived. "Say," Stone

said, "didn't I see you at Little Lake Lodge on a Saturday, just over a week ago? Bringing donuts to a wedding reception?"

I restrained myself from taking a step away from him. "Yes."

Stone's back was to the kitchen, so he wouldn't have been able to see Tom watching us. Stone asked me, "Were you still there when the groom fell ill?"

"Yes. Were you?" I knew that, shortly after Roger collapsed, Stone had been gone from his chair near the delivery door.

Stone's ruddy face turned redder. "Not that I know of. I left about twelve fifteen, and apparently leaving at that hour was enough to arouse suspicion in the minds of Fallingbrook's finest. And the Division of Criminal Investigation's finest, too."

"They have to consider everyone who was there," I said.

"Do they suspect you, too?" I thought I detected a gleam of hope in his eyes.

"I'm afraid so." I was wary of telling our customers that our donuts were suspected, even though the police had to be certain that only a few crullers had been poisoned and that they'd been poisoned after I delivered them to Little Lake Lodge.

Stone asked me, "Do you have an alibi?"

"I had joined the dancing and the party. Lots of people saw me."

Stone looked glum. "I was hoping maybe you'd say you'd driven away around twelve fifteen and saw me driving away, too. I *could* have seen you driving away, you know." He tilted his head and glanced at me from under half-closed eyelids.

Was Gerald Stone actually asking me to make up a story that would give us both alibis?

"You couldn't have," I told him firmly. "I was there until after one thirty Sunday morning, and I didn't drive away. I was taken away in a police cruiser."

He sighed. "I guess I didn't see you, then."

You got that right, I thought to myself. *Sorry.* Except I wasn't sorry. There was no way I would lie to give a possible killer an alibi.

Stone shook his head. "Most folks who were there probably have an alibi, but the best I could come up with, if it wasn't you I saw, was noticing the bride steaming up the insides of a car with someone I figured was the groom. I told the DCI detective that, but she said the bride didn't report seeing me and it couldn't have been the groom. Well, stands to reason the bride didn't see me, the way she and her companion were steaming up the windows. And I told the DCI detective that the car was red, and she didn't believe that, either. She reminded me that I'd said the parking lot was dark."

"The staff parking lot?" I asked. "The one on the hill?"

"That's where I parked. And—get this—that DCI detective checked the phases of the moon, and it was only a thin crescent that night, and had set two hours earlier, besides. She claimed I couldn't tell if the car was red because all dark cars look black at night. But I always carry a small flashlight when I'm working security. I didn't shine it inside the car, but I know that car was red. Bright red."

I wondered if Stone had seen Chad drop Jenn off behind her store on Friday morning. Knowing that the police could be focusing on him, Stone could be concocting stories about Chad and Jenn to make one of them look guilty. Or both of them.

However, if Stone had seen Jenn and Chad together, maybe he could provide both of them with an alibi. He seemed to think that seeing her at twelve fifteen exonerated him, but he was the one who had been, as far as I knew, in the service corridor about the time that the murderer entered the banquet hall's back door with a saucer and about a half cup of arsenic. "How do you know it was the bride in the car?" I asked.

"If it wasn't the bride, it was someone wearing a bunch of white curtains." He shook his head. "That bride. Such a sweet little thing she was."

"She *was?*" Was he saying that she was no longer sweet? Did he believe she had run back into the lodge and poisoned her new bridegroom? Maybe he wanted me to draw that conclusion.

That didn't seem to be it. He explained, "I knew her a long time ago, when she was in grade school." His eyes softened. "She was cute as a button." He leaned closer.

I shot a quick look toward Tom. He was still watching us.

Stone spoke in a lower tone. "No one hired me to work at Little Lake Lodge that night. I went there because I sensed that the sweet little girl, even though she was now grown up, might need someone there to watch over her. Anyone could have whipped out that back entrance with wedding gifts. People sometimes give cash, you know. Completely untraceable if stolen. But when I saw the bride in that car, steaming up the windows with the man I thought was the groom, I decided that, as far as she was concerned, the reception was over and the honeymoon had begun, and all of the wedding gifts were probably in a safe place. It was after midnight, so I went home."

I wasn't about to ask him to explain why, if he thought he was guarding the back entrance of the lodge, he left his post and explored the staff parking lot.

Still, he had told me basically the same story he'd told Suzanne, but it was substantially different from the explanation he'd given Brent. And I knew that Brent hadn't lied about what he'd heard. Apparently, Suzanne hadn't, either. I wanted to ask Stone if he'd explained all of it to the police, but I wasn't sure how to word the question without letting him know I had at least one friend in Fallingbrook's law-enforcement community. Not only that, I didn't want to help a possible murderer tailor his story to make himself look innocent.

The other retired men came in and sat with Stone. I took their orders and then scooted to the kitchen to fill them.

"Everything okay?" Tom asked.

"Yes, but I don't trust him."

"Good. Don't." He lifted a basket of golden-brown donuts from the fryer. They smelled luscious.

Later, cleaning the Knitpickers' table so they could knit without creating sticky sweaters, hats, and scarves, I spotted Chad's car coming from the north on Wisconsin Street. No one was in the passenger seat, and I couldn't see the driver. The car slowed at the driveway leading to the parking lots behind Deputy Donut and Dressed to Kill.

I quickly took the dirty dishes to the kitchen and then went to the office. Dep stretched and meowed. I was going to need to wash my hands after handling dishes, anyway, so I obeyed Dep's command and picked her up. Her fur was warm and soft. She started purring.

Chad's car was near the back of the lot behind Dressed to Kill. Jenn got out of the driver's seat and hurried to her shop's rear door. It was Monday, so Chad should be teaching. Apparently, Jenn's car still hadn't been returned to her and she was borrowing Chad's.

In the afternoon, Misty, Scott, and Hooligan Houlihan all showed up for their breaks and sat together at a big table with a couple of Scott's firefighters. Hooligan blushed when I asked for his order, and I didn't think he was blushing at the sight of me. I hoped I'd made him remember meeting Samantha, and that Samantha was the cause of his blushes.

As always, Scott gave us all equal attention—me, Misty, Hooligan, and Scott's firefighters. When they left, though, Scott held the door open for Misty, and then he walked up Wisconsin Street beside her, trailing Hooligan and the firefighters, who appeared to be carrying on the vehement discussion they'd started in Deputy Donut about which baseball team had the best shot at winning the World Series.

After the last customer left for the evening, Tom and I started cleaning up. Something caught his attention near the front of the store. "Oh, murder," he said.

As I turned to look, the pounding began.

Great. Yvonne Passenmath had returned, and she did not look happy.

Chapter 26

✻

But then, Yvonne Passenmath never looked happy.

"I'll let her in," Tom said.

He unlocked the door and opened it.

Passenmath marched inside. Today's rumpled pantsuit was navy blue, and her curls hadn't frizzed. "I need to talk to Ms. Westhill," she announced in a grumpy voice.

I joined the other two in the dining area and gestured at one of our glossy tree-slice tables. "Have a seat. Would you like a donut?" I didn't tell her that all we had left at the end of the day were crullers dipped in confectioners' sugar. I knew they were delicious and not tainted with arsenic, but I kind of hoped she would turn down the offer, anyway. Discovering that Tom and I did, sometimes, coat crullers with confectioners' sugar might make her decide that on Saturday night we had coated crullers with a powder that resembled sugar but wasn't. "Coffee or tea?"

"I'm not here to eat or drink." She looked toward the office. Dep was puffed up in the window, which apparently made Yvonne less eager to carry on the interview in Dep's domain. Yvonne sat at the table. I sat, too, and so did Tom.

Yvonne glared at him, but she didn't send him away. She took out her notebook and pen. "We checked all of the gloves in the wastebasket you left at Little Lake Lodge, Ms. Westhill."

I smiled. "Emily."

She went on as if I hadn't spoken. "And nearly every single one of them has at least a partial of your handprint and/or fingerprints on what was originally the inside, plus your fingerprints on what was originally the outside."

I nodded encouragingly. "That's not surprising. The person who brought the arsenic could have brought his or her own gloves."

"Could have," she said, "but a few of the gloves that you wore had grains of arsenic on them, some on the insides and some on the outsides." She grasped the cover of her notebook as if she was about to close it and terminate the interview. And perhaps the case.

Tom gave me a look as if to warn me to let him take over. "That's not surprising, either," he said. "You told me you found a plastic bag with arsenic in it inside the wastebasket. Grains of arsenic could have spilled out of that bag when the murderer tossed it. Whose fingerprints were on the bag?"

Yvonne flushed. "No one's. If there were fingerprints on that bag, they were wiped." She didn't close the notebook.

Tom reminded her, "You didn't find arsenic in our shop, our car, or Emily's clothing. Did you check anyone else's car?"

"All of the suspects' cars."

"Gerald Stone's?" I asked. "I saw him at the delivery entrance of Little Lake Lodge around ten that evening, and when I peeked out into that corridor at twelve thirty, he was gone. He was in here this morning." I pointed at the table where he'd sat. "He . . ." I frowned. "He seemed to be asking me to say that I'd seen him driving back to Fallingbrook at twelve fifteen Sunday morning. I didn't see him. I couldn't have. I was at the lodge."

Tom leaned forward, elbows on the table as if he were still a police officer questioning witnesses. "You didn't tell me about that, Emily."

"I was going to when I got a chance."

Tom seemed to be pretending that Yvonne Passenmath

wasn't there. "Let me get this straight. Was Gerald Stone actually asking you to give him an alibi?"

"He didn't know at first, until I told him, that I already had one, and he didn't come right out and offer to give me an alibi if I'd give him one, but that's the way it sounded to me."

"Conjecture," Passenmath blustered.

Tom nodded. "But interesting."

I added, "Stone hoped he had an alibi. He saw the bride and a man inside a car, steaming up the windows at twelve fifteen Sunday morning."

Tom broke in again. "Didn't you just say he wanted you to say you'd seen him driving home at twelve fifteen?"

"Approximately," I answered. "He saw the bride and a man—he assumed it was the groom—when he was on his way to his car in the staff parking lot." I glanced at Yvonne Passenmath. "But he said the bride denied seeing him then. Not that it would have mattered. No one could have been watching him all evening. I'd seen him just inside the delivery entrance around ten, but I didn't look out there again until twelve thirty. He had disappeared by then. In the meantime, he could have come and gone from his car several times. He could have brought a bag of arsenic into the lodge in his briefcase or a pocket. And here's another strange thing." I repeated the reason Gerald Stone gave me for acting as a security guard at Little Lake Lodge during Jenn's reception. "He said when he saw the bride steaming up a car with someone, he figured the wedding presents were safe, and he decided to go home. That doesn't explain why he was already in the parking lot on the way to his car when he made that decision."

The corners of her mouth dipping downward, DCI Agent Passenmath reclaimed control of the interview. "I'm not going to make baseless guesses about people going to and from their cars, and I'm not going to tell you whose cars and homes we've searched. I don't give civilians details that should remain secret."

Nodding in apparent approval, Tom slipped back into his role as a civilian. "We appreciate that. I'm guessing that if you found even the slightest bit of arsenic in a potential suspect's car or home or on their clothing, you'd be looking very carefully at that person." Well, maybe he hadn't completely gone back to being only a civilian.

She gave him a withering glance. "Of course we would."

Tom persisted, "But you haven't found any arsenic other than at the scene and in and around the victim."

Passenmath's face reddened again. "I didn't say that. And your shop was thoroughly cleaned before the investigators could have gotten here. I'll let you detect your own conclusions from *that*. Meanwhile, I suppose you two will find out all you want from some loose-lipped detective on the Fallingbrook force."

Tom turned on his police-chief stare and aimed it at her.

I wanted to laugh. *Brent, also known as Mr. Mmp, loose-lipped?* To be fair, Brent probably did tell me more than he would have told a random person wandering around the streets of Fallingbrook. Brent had thanked me for some of the information I'd given him. But, I thought uncharitably, Yvonne Passenmath would probably rather have a murder go unsolved than let a civilian, especially one she disliked, help solve it.

Maybe I was being a smidge unfair. Besides, as far as I could tell, Yvonne disliked nearly everyone.

She wasn't done with me yet. "I understand that you took donuts to an event last night, Ms. Westhill. Am I correct?"

"Yes, I did."

"What were the ingredients?" she asked.

Tom could probably tell from the look on my face that I was struggling not to make sarcastic remarks about poisons. He quickly listed the ingredients.

Passenmath asked me, "Did anyone eat a lot of them?"

"Most women ate only one or two. Some might have had as many as half a dozen, while others didn't get any."

Jenn had been right in her description of Passenmath. The surly detective really did have beady eyes, and they were getting beadier by the second. "One woman, who had not eaten dinner while there, collapsed after eating your donuts, is that right?"

"Jenn Zeeland's half-sister."

Passenmath corrected me. "Jennifer Zeeland's last name is now Banchen."

I nodded. "Thank you, Detective Passenmath." I didn't think it came out as sarcasm, but Passenmath glowered as if I'd insulted her. I ignored the glower. "Suzanne ate a donut, only one, as far as I could tell, and she collapsed, but I doubt that the donut had anything to do with her fainting. The room was stuffy, and she might not have had anything to eat or drink for hours."

Passenmath demanded, "Do you have any of those donuts left?"

"No," Tom answered, "but I could whip up a batch for you."

Passenmath placed her palms on the table, her fingers pointing at each other, her arms out from her shoulders, and her elbows bent as if she were trying to make herself look bigger and more powerful than Tom. And if that weren't menacing enough, she leaned forward. "That would be completely useless. I want to test the donuts that were at the event, not a new batch. And unfortunately, the victim did not present herself at the hospital after she became ill, or save part of her donut for us to test."

It seemed to me that saving a piece of food in case one became ill from it later would be a little strange, but I only said that Officer Houlihan had taken the bakery boxes that had contained the donuts as evidence. I asked, "Did any crumbs in those boxes contain anything that might make someone faint?"

Passenmath snapped, "I'm not answering that."

Tom was braver than I was. He had a quick comeback. "In

other words, the boxes that Emily took from here to the event tested negative for toxic substances."

Passenmath stood up. "I have work to do." In her heavy shoes, she stomped out without doing what I'd feared she'd come to do, especially after she'd said that some of the gloves I'd handled had arsenic on them. She didn't arrest me.

Tom locked the door behind her. Passenmath struggled into the driver's seat of an unmarked cruiser. Shaking his head and muttering words, some of which sounded like "big" and "britches," Tom returned to the kitchen.

We finished tidying and then joined Dep in the office. Dep brought Tom a bedraggled catnip mouse to admire. The three of us, minus the soggy toy, put in an order for flour and sugar, and then Tom left, promising to say hello to Cindy for me.

Suzanne had said that she and Jenn and I should get together after the previous evening's presentation to discuss anything we might learn in Vanessa Legghaupt's studio, but then Suzanne had fainted and gone home to rest and Jenn had canceled the meeting. Although we'd texted each other after my presentation, Jenn and I hadn't planned another tea party in the office of Dressed to Kill.

However, I saw no reason not to present myself, with a box of donuts, at the shop's back door.

Chapter 27

I double-checked, and we truly didn't have any donuts besides crullers coated in confectioners' sugar. Hoping that I wasn't being insensitive and that seeing crullers wouldn't remind Jenn too strongly of Roger's death, I tucked six of them into a bakery box. In the office, I put on one of the cardigans I'd bought from Jenn, a heathery gray fisherman's knit. I told Dep, "I'll be back soon."

Dep climbed up to the catwalk encircling the room above the windows.

I locked her inside and went out. Chad's car was still in the back of the parking lot.

Through one of the back windows of Dressed to Kill, I saw Suzanne sitting at her desk and hunched over, apparently concentrating on her computer screen. I waved. Her head jerked up as if I'd startled her. Maybe she wasn't expecting me, after all.

I pointed at the bakery box. She nodded, stood up, and left the office.

Seconds later, the door's bolt scraped back with a noise that made my teeth feel furry.

Suzanne opened the door and stood back for me to enter. She was in the blue and white floral-printed dress she'd been wearing when I first saw her, the day before Jenn's wedding, when Suzanne was dashing out of Dressed to Kill after her argument with Jenn. This time, though, Suzanne's stiletto-heeled boots were zipped up. I asked how she was feeling.

"Fine."

"No lingering effects from fainting last night?"

"No."

"Do you have any idea what caused it?"

She shrugged and turned around. Surely, she didn't believe that any of the tiny vegan donuts I'd taken to Vanessa's had been poisoned. I couldn't figure out a way of asking her that wouldn't sound rude or accusatory, so I silently followed her into the office. The table wasn't set.

I explained, "We didn't have a chance to get together last night after we were at Vanessa's, so I brought these in case you two had time for one of our tea party meetings tonight. If not, I'll just leave them here." I set the box of crullers on the bare white table. "But I need to tell you what Gerald Stone asked me today."

"We have time, if Jenn can pull herself away from those chattering women out front." She went back to her desk and shut down her computer. "Did Gerald ask you out?"

I shook my head so swiftly that my neck hurt. "Nothing like that!" Maybe my denial was too forceful to be believable, but going out with Gerald Stone, who was old enough to be my father? Ew. "Gerald Stone doesn't have a good alibi for early Sunday morning, and he seemed to be offering to provide one for me if I'd reciprocate."

She stood up from her computer. "Did you agree?"

"Of course not. But he came across as desperate for an alibi."

"Getting someone to lie to give you an alibi is illegal. It's one more fact we have against him."

"He didn't come right out and try to make a bargain with me, but the hint was definitely there."

"He did it," Suzanne stated. "He killed Roger, and he doesn't care if Jenn's blamed, and he'll kill her, too, if he can."

Based on the fondness I'd thought I detected in Gerald

Stone's eyes when he was talking about Jenn as a little girl, I wasn't sure that Stone was a threat to Jenn. Maybe, in addition to killing Roger to end Roger's blackmailing, he had killed Roger in a misguided attempt to protect Jenn. But that would still have been creepy, and again mentioning Stone's possible stalking could increase Suzanne's worries about her younger sister. I changed the subject. "Is Jenn driving Chad's car to and from work?"

Suzanne opened a drawer underneath the kitchen counter and took out turquoise place mats. "What do you mean?"

"That red car in the back of the parking lot. I thought it was the one that Chad drove on Friday when he came to Deputy Donut."

She slapped three place mats onto the table. "Could be. I don't pay attention to cars. So what if it is? That doesn't mean that Chad harmed Roger. He didn't have to if he wanted Jenn back. Chad's a good guy."

I agreed.

She went to the office doorway. Standing on one foot with the other knee bent at a right angle and held out behind her as if for balance, she clutched the doorjamb and peered around it toward the front of the store. Jenn and other women were talking and laughing out there. Hanging on to the jamb with both hands, Suzanne put her foot down and turned halfway back toward me. "I warned Jenn to stay away from Chad until they incarcerate Roger's killer. I also told her, long ago, that Roger was bad news. But I have to give her some credit. She is sensible, most of the time. Roger obviously had some good points or she would not have married him." She came back into the office. "That beady-eyed detective was here again today, and I think she went to your shop right afterward."

"Yvonne Passenmath was talking to Tom and me a few minutes ago. That's why I'm late to our usual meeting."

"Did you tell her that Gerald wanted you and him to give each other alibis?"

"I told her that he'd made that hint."

"What did she say?"

"I don't think she took it seriously." My face probably showed my frustration.

Suzanne seemed to be listening to the women in the shop, but she must have given up on making out their words. She spoke again, in a low voice. "That female detective is still convinced that spouses are the most likely killers. In her mind, that means that no one besides a spouse would kill, so she doesn't have to take any other suspects seriously."

"She does seem to have a one-track mind, but maybe what I said about Gerald will start her thinking more about the evidence against him."

"Maybe." Suzanne's face went blotchy. Was she embarrassed? Or was she angry? "Did you tell her about Jenn driving—allegedly driving—Chad's car?"

"I'm sure the police have already figured out a lot about everyone who was at the reception. Have they given Jenn's car back?"

"No."

"So they won't be surprised if they find out that Jenn's borrowing a friend's car. Do they still have your car, too?"

Suzanne came back into the kitchenette portion of their office and peeked into the bakery box. "Yes, and I don't know why they're keeping them so long. That beady-eyed detective said they haven't found anything in our cars. Keeping them this long is just another way that female detective is harassing Jenn." Suzanne opened a cabinet above the counter, took out clear glass plates with scallops around the edges, and put them on the place mats. "Did they test *your* car and home?"

"They tested the car I was driving that night and our shop, but not my home." Ignoring Suzanne's frown of disapproval, I asked, "Did investigators test your home, and Jenn's?"

"Yes. Of course they didn't find anything." Suzanne turned

the three glass plates so that their scalloped edges lined up on the place mats the same way, the division between two scallops on the plates neatly centered with the middle of the backs of the chairs. "I noticed that the beady-eyed detective kindly waited to go to your shop after you closed," she said, "but she came into ours and insisted on questioning Jenn here, in the office, while we were still open. For some reason, she thought that would be okay, and that I could cope with customers by myself while she interrogated Jenn. We probably lost at least one sale, since I'm not as good as Jenn is at manipulating people into buying things they don't need."

"I'm sure you did fine." I was sounding as encouraging as Vanessa Legghaupt usually did. Was I becoming a phony?

Suzanne shivered. "That female detective is cherry-picking things to make Jenn look guilty, and ignoring every fact that points to anyone else."

"I think she also suspects Gerald Stone, but not maybe as much as she suspects Tom and me, especially me."

"You'd never know it by the things she asks us and says to us. For instance, on Saturday night, Jenn and I were under a lot of stress. Roger was drinking too much, and maybe Jenn had too much to drink, also, and I'm not used to even those few sips of champagne I had during the toasts. Plus, we were tired from weeks of working hard to make certain that everything about the wedding, reception, and honeymoon would be perfect, and Jenn was stressed about the packing she still had to do before their trip. Jenn and I left the reception around midnight. That DCI detective seemed to think that meant we were up to no good. We only went to the ladies' room. We were in cubicles, and people were coming and going, and I didn't feel well, and I stayed there for a long time. Maybe I even fell asleep for a few minutes. When that male detective asked me where I was during that time, I told him, but I also said that Jenn was with me the entire time. I thought she was. We were talking to each other when we first got to the ladies' room and also about the time I started feeling well enough to leave."

I'd never heard so many words in a row pour out of Suzanne's mouth.

Although breathing heavily, she kept talking. "It turned out that Jenn had tried to get Roger to stop drinking by going out and waiting for him in his car. I didn't know when she left the ladies' room, and as far as I knew, she'd done what I'd told the police, stayed to keep me company since I wasn't feeling well. So those detectives think I was lying to give Jenn an alibi when, as far as I knew, I was telling the honest truth."

Brent and I had noticed that a black sports car had been fogged up, and Brent had later confirmed that the black car had belonged to Roger. Did Jenn actually go to Roger's car right away, or did she first spend time in Chad's car with him? Chad's car was bright red. If Gerald Stone was to be believed, which could be a big if, a woman wearing lots of white was helping steam up the windows of a bright red car at about twelve fifteen.

Jenn probably hadn't wanted to admit, even to the police during a murder investigation, that she'd been with her old boyfriend in his car while her wedding reception was still going on.

Suzanne tapped the corner of the box of crullers, nudging it closer to the center of the table. "And then there's the money. Jenn knew that Roger had money, but she never dreamed it would be so much, and even if she had, she wouldn't have killed the man she loved for it."

The evening before the wedding, Jenn had told me that Suzanne had tried to get Jenn to cancel the wedding and had called Jenn a gold digger. For very good reasons, Suzanne was probably not about to repeat the accusation that she'd made in the heat of an argument.

Suzanne folded three paper napkins into rectangles and set them beside the plates. "Before the wedding, Jenn started looking into renting a larger retail space in a mall south of town."

"You're moving away from here? I'll miss you." I wasn't sure about missing Suzanne. I meant the store and Jenn and Jenn's wonderful sweaters. "Though maybe I'll save money if I can't pop into Dressed to Kill and buy another sweater every few days." It was an exaggeration. Not a huge one.

Suzanne unfolded the napkins and refolded them in triangles. "It's not finalized yet. Jenn was toying with the idea, and maybe she won't do it, now that Roger's gone, or maybe she'll buy a building instead of renting one. I'd pitch in my half. I have savings from my days in an accounting firm." She placed the napkins neatly beside the plates again. "We'd get a larger space than this so we could sell shoes and boots, too. I don't know a thing about selling sweaters and jeans and cocktail dresses and down-filled jackets, but I do know about footwear. I would run that part of the business, displaying the shoes temptingly, helping people find exactly what they wanted, and I would still have plenty of time to do the books. I feel like I'm not contributing enough, since Jenn's the one with the creative ability."

And the people skills. But I didn't say it. Maybe Suzanne took a while to warm up to people. For the first time in our short acquaintance, she was talking to me like she was a friend, not the prickly older sister of a friend. But how would she treat strangers who came into her store wanting shoes, boots, and slippers? I knew from experience that she could veer from silent to abrupt to socially awkward to visibly annoyed, hardly traits that were helpful in retail sales.

Her stiletto heels resounding against the tile floor, Suzanne circled the table and rubbed her thumb along the napkins' creases. "So that female detective got wind that Jenn was looking at larger retail spaces, and the detective had the gall to suggest that Jenn was shopping around because Jenn was planning to kill Roger so she could inherit his money. Jenn got hot under the collar and told that detective that Roger would have lent her money if she needed it." Suzanne's hands balled into fists. "But that DCI detective starts seeing things one way, and she doesn't change her opinion, no matter what really happened. She should be going after Gerald Stone, especially after what you just told me about him, and if those two women we saw last night truly have the alibi that the life coach said they did."

"Maybe Detective Passenmath will spiral in on Gerald Stone yet," I said. "This morning in Deputy Donut, after I made it clear to Stone that the police already knew where I'd been early Sunday morning and that I could not have seen Stone driving away from Little Lake Lodge, he basically told me the same thing he'd told you, that he'd gone to the reception to look after Jenn and her wedding presents."

"Totally a fiction. I went out with him last night after I started feeling better."

"Suzanne! He could be dangerous."

"You and Jenn keep harping on that."

"Does he know where you live?"

"Not unless someone told him." She pierced me with a look. "I didn't."

"How about where you work?"

"Of course he knows that. He walked me here after I hurt my ankle in your shop. He's picking me up here tonight. If you and Jenn are still around, you can protect me."

Glad that my phone was in my jeans pocket, I said dryly, "We can all try to protect each other."

"Getting to know him has paid off. He's started telling me his secrets, and he doesn't realize that I can put two and two together and come up with murder." She cocked her head toward the front of the store again. "Jenn will likely be half the night with those gabby women, and besides, I didn't know for sure you were coming tonight, so I already told her what I found out from him last night. He confided that before he retired, he kept a stash of cash in the safe at Stone Drugs, and someone, and he's pretty sure he knows who, must have watched him key in the combination to his safe, and then that person helped himself to the cash when Gerald wasn't looking."

"Who was the person?"

"He wouldn't say."

Maybe because admitting that the thief was Roger would be the same as confessing to murdering Roger....

"How did he know who it was?"

"He said the person told him, but not in so many words. He said the person got away with stealing hundreds of thousands of dollars."

"Why would Stone have kept so much cash on hand in a pharmacy?"

"I asked that, too. He said he didn't trust banks. He was lying, I could tell. I don't know what extracurricular business he was carrying on in that drugstore, but I suspect it wasn't legal."

"And if that was true, maybe the 'not in so many words' was a blackmail threat, and Stone had to pay the thief, or the thief would tell the police about Stone's possibly illegal activities. So, in addition to the cash stolen from the safe, the thief-turned-blackmailer kept the pressure on, and Stone had to sell his drugstore, his mansion, and his expensive car."

Suzanne thinned her lips. "That's my guess."

"And there's no end to blackmailing," I pointed out, "unless there's an end to the blackmailer."

She wrapped her arms around her middle as if she were trying to defend herself from murderers. "We were talking about motivation, means, and opportunity. Gerald Stone had all three."

"Don't go out with him again, Suzanne,"

"I'll stop seeing him as soon as I get enough information from him. Like why, if someone robbed him of hundreds of thousands of dollars, he didn't go to the police about it."

"Asking him that question could be dangerous."

"I don't ask him things point-blank."

Ignoring the criticism, which I probably deserved, I gamely went on. "With what you just told me, I think you already have enough information about him. I hope you told Detective Passenmath everything you've learned from Stone."

Suzanne made a face like she was smelling rotten eggs. "You've got to be kidding. Everything I say, she thinks I'm coming up with something new to try to get Jenn off the hook."

"It's not too late to tell Passenmath, especially now that she knows about Gerald hinting to me about possibly providing alibis for each other. And think about other witnesses. You never know what they might have already said that will corroborate what you tell Detective Passenmath. She might even believe what you say. We all need to tell the police what we know so the police can put the pieces together, or the killer might strike again."

Paling, Suzanne whispered, "And we don't know for sure if Roger was the original target. It could have been Jenn, and Gerald might still be after her. He claims he remembers Jenn being inside his store, and she certainly remembers being there before our mother became too ill to go to the pharmacy for her prescriptions. What if he thinks that Jenn saw or heard something incriminating about him when she was a child, and if she remembers it, she can put him behind bars? That would explain why he's been stalking her all these years, and why he posed as a security guard outside her wedding reception. He saw his chance and took it, but Roger ate the crullers that were destined for Jenn."

It was a plausible theory, although not as believable as the one about Roger stealing from Stone and then blackmailing him. I urged, "You have to tell Detective Passenmath this, Suzanne."

"I will, after one more so-called date with Gerald tonight. We're going to walk from here to the Fireplug Pub together. I'll ditch him and walk home by myself, though."

"That could be easier said than done."

Jenn popped her head into the office. "Emily! Great. I thought I heard your voice." She glanced toward the table. "And I see you brought donuts. And no tea, yet?"

"I didn't think you were ever going to get yourself free from all those women milling around in the store," Suzanne said.

Jenn grinned at her. "Those women are called customers, Suzanne. They pay the bills." She became serious again. "Emily, after listening to your talk last night, I decided to change our window display. You have such good ideas. Can you come help me figure out what to do?"

"Don't take forever," Suzanne warned. "Making tea is not a long process."

Chapter 28

Jenn led me toward the front of the store. She was in jeans, boots, and a gorgeous navy blue and turquoise sweater she'd designed. "I'm not sure that the antique skis, sleds, and skates are sending quite the right message," she told me. "Do you think they're making everything else look old?"

"No, but there's nothing wrong with changing the look of your windows just because you want to."

"I feel like the antiques are too brown. All that old wood, you know? And they're scratched up in places."

"If you're not afraid of destroying their value as antiques, you could paint them."

"That might work. I've been putting clothes in the window displays to replace the ones that customers buy, so at first glance, passersby might think that nothing in the windows or in the store has changed, and they might just keep walking."

"Welllll," I drawled in a humorous voice, "if they're buying the clothes they see in the window . . ."

She laughed. "I get that. The displays are bringing in customers and sales." She opened the front door. The bells jingled, and we went out onto the sidewalk. The door closed behind us.

I studied the windows for a few seconds. "I see what's happened," I said. "When you take out a sweater, you put in a new sweater. Same with everything else. At first the colors were all warm autumn colors, but now you've got pastels and primary colors mixed in with them, and it no longer looks as harmonious and enticing. How about going through the store and finding clothes in fall colors again, and replacing the pastels and primaries? Also, Halloween's coming. How about adding some pumpkins and whimsical gourds?"

Her eyes brightened. "And the pumpkins I put in now could transition to Thanksgiving, and after Thanksgiving I'll hang hand-knit stockings on the mantel and decorate the windows for Christmas, with clothes in colors that match the season, and I could even paint the skis and snowshoes to match. They'd look great all white. Thanks, Emily. That's very helpful, but it's not really what I wanted to talk to you about." She glanced toward the window in the door and took a deep breath. "Suzanne doesn't like that detective from the DCI, so she refuses to tell her things that the detective needs to know. Meanwhile, Suzanne's putting herself in danger by continuing to try to gather more evidence against Gerald Stone."

Pulling my beautiful heathery gray cardigan tighter against a breeze whipping leaves up off the sidewalk, I told Jenn about Stone hinting that he and I could provide bogus alibis for each other.

"That man has no morals," Jenn said.

"I again tried to get Suzanne to stop seeing him, but she says she's going out with him again tonight, to the Fireplug Pub."

Jenn gazed northward, toward the town square and the pub. "She never tells me where they're going. Maybe I should just happen to go to that pub tonight. Chad might be willing to come with me."

"I could do something similar. If she's not working, I could bring Misty, the tall blonde who was with me last night at Vanessa's. She's a police officer."

"And your father-in-law used to be police chief, right?"

"Yes."

"Would your father-in-law or your friend know anyone from the Fallingbrook Police Department who's *not* from the DCI that we could talk to? Maybe you and I could tell them everything that Suzanne has told us."

I'd already mentioned a lot of it to Brent, but hearing it also from Jenn might help him find a way to prove that Jenn did not kill Roger. "Alec's former partner is helping Detective Passenmath with the case. How about if I call him?"

"That sounds perfect."

I phoned Brent's personal number. It went straight to message. "It's Emily Westhill," I said, mostly for Jenn's benefit. Brent or his phone recognized my number, and Brent knew my voice, besides. "I talked to Gerald Stone this morning. I told Yvonne about our conversation, but . . ." I was afraid that Yvonne wouldn't pass the information along to the rest of the investigators, and maybe Brent should know that Suzanne and Stone were planning to go to the Fireplug Pub that night. Brent might want to send a plainclothes officer to keep an eye on Gerald. "I'd also like to talk to you about what Stone said to one of my neighbors. Call me back, or come over to my place if you can. I should be home in about an hour."

Jenn thanked me for contacting Brent, and then her eyes reddened. "I don't think I can take this smothering from Suzanne anymore."

"She cares about you."

"I know, but she goes too far. I guess she didn't trust me to have an alibi for Saturday night, and we didn't get to compare our stories before police officers separated us at the hospital and questioned us. She told the police I was with her in the ladies' room at the lodge on Saturday night, but I wasn't there as long as she said I was, and I told them where I actually was. I was . . . well, this is embarrassing . . . I was with Chad. He and I danced a few times during the reception, and I realized that I'd made a big mistake, and he pretty much agreed."

And after that, Chad flirted and danced with me. I kept my mouth shut.

Jenn went on. "After Chad danced with you, he and I decided to meet at his car to talk about what we could or should do."

I hadn't taken Chad's flirting seriously, and the pain in his eyes about losing Jenn had seemed real. At that point, despite agreeing with Jenn that marrying Roger was a mistake, Chad could have felt that he'd lost Jenn. I couldn't believe that his sadness was due to planning a drastic way of freeing Jenn from Roger.

Jenn explained, "After I left the reception with Suzanne, she and I went to the ladies' room, but I didn't stay long. Suzanne was still in a cubicle when I left. I went outside and met Chad at his car. He was one of the guests I'd told to park in the staff parking lot to leave enough space in the main lot for everyone else. It was cold, so we got into the back seat, and . . . we ended up kind of making up for lost time, not that there was much I could do in that constraining dress. We thought we'd been caught around twelve fifteen when a security guard with a flashlight walked by, but he just kept going, got into his car, and drove away. Maybe the security guard was Gerald Stone."

"Probably. I think Stone was the only security guard at Little Lake Lodge that night. Did you tell the police about seeing the security guard at that time?"

"Of course. Chad did, too. Both of us, separately, told the police they needed to investigate the security guard. But then that woman detective came along and decided to prove that murders are nearly always done by spouses. She started trying to tailor the facts to make me look like someone who would murder my brand-new husband. Maybe I did make a mistake in agreeing to marry Roger, but I did love him. I still do. I just didn't realize that I loved Chad more."

"The day before your wedding, you told me you'd invited your ex-boyfriend to your wedding and reception because he was one of your best friends. I didn't realize you were still in love with him."

She gave me a rueful little smile. "Neither did I, and I should have. Chad left in his car shortly after we saw that security guard. Gerald Stone."

"Did Chad, by any chance, follow Gerald Stone to see where he went?"

"Why would he? We didn't have an inkling who the security guard actually was or that he could have harmed anyone." Her eyes softened. "Poor Chad. After we said our truly reluctant goodbyes, he thought he'd lost me for good. He got so . . . so teary a few miles down the road that he actually had to pull onto the shoulder until he could get control of himself enough to drive. Meanwhile, after Chad left that parking lot, I had the brilliant idea of waiting for Roger in Roger's car, which was also in the staff parking lot. We'd been planning to leave about twelve thirty, and I hoped that he would stop drinking and come looking for me, and we could go home and pack so we could get to the plane on time and go on our honeymoon. Or if he sniped at me one more time, I was going to send him to the airport by himself, and I'd go back to Chad and start divorce or annulment proceedings. But I got cold and Roger didn't show up, so I went looking for him. First, I needed to check my makeup. I went through the back way to the ladies' room. My makeup was a little smeared, but not more than happens to any bride after hours of people hugging and kissing her. Suzanne was still in the ladies' room, locked in a cubicle. I recognized her shoes under the door. She wasn't well. I talked to her, which is why she could have believed I was in there all along. She told me we were all supposed to leave the lodge. I went out the way I'd come in, through the back door. Then I walked around to the front of the lodge, and you know the rest."

"Has Chad backed you up on all of this?"

She nodded. "Everything except me being in the ladies' room before I went out to talk to him, or going back, after.

He knew that I planned to wait in Roger's car, but he didn't necessarily know that I actually went there. He's a wonderful person, and I don't know why I fell for Roger and dropped Chad." She was nearly wailing. "But because of what Suzanne told them, the police don't believe that either of us was in the ladies' room. And they don't believe us about Gerald Stone probably having harmed Roger before he came out and shined his flashlight around the staff parking lot."

I believed it, and I was sure that Brent would, too, after I explained it all to him. I looked up and down the sidewalk. I saw several pedestrians, but not Gerald Stone. "Suzanne told me that Stone is going to pick her up here this evening."

"Did she say when?"

"No."

Jenn opened the shop's front door for me. "If I wasn't afraid I might miss out on a customer, I'd be tempted to lock up as soon as we're inside."

Although I could tell she was teasing, I said, "The back door is probably still unlocked. Suzanne unbolted it to let me in."

"Did you see anyone go up the driveway toward our parking lot while we were out on the sidewalk in front?"

"No, did you?"

"No."

I pointed out, "Someone could have gone up the driveway before that, while we were walking from the office to the front of the store." We were both bantering, and not really expecting Gerald Stone to jump out from behind a rotating clothing rack. However, I was extra alert, preparing to dodge him. I pulled my phone out of my pocket and held it in my hand.

We took our time going back to the office, pointing out the clothes that we thought would look great in Jenn's autumn-themed windows.

In the office, the tea was cooling in three cups on the table, and Suzanne was sitting at her usual spot at the table, with her back to the two desks. Although we usually served ourselves from the bakery boxes I brought, Suzanne must have had extra time while Jenn and I were planning display windows and talking about Saturday night and early Sunday morning. Each of the scalloped glass plates had a cruller on it.

The cruller on the plate where I usually sat was coated in thick white powder.

When I'd brought the crullers to Dressed to Kill, none of them had that much confectioners' sugar on them.

Chapter 29

✻

Had Gerald Stone arrived when Jenn and I were in the front? When Suzanne wasn't looking, had Stone coated a donut with a white powder that might or might not be sugar?

The only car I could see outside the back window was Chad's, but most of the parking lot was not visible from where I was standing, just inside Dressed to Kill's combination kitchen and office.

I wanted to be able to watch the back hallway and also keep track of vehicles that came through the rear of the parking lot. I sat in the chair where Jenn had sat other times.

Suzanne jumped up and banged into her chair, pushing it back farther than she'd probably intended. Her face red and splotchy, she threw herself into my usual seat, in front of the cruller that was covered with too much white powder.

If she made a move to touch that cruller, I was going to stop her.

Shrugging, Jenn sat in the chair that Suzanne had vacated and pulled it closer to the table.

I asked Suzanne, "Has Gerald Stone arrived yet?"

Looking puzzled, Jenn studied my face as if she'd noticed the unsteadiness of my voice.

Suzanne dismissed my question. "Too early."

Who had put that too-white cruller at my usual place? Jenn

and Suzanne knew I'd sat there during our other tea-and-donut information-sharing sessions. Who might they have told?

I asked Suzanne, "Is Chad here?"

She gave me a look that was one part disbelief and three parts disgust. "Why would men be hanging around the back of a women's clothing store?" She made a show of staring at all four corners of the room, and then she threw her palms upward. "Do you see them here?"

"Suzanne . . ." Jenn was obviously trying to tone down her half-sister's sarcasm.

I defended myself. "I wondered if someone had arrived while Jenn and I were outside, that's all."

Suzanne informed me in frosty tones, "The only other people would be customers, and if there were any, they'd have come in the front, and you two would have seen them and sold them something."

Unless she was lying, and Chad or Gerald had left or one of them was hiding somewhere in the back hallway or the basement, Suzanne was the only person who could have put the obviously doctored cruller at my usual place. What was the extra white powder on it? And had she been hoping that I would eat it?

But I'd sat in Jenn's usual seat, and Suzanne had immediately switched to the chair I'd occupied other evenings, and she'd been in such a hurry that she'd nearly tipped over her own chair. And her face had developed those red splotches that seemed to show that she was angry or upset.

The only Deputy Donut treat that I'd ever seen her eat, besides coffee with Gerald Stone, was that one tiny donut at Vanessa's studio. Other than that, she had never touched one, not even to remove it from a box and put it on a plate, at our afternoon tea parties.

So, either she wanted that sugary-looking cruller for herself, or she was afraid that Jenn might sit in my usual place, and she didn't want Jenn to eat that particular cruller.

My own face seemed to flame, and I could hardly breathe. I tried not to stare at Suzanne.

Had Suzanne, not Gerald, coated crullers for Roger in extra white powder?

The alibi that Suzanne had provided for Jenn would have been Suzanne's alibi, also, if Jenn hadn't told the police a different story when they questioned her in the hospital.

I barely noticed Jenn and Suzanne discussing ideas for changing the displays in the store's front windows. I was pondering the supposed alibi that Suzanne had given the police.

Maybe Suzanne had left the ladies' room shortly after Jenn did. Before Jenn returned to the ladies' room, Suzanne would have had plenty of time to poison the crullers the way I'd described to Yvonne Passenmath and then sneak back to the ladies' room. Suzanne might not have known that Jenn would return. She would only have needed someone else to notice her in the ladies' room, and if she had to later, she could claim she'd been in that cubicle from midnight until whatever time she needed for a believable alibi. Maybe she'd hoped that Roger would die after he left the lodge, the saucer of arsenic would be discarded when the banquet hall was being cleaned up, and no one would realize that Roger had ingested poison at the lodge.

But why would Suzanne have wanted to kill Roger?

The day before the wedding, Jenn had told me that Suzanne had hated Roger and had been adamant that Jenn should cancel the wedding.

Also, it had seemed to me that Suzanne's description of buying a bigger store and adding footwear to the inventory had been enthusiastic, especially for Suzanne. Had she figured out a way of eliminating Roger and benefiting from his wealth?

And had Suzanne's "information gathering" really been an attempt to discover whatever she could about other suspects—Gerald Stone, Vanessa, April, and me—that could divert attention from her and point to one of us as a murderer? Had her fainting after she ate one of Tom's and my tiny donuts been faked, another ploy to make me, and possibly Tom, look guilty?

If she truly believed that Gerald Stone was a killer, would she have gone out alone with him? Wouldn't joining him for coffee in Deputy Donut with Tom and me plus a room full of coffee- and donut-mongers, many of them police officers, have been enough? Her lack of caution around Gerald Stone could mean that she knew he had not murdered Roger. One surefire way for her to be positive about that would be if she herself were the sole killer.

I was definitely not going to eat or drink anything in Dressed to Kill.

Suzanne was arguing that the antique sleds and skis in the front windows should be painted red and green, not white, for the Christmas display.

She didn't touch the extra-white cruller on the plate in front of where I usually sat, and I didn't touch the one at Jenn's place, although it looked fine. The tea was still hot. I cradled my cup in both hands as if trying to warm them. Conjectures and plans collided in my brain.

Jenn asked, "Emily, aren't red and green together sometimes a little much? They almost clash."

"Just red then, or just green," Suzanne snapped. "The white could be blinding."

"You might try the palest of blues," I suggested, "like snow at dusk."

Looking somewhere beyond my head, Jenn smiled.

"No," Suzanne stated firmly. "I don't like that."

My phone rang. I set the teacup down and checked the display.

Brent.

"Sorry, I'll have to take this," I told Jenn and Suzanne.

Jenn nodded.

Suzanne simply watched me. Were her eyes always that cold?

I considered telling the two sisters that reception was bad and I had to take the call outside, but if that one cruller was as dangerous as I suspected, I wasn't about to leave it behind for Jenn or Suzanne to eat, and I wasn't about to touch it or take it anywhere with me, either. "Hi, Brent," I said, trying to sound cheerful. In front of Suzanne, I couldn't tell him that I was afraid she was trying to poison me, so I merely stammered, "I found out more about Gerald Stone. I'm with Suzanne and Jenn at Dressed to Kill. Suzanne talked to Gerald Stone, and what she found out makes us suspect that someone had been blackmailing him."

Brent spoke more quietly than usual. "You and I already discussed that possibility. Does she have hard evidence?"

I couldn't send him the visual signal—brush my hair off my forehead and then tug on my earlobe—that he knew for "rescue me." I said, "You're right. I'm conking myself on the forehead. Next thing you know, I'll be tugging on my—"

"Em!" His whispered interruption was urgent. "Do you need help?"

"Good thinking!" I was still trying to sound upbeat, even though my involuntary trembling was undoubtedly affecting my voice. "Talk to you later."

"See you *soon*," he said in a quiet voice. "I'll call for backup on my way. Stay on the phone."

I wasn't sure I could, considering that I had a more pressing need for my phone. Not wanting Brent to worry, I chirped, "You're breaking up."

I put my phone, its camera face up, on my lap and set it to record a video. Nothing would be visible in the video besides the underside of Jenn and Suzanne's cute table, but anything we said might be audible. With luck, when Brent attempted to return to our call we'd still be connected and he'd hear what was going on in the office of Dressed to Kill, but I feared that when I started the video, my phone had switched to camera mode. However, staying on the line with Brent wasn't crucial. He would worry if I disconnected, but he was on his way. All I had to do while I waited for him was pretend to enjoy a companionable tea party.

Jenn reached for the extra-white cruller on the plate in front of Suzanne.

Suzanne snatched the plate away with the cruller still on it. "If you need two at once, get your own from the box," she ordered, every inch the bossy big sister from TV and films.

"I want the sugary one. Trade you!" Jenn spoke in a singsong like a sassy little sister.

Suzanne plunked the too-white cruller onto my plate along with the one that I hadn't touched. "Emily brought it. She should have it." She stood, picked up her plate, and walked with a self-conscious and slightly jerky motion to the sink. She set the plate in the sink, washed her hands, and turned off the water. "When will you learn to let our guests have the best, Jenn? Why do you always have to grab the biggest, the juiciest, the sweetest of everything?"

Her openmouthed gape matching the expression that I suspected was on my face, Jenn got up and came around the table toward me and my plate. "Since you spoiled me, Suzanne." It was said in a singsong again, but I thought I saw the beginnings of panic on Jenn's face.

I was ready to move the plate out of Jenn's reach or push her hand away if she came too close to the whitest cruller, but Suzanne swooped to the table, grabbed my plate, and threw the two crullers into the trash, pretty glass plate and all.

Jenn accused, "You threw out Great-Grandma Zeeland's plate!"

"Oh, sorry." Suzanne's scowl had more to do with anger than apology. "I forgot those ugly plates once belonged to your father's grandmother. I'll get it later." She leaned back, resting her hips against the counter.

But Jenn burst out crying. "You poisoned Roger and now

you're trying to poison Emily. Roger was my husband and Emily is my friend."

Suzanne taunted, "There you go again with your crybaby act. I was just testing Emily with a donut covered in extra sugar to see if she suspected us of poisoning Roger. She avoided sitting at the place where I put it, so obviously, she does suspect us."

Jenn asked through her tears, "Why would you think you need to test Emily's suspicions unless you're guilty yourself?"

Her big sister told her, "Don't be silly."

I suggested as evenly as I could with my teeth clenched together, "You can prove you weren't trying to poison me by retrieving those crullers and eating them yourself."

Suzanne lifted one bony shoulder. "I don't eat garbage, which, by the way, your donuts are even before they're thrown out."

Jenn scolded, "Suzanne!"

"I'm only speaking the truth."

Jenn retorted, "You're being rude."

Suzanne folded her arms. "How do you know that Emily didn't poison the crullers that Roger ate, the donut I ate last night, and the crullers she brought over just now, when she wasn't even invited?"

"Because she wouldn't."

"You're standing up for a stranger while accusing me, your own sister."

Jenn wiped the sleeve of the pretty navy and turquoise sweater across her eyes. "I can always tell when you're lying, Suzanne. There's a reason you wouldn't let me have the sugariest donut, and that's because you put something on it that's not sugar." She headed for the wastebasket underneath the sink. "*I'll* eat it."

Suzanne stopped her with both hands and held the cabinet door shut with a knee. "I never thought I'd have to tell you all these years later, when you are *supposedly* no longer a willful child, not to eat food out of the garbage."

Jenn backed away from her, toward their desks and the room's rear windows. "You did it. You planned it ahead of time. You took arsenic to the reception, put it on some crullers, and fed them to Roger."

Suzanne stayed where she was, blocking the cabinet door in front of the wastebasket. "I did not *feed* them to Roger."

Jenn demanded, "What did you do, leave them somewhere for him to find? How could you be certain that no one else would come along and eat them?"

"That wouldn't have mattered. You weren't anywhere near, and if someone else got sick, we'd have found a way to blame Roger. He would have gone to prison, and I'd have saved you from him by one method or another."

Jenn sobbed out, "You were going to let someone die, and then blame Roger? Like you've been blaming everyone else for Roger's death?"

"I told you to cancel the wedding, but you refused. I had to protect you."

Jenn shook her head. "No, you didn't. And you didn't have to try to hurt Emily. That makes no sense."

Suzanne pointed a long, bony forefinger at me. "She was figuring out too much, and she was going to tell her father-in-law or one of her cop customers, and I'd be charged with murder. Is that what you want, Jenn? Your big sister in jail?"

"Of course not! But I also didn't want my bridegroom to die and I don't want Emily to be hurt. She's been trying to help us, and you pay her back by trying to kill her?"

"She's a danger to us," Suzanne said, almost offhandedly, as if I were an object, not a human. She strode past the back of my chair. Not wanting her to see my phone and possibly guess that I was recording the conversation, I leaned forward to hide my lap.

Suzanne grabbed my left arm above the elbow and wrenched it up and back. Pain screamed through my shoulder, making it impossible for me to do anything besides gasp.

She lifted me out of my chair. My phone slithered off my

lap and landed on the tile floor. I hoped it had recorded the conversation so far. My chair wobbled and crashed down.

Brent was on his way, I reminded myself.

But Suzanne could do a lot of damage before he got there unless I stopped her.

She was much taller than I was, but very thin and probably not as muscular or fit. Both hands grasping my upper arm, she pulled me toward the hall outside the office. I tried to hold back, but the soles of my shoes slid along the shiny tile floor. At the doorway, I grabbed at the jamb with my right hand. Suzanne stomped on my left instep with one of those stiletto heels and brought the heel of her left hand down hard on my right wrist, knocking my hand away from the jamb.

Jenn shouted, "Suzanne, stop it!"

"Too late." Suzanne continued tugging me toward a closed door that I guessed led to the basement.

Jenn dashed to me and yanked at my right forearm. "Let go, Suzanne. Think! What are you *doing?*"

Now I was certain that rage, and not embarrassment, was causing the blotches on Suzanne's face. "I am thinking. I always am, as you should know. I'm going to lock her in the basement. Gerald's due any minute. He's going down there with her, and you and I will tell the police that Gerald confessed to killing Roger and when Emily tried to stop him from hurting all three of us, they both fell down the basement stairs, and he set a fire down there, and they couldn't get out."

Tears streamed down Jenn's cheeks. "No, Suzanne, no. You'll just make everything worse for yourself. You can't hurt Emily and Gerald Stone. You can't burn up everything that you and I worked for."

"Watch me. It's not like we don't have fire insurance. You'll be covered."

Strands of Jenn's hair stuck in the tears streaking down her face, probably making seeing difficult. With her free hand, she brushed the hair back. "But all those beautiful garments that I worked so hard to design and create. It's like burning up my babies."

"Hardly." Suzanne was panting, but her voice came out like ice.

I was short of breath, too. I managed to ask Suzanne, "Did Gerald Stone have anything to do with poisoning Roger?"

"Gerald harmed Roger years ago by tempting him with all that cash. He's the one who turned Roger into a blackmailer, and into someone who thought that money was more important than everything else, including his fiancée."

I argued, "That isn't what I asked."

But Suzanne ignored me and glared at her little sister. "You'd have been miserable with Roger."

Jenn let go of me and stood straighter, facing Suzanne. "That wasn't your decision to make."

With only me struggling against her, Suzanne hauled me the rest of the short distance to the basement door. Holding my left wrist and twisting my arm high on my back, she reached up and undid the substantial bolt near the top of the frame. The door swung back against the wall and revealed a wonky wooden stairway leading down to a dark and gloomy basement.

Chapter 30

✣

As if suddenly shaken out of her shock, Jenn shouted at her sister, "If you throw Emily down there, I'm going, too!"

Suzanne's grasp on my left arm faltered.

She was closer to those stairs than I was.

I hooked my left foot around her ankle and pulled it toward me while shoving hard at her shoulder with my right hand.

Jenn rushed us.

To my surprise, Jenn seized my arm again, pulling me away from the top of the steep stairway, and she also pushed Suzanne's shoulder. I pivoted away from Suzanne, whose grip on my left arm had been the only thing keeping her balanced on the edge of the top step. She stumbled backward down one step. Another . . .

Her arms flailed. She grabbed the handrail.

Her mouth grim and her eyes blazing, she started upward.

I slammed the door and held it shut, but I was too short to reach the bolt. Shaking with sobs, Jenn worked it into place.

Suzanne pounded on the door and rattled the knob. "Let me out!" She must have planned that I would tumble all the way down the steep stairs and end up unconscious or with too many broken bones to be able to find a way out. And then she was going to incapacitate Gerald Stone down there with me and start a fire.

Suzanne was definitely not unconscious, and I didn't know how long the door would resist her assault on it.

I clutched Jenn's arm. "Come on. Let's get out of here."

Fresh tears cascaded down Jenn's cheeks. "No," she whispered. "I have to stay with her."

Dashing into Dressed to Kill's office, I shouted, "You need to leave! You're not safe here!"

Jenn refused to budge.

My phone was still on the floor underneath the table. I picked it up. Despite having landed on the hard tile floor, it had continued recording a video. I ran to Dressed to Kill's back door and opened it. Chad's car was still the only one in the parking lot. I wanted to sprint across the driveway and lock myself into Deputy Donut with Dep, but I couldn't leave Jenn alone with her sister's fury. Suzanne was hammering on the basement door with her fists, and I didn't know how well the bolt would hold. Or the hinges.

"Open the door!" Suzanne shrieked.

As I'd feared it would, my phone had dropped the call with Brent when it went into camera mode. My hands trembling, I speed-dialed him.

He answered immediately. "Are you okay?"

"I'm fine. Jenn's half-sister Suzanne admitted to poisoning Roger. She tried to poison me and then she tried to push me down the basement stairs, but Jenn and I shut her into the stairway instead. But Suzanne might be able to break down the door."

"Is Suzanne armed?"

"I don't think so, but she's wearing stiletto-heeled boots, and I don't know if she has more of the white powder she put on a cruller she planned for me to eat."

"I'm almost there." Over the phone, I heard the soles of his shoes slapping pavement. Although Brent didn't sound out of breath, he was apparently jogging. "Yvonne plans to block off the street in front of Dressed to Kill."

"Suzanne's near the rear of the store."

"Patrol cars are on their way there."

"Let me out!" Suzanne screamed.

"Not until you calm down!" Jenn yelled.

Brent demanded, "Are you inside their shop, Em?"

"I'm outside their back door."

"Emily, get away from there. Stay on the phone, go to Deputy Donut, and lock yourself in."

Surely, after all Suzanne had done to supposedly protect Jenn, she wouldn't harm her little sister now. I strode across the driveway.

A Fallingbrook Police Department cruiser squealed into the driveway. I ran up the steps of Deputy Donut's back porch. Beyond the door, Dep meowed.

Misty was driving the cruiser, with Hooligan beside her. My phone still in my hand, I waved toward the lot behind Dressed to Kill. Misty parked facing the back door. Neither she nor Hooligan got out of the cruiser. Hooligan sat watching the back of Dressed to Kill. Misty fiddled with the computer between them.

I could still hear Brent running. I told him, "Misty and Houlihan are here."

Misty glanced toward me, jabbed her index finger in the direction of Deputy Donut's office, and lowered her window. "Go inside and get down!" she hollered.

Knowing that Misty and Hooligan would be able to help Jenn much better than I could and that I'd be in trouble with both Brent and Misty if I stayed outside, I went into our office and double-locked the door. "I'm locked inside," I said into the phone. I could still hear Brent running. With my free hand, I disarmed our alarm.

"Meow!" Dep said.

I picked her up. My hands were shaking.

With my cat purring comfortingly in my arms, I backed

away from the windows and sat on the couch. In a way, I regretted how we'd designed our office, surrounded by windows that might not survive a gunfight. However, I would have felt trapped if I couldn't see what was going on.

Another cruiser pulled into the lot and parked facing the back of Dressed to Kill. I couldn't help it. I popped up again, but I stayed back from the room's outside windows. All four officers got out of their cruisers. Misty and the other driver started toward the back door of Dressed to Kill. I was glad I'd left it open. The officers could see—and hear—at least part of what was going on inside. Guns drawn, the two cops who had been passengers covered their drivers and followed them toward the building.

Someone pounded on our front door.

I jumped and turned around.

Brent was standing in our front entryway with his face nearly pressed against the glass and his hand shielding his eyes. Store windows across Wisconsin Street reflected strobing red and blue lights.

I set my phone on the desk. Clutching Dep, I ran out of the office and through the dining room. The strobing lights were from a black unmarked police cruiser parked in front of Dressed to Kill. I couldn't tell if Yvonne was inside the cruiser.

I unlocked the door. Brent rushed in. Despite having jogged several blocks, he didn't seem out of breath. Gently, he grasped my shoulders. "Are you okay?" His hands were warm.

"Yes."

Dep added, "Meow."

For once, Brent hardly noticed the attention-seeking cat. He glanced past us. "Is anyone else inside this building?"

"No. Two cruisers are behind Dressed to Kill. Misty, Houlihan, and two officers from the other cruiser headed toward the back door. At least two of them had their guns drawn."

"And Suzanne is still near the back of the store?"

"Probably."

Brent let me go and strode through the dining area to the office. Carrying Dep, now purring more loudly, I followed.

Brent stepped out onto the back porch. "Lock this door after I leave and stay inside, away from the windows, until I give you the all clear." He stalked toward Dressed to Kill.

I obeyed Brent, mostly, but I continued watching. Brent disappeared on the other side of Dressed to Kill's open door. I backed away from the windows. I must have been holding Dep too tightly. She squirmed. I set her down. She scrambled up to her catwalk.

Tensely, I watched and listened. No shots were fired, but within seconds, Hooligan and the officer who had been a passenger in the other cruiser came outside. They had holstered their weapons and were walking Suzanne between them, holding her by the arms. She was barefoot, but she held her head high. Her wrists were cuffed behind her back.

Dep dropped a ball from the catwalk. It bounced off my phone onto the desk. A sodden catnip mouse thumped down onto the phone. I hoped my phone had captured a video in Dressed to Kill and that, despite the kitty toys hailing down, I would be able to retrieve the video.

Misty and the other cruiser driver came outside with Jenn between them. Each of them held one of Jenn's elbows. Jenn was crying, but she wasn't handcuffed, and Misty appeared to be trying to comfort her.

Brent followed them.

A balled-up piece of paper that I'd thrown into the trash a couple of days before flew off the catwalk, hit me on the head, and landed on Dep's favorite spot on the couch.

A vehicle careened up the driveway.

The police officers hustled their charges to the other side of the parked cruisers.

A black unmarked police car parked in an angle, blocking the rear of the driveway completely. Anyone familiar with the parking lots behind the stores on Wisconsin Street would know about the other exits.

Yvonne Passenmath flung herself out of the driver's seat and clumped toward the group behind the two marked cruisers.

She was heading for Jenn, not Suzanne, and she had a sheaf of papers in one hand.

Chapter 31

✺

I figured that Brent was too busy watching Yvonne Passenmath to give me the all clear he'd promised. I picked up my phone and tiptoed outside. Dep was up on the catwalk, so I had no trouble keeping her inside and closing the door. Holding my breath, I stayed on the porch.

Passenmath yelled, "Jennifer Zeeland Banchen!"

All five of the officers from the Fallingbrook Police Department stared at Passenmath with something like horror.

Suzanne shouted, "No! Jennifer is innocent. She wanted to marry Roger, and I had to stop it any way I could."

Jenn wailed, "*Why?*"

Passenmath wavered as if unsure which of the two sisters to approach.

Suzanne raised her chin. "I promised our mother on her deathbed that I would look after you, and that's what I did, for all the appreciation I've gotten. In the early years after our mother's death, I was the one who made the important decisions. I guided you through your childhood, your teens, and your young adult life. I tried my hardest to be a mother to you."

"You were." Jenn's voice broke.

I tiptoed down the porch steps.

Suzanne glared at her sister. "And then when you were grown, I let you make your own decisions. Many of them weren't great, but deciding to marry Roger was the worst. He was a control freak and wanted to run your life. He called himself a life coach, but he kept flying into rages. He could have harmed you physically. He would have crushed you." Suzanne straightened her shoulders as best she could, considering that her wrists were cuffed behind her back. "I knew how to protect you. And I succeeded." Suzanne turned toward Yvonne Passenmath. "Go ahead. Take me away and lock me up. My sacrifice was worth it."

Passenmath answered, "You're saying that you worked alone, and that Jenn Zeeland Banchen did not help you poison Roger Banchen?"

Suzanne glowered at Passenmath. "Weren't you listening? I just *said* that."

Passenmath gave Brent a smug look as if to say that only she knew how to cajole a murderer into confessing.

"What's going on?" a man asked. Wearing a beige blazer, a white shirt unbuttoned at the neck, no tie, gray slacks, and white loafers, Gerald Stone was walking up the driveway toward Passenmath's unmarked cruiser. Bright red and orange Gerbera daisies peeked out of the top of a large paper cone in his hand.

"What are you doing here?" Passenmath asked him.

He stopped walking. "Picking up my date."

Brent ordered him to drop the flowers and put his hands up.

Looking confused, Gerald Stone complied.

Passenmath flicked a glance at me, and if anything, she looked more smug. "Who's your date, Mr. Stone?"

Gerald Stone nodded toward the woman Hooligan and the other officer were holding by the upper arms. "Vinnie."

Passenmath demanded, "Who's Vinnie?"

Gerald Stone pointed at Suzanne. "Her, in the blue-flowered dress."

"Ha!" Passenmath was the most amused I'd ever seen her. "I'm afraid she's already been picked up."

Gerald Stone spluttered "Why, what, huh?"

Instead of answering, Passenmath turned toward Suzanne. "Is this your accomplice? Did he help you poison your new brother-in-law?" Passenmath seemed to be enjoying herself.

I felt a little sick, and Misty looked the same way.

Still watching Gerald Stone, Brent hadn't unholstered his revolver. I knew he could do it quickly if he had to.

"I just told you." Despite the difficulties she was in, Suzanne flaunted her usual sarcasm. "No. The man didn't know a thing about what I was doing. He didn't even see me. He was snoring when I crossed the corridor from a meeting room to the banquet hall with my bag of rat poison and a saucer. I could see enough through the white drapes to recognize Roger. He was standing—if you could call it that; he was already three sheets to the wind—near a plate of crullers, stuffing them into his pockets. I squeezed one hand into a plastic glove I found, opened a bakery box, took out a cruller, coated it with arsenic, reached between the curtain and the donut wall, and put the cruller on the plate with the ones Roger had been taking. I did that with four other crullers, and then peeked between the curtains. Roger outdid my highest hopes. He gobbled all five of the poisoned crullers. I threw out the empty bag, hid the saucer under Emily's silly hat, and tiptoed back out into the hallway. Doing all of that took me only about a minute or two, but during that time, Gerald Stone disappeared, and I heard the outer door close. I went through a conference room to another corridor, and from there, I returned to the ladies' room." Her eyes glittered with something resembling pride. "I saved my sister."

"And," Passenmath added, "you threw out a disposable glove in a wastebasket in that other conference room. Your hand was too big, and you tore it slightly. We'll find a handprint inside that glove, and it will be yours."

Suzanne sneered at her. "So? I already confessed. You don't need to be digging up more evidence."

"That shows how much you know," Passenmath told her. She aimed a forefinger at Hooligan and the other officer gripping Suzanne's upper arms. "Take her to the station."

The driver of the second cruiser let go of Jenn and helped Suzanne into the back seat of that cruiser, and then he and his partner climbed into the front seats, leaving Misty and Hooligan behind with Jenn. The cruiser carrying Suzanne headed toward one of the lot's other exits.

Passenmath pointed at Gerald Stone. "You're riding with me. I have some questions for you, about Saturday night and also about some very questionable practices when you ran a pharmacy." She helped Stone into the back seat of her unmarked cruiser and shut the door. The way those cars were set up, Stone wasn't going to be able to unlock the door or escape.

Passenmath didn't get into her car. She leaned against it, folded her arms, and stared at Jenn. Misty's arm was around Jenn, who was crying. Hooligan reached into his and Misty's cruiser, brought out a box of tissues, and handed them to Jenn.

Brent eased around the front bumper of Passenmath's unmarked car and started toward me.

I stared down at the phone in my hand in dismay. Suzanne had confessed again, and this time I hadn't even attempted to record it.

I looked up. Misty was frowning at me. Then she gave me a half grin and pointed at her vest. She was wearing a body cam and must have recorded all of it. Besides, six police officers had witnessed the confession. I smiled back and stuck my thumb up. Her smile broadened.

I hoped her broadening smile wasn't because Brent was now standing right beside me. He was definitely on duty. All business, I apologized because my phone had dropped our call. "I set it to record a video and I guess these things don't always multitask."

"Did you manage to record anything before the officers got here with their dash and body cams?"

I fiddled with my phone. "I hope so." I started the video of the underside of the table and turned the volume to its highest.

Passenmath came and stood on my other side. All three of us stared at my phone's screen. We heard Suzanne's first confession, and then the video became a blur of movement as my phone slid off my lap. Hitting the floor, it made a jarring crash. We heard the shuffling of feet and Suzanne's threats to lock me in the basement and set fire to the store, and we heard the noisy struggle between Suzanne, Jenn, and me. We heard me run toward the phone and yell at Jenn to leave Dressed to Kill. We heard Jenn refuse, and then we heard the two sisters argue with each other while I inadvertently filmed my sneakers running outside to the parking lot. The recording ended when I called Brent.

Brent gave my shoulder a quick squeeze.

Passenmath ordered him to e-mail the video to her. She jammed herself into the unmarked police car and steered into the parking lot. Tires squealing, she turned around and then zoomed down the driveway, missing Gerald's bouquet by inches. The paper around the flowers rustled in the breeze of the passing car and then went still.

Chapter 32

After the sound of Passenmath's car died away, Jenn turned to Misty and asked in a small voice, "Can I go to the police station, too?"

"Yes, we'll need your statement, but I'm afraid you won't be able to be with your sister."

"I can call a lawyer for her, can't I?"

"Yes," Misty said.

"I need to lock the store."

"It's a crime scene," Misty told her. "My partner will guard it until the investigators get here."

Jenn's head drooped. "Okay."

Misty pinioned Hooligan with a stare. "And then he can walk back to the station."

"It'll be hard, but I'll manage." He not only had adorable freckles. He also had dimples. I grinned, too, more convinced than ever that Hooligan and Samantha belonged together.

Misty helped Jenn into the back seat of her cruiser, and then she drove down the driveway at a reasonable pace.

I started up the porch steps to the office door of Deputy Donut.

"Where are you going?" Brent asked.

"To get Dep, lock up, and take her home."

"You're limping, and there's blood on the top of your shoe."

I looked down. "So there is. I . . ." I gazed up at the sky. "I forgot that Suzanne stomped one of her stiletto heels into my foot, but thanks for pointing it out." I smiled to show I was teasing. "Now I'm feeling it, and I'm also feeling where she karate-chopped my right wrist."

"Let me see."

I pushed up my sweater sleeve, unbuttoned my shirt cuff, shoved that sleeve up also, and held out my arm. He touched the reddened patch on my wrist.

"That doesn't look too bad," he said, "but let's get you to the hospital and have it and your foot checked. I'll have a police photographer meet us there."

"You came on foot, didn't you?"

"I was about a quarter mile north of the police station. I knew that running here would be quicker than running to the station, signing out a car, and driving over, and I didn't want to delay Yvonne or the others."

I hid a grin. He probably also didn't want to ride with Yvonne or let her keep him in front of the store while other officers arrested Suzanne in the back of the store.

Not knowing what I was thinking, he remained serious. "I can call an ambulance or commandeer a patrol car to take us to Emergency. Your car isn't here, is it?"

"Not my own car, but the donut car is in the garage."

"Do you have the keys?"

Dep was having a meowing fit on the other side of the door. "Come inside," I offered. Brent followed me into the office, picked up the noisy cat, and hugged her. I opened the desk drawer and handed Brent the Fordor's keys. "You keep finding new ways to drive that 1950 Ford, don't you?"

He smiled down at me. "You got it. Maybe I'll apply for a job as your delivery person." Dep purred.

"*My* delivery person?"

"The Deputy Donut delivery person, though I'm quite happy to deliver you anywhere you want to go."

"Should we drop Dep off at my house before we go to the hospital?"

He gave Dep a knuckle-rub. "You'll wait, won't you, Dep, for Em to have her wrist and foot examined?"

"Mmp," Dep grumbled.

"And then you'll drive us both home," I suggested, "and stay for dinner with some delicious sugar-coated crullers for dessert?"

"Yes," Brent said. "A quick dinner, I'm afraid. It's bound to be a long night back at the station, so I'll even accept a cup of coffee. Did you lock the front door after you let me in a while ago?"

"I don't think so."

He handed Dep to me. "Sit down and rest that foot. I'll do it. What about the door near the loading dock?"

"I'm sure it's locked."

He locked the front door, checked the loading dock door, and returned. "I'll bring the car around."

"I can walk. The donut car is only right there, in its garage."

"And you only have a hole in the top of your foot. I'll be back."

He brought the donut-topped delivery car as close as possible to the back steps. I armed the building's alarm system, went outside, and made certain that the back door was locked. Dep would be secure until we returned for her and our crullers.

Brent ran up to the porch, put an arm around my waist, and half-carried me down the steps. I didn't really need help, but I didn't complain. He eased me into the passenger seat, got in behind the wheel, and drove down the driveway, carefully, for the sake of my foot and the lovely old car.

At the street, he pressed down on the gas pedal and turned on the donut's sprinkles. Colored reflections splashed across store windows. Brent smiled. The 1950 Ford couldn't possibly attain the sorts of speeds he was used to, but he was apparently enjoying driving it, dancing lights and all.

I thought of broadcasting the siren through the loudspeaker on the roof. Instead, I started the 1950 soundtrack playing inside the car.

A male singer crooned "The Tennessee Waltz." I couldn't help a small gurgle of laughter.

Brent looked over at me. "Does your foot hurt a lot?"

"I'll be fine." I knew it was true.

Recipes

Honey-Glazed Crullers

Light and eggy crullers are popular in many countries—and they all seem to use the same basic recipe, the French pastry known as *pâte à choux*. Don't be intimidated by French cuisine. These are quick and easy. If you're the sort of person who wakes up before the rest of the family, whip up a batch and surprise everyone when they arrive at the breakfast table. And *pâte à choux* is also used for eclairs and cream puffs, so master this dough and you can make all sorts of exotic-seeming pastries. *Pâte à choux* is light on sugar and flour and heavy on butter and eggs. Sounds healthy, doesn't it . . . ?? This makes a small batch and can be doubled.

½ cup water
3 tablespoons unsalted butter
1 teaspoon confectioners' sugar
Dash of salt
½ cup all-purpose flour, sifted
2 large eggs
1 egg white
Vegetable oil with a smoke point of 400°F or higher, or
    follow your deep fryer manufacturer's instructions

Place the water, butter, sugar, and salt in a heavy-bottomed pot on medium-high heat. Stir to melt butter, if necessary. When mixture simmers, add the flour, lower the heat to medium-low, and stir with a wooden spoon. You might be afraid the flour will clump, but keep stirring over medium-low until a ball of dough forms. Continue to cook and stir for a couple of minutes to dry out the batter. The dough is ready for the next step when a thin film coats the bottom of the pan.

The next step can be done with a mixer or by hand. Transfer the dough to a mixing bowl. Stir the dough until it cools slightly, a minute or two. Add the eggs, one at a time, and mix on medium speed, scraping down the sides of the bowl. Add some of the egg white bit by bit until when you draw a spatula through the batter, the channel you made begins to close quickly. The batter will be glossy and damp, but not wet.

Transfer the batter to a pastry bag fitted with a ½-inch star piping tip or to a plastic bag with one corner cut off (try cutting it in a star shape).

Pipe circles of batter onto parchment paper or a silicone baking pad.

Heat at least 2 inches of oil to 370°F.

With a smooth metal spatula, slide crullers into hot oil. Fry only a few at a time until golden, 1½ to 2 minutes per side. Remove with chopsticks, a slotted spoon, or a spoon handle and drain on a paper towel.

You can also bake these crullers, and they'll come out with a texture more like cream puffs or eclairs (so who's complaining?).

Preheat the oven to 450°F. Line a baking sheet with parchment paper or a silicone pad and pipe the crullers onto it, at least 1 inch apart. Bake for 5 minutes, then reduce heat to 350°F and bake for another 10 minutes. Turn off the heat, open the oven door a whisker (prop the flat side of a fork handle in the top of the door), and let the crullers sit in the cooling oven for 5 minutes.

While the crullers are still warm, spoon honey glaze over them.

Honey Glaze

⅛ cup honey
Confectioners' sugar, sifted

In a small bowl, warm the honey in your microwave oven. Add confectioners' sugar by teaspoonfuls and stir, dissolving the sugar until the glaze is as white as you'd like.

Black-and-Whites

These little gems are baked, not fried, and they're very rich and sweet.

Donuts

Melted butter or unflavored coconut oil
⅓ cup black Dutch process (alkalized) cocoa powder, pressed
    through a sieve to break up clumps
⅞ cup all-purpose flour, sifted
⅝ cup light or dark brown sugar
½ teaspoon baking powder
½ teaspoon baking soda
1 large egg
⅜ cup milk
1 teaspoon vanilla extract
1 teaspoon white vinegar
¼ cup (4 tablespoons) melted butter

Preheat the oven to 350°F. Lightly brush melted butter or unflavored coconut oil in the cups of a regular-sized donut pan.

In a large mixing bowl, whisk together the cocoa, flour, sugar, baking powder, and baking soda.

In a small mixing bowl, whisk together the egg, milk, vanilla, vinegar, and melted butter or vegetable oil. Don't worry if the vinegar curdles the milk and melted butter.

Add the wet ingredients to the dry ingredients and stir until blended

Spoon the batter into the prepared pans, filling them about ¾ full.

Bake the donuts for 10 to 12 minutes, or until a toothpick inserted into the center of one comes out clean. Do not overbake.

Remove the donuts from the oven, allow to cool a few minutes, invert cooling rack over pan, and turn pan and cooling rack together right side up. If the donuts do not fall out of the pan, loosen the edges carefully with a narrow silicone spatula and try again.

Let donuts cool. Using a serrated knife, carefully slice donuts in half horizontally so that you have two circles from each donut.

Form vanilla filling (see below) into ball.

Using a rolling pin, roll filling between two sheets of parchment paper to about 1/4 inch.

Using a donut cutter, cut out rings of filling.

Slide a thin metal spatula underneath rings and gently place them on the flat side of the donut half that was on top in the oven.

Make a "sandwich" by gently pressing the other slice on top. Serve rounded side up.

This makes six regular-sized donuts. These are so rich that you might prefer to make them as mini-donuts. If using a mini-donut pan, bake for about 7 minutes or until a toothpick comes out clean. Do not overbake.

Recipe can be doubled.

Vanilla Filling for Black-and-Whites

1¼ cups powdered sugar
½ teaspoon granulated sugar
¼ teaspoon vanilla extract
5 tablespoons refined (non-virgin) coconut oil, softened (warmed until workable, about 80–100°F). If you substitute virgin coconut oil, your filling will have a coconut flavor. Do *not* substitute liquid coconut oil.
2 teaspoons hot water (Try mixing the hot water with the coconut oil to soften it.)

Place ingredients in bowl and beat until combined. Filling will be stiff, but it rolls out well at room temperature.

Recipe can be doubled. Excess can be stored in refrigerator.

Connect with Us

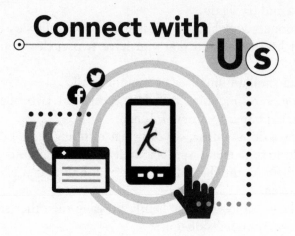

Visit us online at
KensingtonBooks.com
to read more from your favorite authors, see books
by series, view reading group guides, and more.